Trinity and Blane and Jay cap
first scene. This story is full of _ _  ل
and surprises ... especially for someone like me who
didn't think she'd be interested in wrestling! Good job,
Heather Greer!

— HOPE TOLER DOUGHERTY, AUTHOR OF
*IRISH ENCOUNTER*

At the heart of *Love in the Squared Circle* is the truth that
God looks at our insides, not outsides. Gotta love that.
And the sweetness. Gotta love that too. Sweetness with
a message of wrestling judge-y-ness, embracing love-
y-ness. This one is such a heart-hug of a book.

— RHONDA RHEA, TV PERSONALITY,
AWARD-WINNING HUMOR COLUMNIST,
AUTHOR OF 19 BOOKS

# Love in the Squared Circle

## Heather Greer

Scrivenings
PRESS
Quench your thirst for story.
www.ScriveningsPress.com

©2022 Heather Greer

Published by Scrivenings Press LLC
15 Lucky Lane
Morrilton, Arkansas 72110
https://ScriveningsPress.com

Printed in the United States of America

Paperback ISBN 978-1-64917-199-3

eBook ISBN 978-1-64917-201-3

Cover by Linda Fulkerson
www.bookmarketinggraphics.com

Scripture taken from the NEW AMERICAN STANDARD BIBLE(r), Copyright (c) 1960,1962,1963,1968,1971,1972,1973,1975,1977 by The Lockman Foundation. Used by permission. www.lockman.org.

All characters are fictional, and any resemblance to real people, either factual or historical, is purely coincidental.

*1 Samuel 13:14b NASB "The LORD has sought out for Himself a man after His own heart."*

*For all who try to look beyond and see the heart. And those who desire to be people after God's own heart.*

# ACKNOWLEDGMENTS

Every book is a team effort.

First and foremost, thanks to God for allowing me to tell stories that encourage and challenge others to grow in their faith.

To my husband Andy for being my biggest cheerleader and tag team partner in life, no matter what.

To Reatha and David, without your friendship and regular wrestling night invitations, this book would not exist.

Last but not least, to Amy and Erin who I bounce ideas off and vent to on a regular basis. This writing journey wouldn't be nearly as fun without you guys. The Carbondale Christian Writers group who've been beside me since book one, making me better and celebrating with me. And the team at Scrivenings Press who have worked so hard to make this book the beautiful story it is. Thank you!

# 1

"Please be there. Please be there," Trinity Knight begged under her breath as she fought through the throng of people exiting the conference room. As Jay's small hand slipped from hers, she tightened her grasp and kept moving. She wouldn't take the chance of getting separated from her eight-year-old son.

Trinity slowed her stride as she broke through the last of the departing masses and over the room's threshold. Even with so many retreating, people filled the space, jostling Trinity and Jay, stalling their movement through the room. A grunt escaped Jay's lips as he ran into her. She stepped to the side allowing him space to right himself.

"Where is he mom? Where's Maverick?"

Trinity scanned the room. She stopped, catching sight of the backdrop designed to look like a wrestling ring complete with an excited crowd filling the stands. A sign on the table to the right confirmed it was the area for photo ops with Maverick. Her heart sank. Her son's favorite wrestler was nowhere in sight. Other wrestlers had tables scattered throughout the room, but it wouldn't matter. They'd come to see Maverick.

"Oh, no," Trinity whispered to herself. How could she let this happen? She'd endured an overflowing schedule for the last week. Pennies were pinched to make sure the trip wasn't going to be too taxing on her budget. She smiled through the four-hour car trip from Cape Girardeau, Missouri, to Nashville, Tennessee, with an over-the-moon excited boy. Everything was to get him here for this moment, and she'd failed.

The noisy crowd wasn't conducive to the heart-to-heart Trinity was about to have with Jay. Finding one relatively unoccupied and quiet corner, Trinity wove through the people with her son in tow. Kneeling in front of him, she focused directly into the jade green eyes, so much like his father's, as she delivered the heartbreaking news.

Such a small thing to anyone else, but her son had experienced deeper disappointments in the last year than anyone should have to face, much less an eight-year-old. Already, the spark of excitement he'd had since breakfast was cooling. He knew what was coming. The last eighteen months of his young life had prepped him too well for times like this.

Emotion clogged her throat, and she sucked in a deep breath. "I'm sorry, buddy. I think we've missed him."

His gaze darted around the room before settling back on her. "But we're supposed to see Maverick. Are you sure he's not here?"

"I'm sure." She nodded, fighting her own tears as one escaped down her son's cheek. "I'm so sorry. I should've given us more time. I didn't realize how busy the roads would be this morning. It looks like Maverick is done for the day."

Jay wiped a tear from his cheek. Clearing her throat, Trinity blinked away the urge to let her own tears flow. A thin smile appeared, forced but present, nonetheless. He shrugged a shoulder.

"It's okay, Mom. We still get to watch him wrestle tomorrow night. Don't be sad."

————

The wind knocked out of Blane as surely as if he'd been gut-punched. What little boy put his disappointment aside to console his parent? What prompted his understanding of such complex emotions that he even understood the need?

If the voice asking after Maverick's whereabouts had been whiny or demanding, it would've faded into obscurity along with the other similar-sounding voices Blane Sterling heard all day at these meet-and-greet events. But it was neither, and for that reason alone, it snagged his attention. Turning from the table where he waited for his photo op times with the fans to begin, he glanced toward the plaintive voice's origin.

Blane raised one eyebrow as he found the little boy with the sad voice. The child had addressed his mother, but he hadn't expected the woman and son to be alone. Fathers and sons were a staple at events like this. Moms joined them on rare occasions. Sure, there were plenty of female fans, but generally they didn't attend these events on their own. And it didn't take one hand to count the number of times he'd seen a mother-and-son combo coming to enjoy the show.

Without thinking it through, Blane moved to stand behind the pair. Whether it was the wide eyes that stared up at him or the not-so-subtle way the boy edged closer to his mother, the woman was alerted to his presence. She looked over her shoulder. He knew the moment she saw him because she stood, turned to face him, and pulled her son closer to her side in one graceful move.

She eyed him warily and pushed a wavy strand of strawberry blond hair over her shoulder. "Can we help you?"

The boy tugged on her hand. "Mom, that's Blane Sterling."

While her son spoke his name with something near awe, the woman seemed unimpressed. The look on her face didn't telegraph fear, but it did border on cautious nervousness. He'd seen it a million times before when meeting people in person. From his hair to his height, everything about him was carefully planned to intimidate in the ring, but that often translated to life outside the ring too.

Blane stuck out his hand with what he hoped was a reassuring grin. The woman paused before offering her delicate hand for a brief shake. If he focused on her son, maybe she would see there was nothing to be concerned about. He looked down at the boy and grinned.

"So, you know who I am, do you?"

"You're the champ." His brown head bobbed emphatically with his words. "My dad and I watched you win on TV, but I'm going to see Maverick wrestle tomorrow. We're going to Ring Wars 24. I won't have to watch it on TV. I get to be there."

Blane smiled at the way the child specified the title of the company's biggest show of the year. He'd probably been counting down the days with his father.

"And is your dad going to watch Ring Wars with you tomorrow? That sounds exciting."

The woman's posture stiffened as she slid an arm around her son's shoulders. Blane wasn't sure if the motion was meant as support or a shield. A sick feeling twisted his stomach into knots as the boy's eyes filled with tears that didn't fall. The quivering lip returned as he spoke.

"My dad's in heaven."

He looked up at his mom. The protectiveness that had first drawn his attention crept back into the boy's posture. A slight tremor in his voice belied the child's smile, revealing the emotions churning underneath. "But Mom's going to watch with me. We're going to have fun, aren't we, Mom?"

She cleared her throat. "Yes, baby. We're going to have a great time."

"Mo-o-om! I'm not a baby."

Despite the seriousness of his faux pas, Blane fought a grin at the horrified tone. The woman smoothed her son's hair with her hand.

"Of course, you're not, Jay. I shouldn't have said it that way."

With a clear picture of the situation, Blane folded his six-foot five-inch frame down to squat in front of Jay. "Let me see if I've got this straight. You and your mom came to see Maverick today, but you ran a little late? And you and your mom are going to the stadium tomorrow to see him wrestle?"

"Yes, sir."

"So, you didn't come to watch me defend my title, huh?"

Light brown curls danced as he shook his head. "Nope. I came to see Maverick."

"Jay!"

Blane laughed as a deep blush bloomed on her cheeks. "It's okay, really. We've all got our favorites." He winked at Jay. "Maverick is one of my favorites, too, just as long as he doesn't try to take my belt."

He stood and addressed the woman whose cheeks still held the color of her embarrassment. "Can I talk to you a minute Mrs. ...?"

"Knight. But please, just call me Trinity." She got Jay's attention before continuing. "Mr. Sterling and I are going right over there and talk for a minute. I want you to sit on the floor right here and don't move. You can play one of your games on my phone while you wait. Got it?"

He nodded and took the phone, then sank to the floor with his legs crossed in front of him. "Got it."

Blane moved them far enough away that Jay wouldn't be able to overhear and close enough that Trinity would have no reason to be nervous. As it was, she didn't take her eyes off her son, not even when Blane spoke.

"First of all, it's Blane. None of this Mr. Sterling stuff. Second, I want you to be my guests tonight. In fact, I'd love it if you'd come back in two hours, after my meet-and-greet is finished. We'll go over to the stadium. I think Jay would love a backstage look at what happens at these events. He can meet some of the other guys. Maverick might even be there. What do you say?"

———

When she'd turned to find this bear of a man with his long, black hair pulled back at the nape of his neck and his dress shirt straining with the responsibility of containing his muscled chest, Trinity had to consciously hide her surprise. She wasn't sure it worked, however, since he'd immediately stuck out his hand and smiled at her.

How did one simple gesture transform someone so completely? His clear, turquoise blue eyes lit up with his smile, and not even his dark beard and mustache could hide the deep dimples framing his mouth. Standing beside him, her five-foot four-inch frame made her feel like a child instead of a perfectly capable woman. Her late husband hadn't been a small man, but even Tucker would have seemed slight compared to Blane Sterling.

But he'd asked her a question. True, his smile undid some of her unease, but he was still a stranger. A famous stranger. If he were not to be trusted, would he be out schmoozing the public? Would the Universal Wrestling Organization hire someone shady? Then again, what did she even know about the world of wrestling? No. She should stop being silly. Of course, the company vetted the wrestlers they employed.

And this wrestler wanted to spend the afternoon giving her son the time of his life. Didn't Jay deserve a little spoiling? There'd been little of that recently.

His eyebrows rose. Oh no, she'd been staring at him while he waited for her answer. She wouldn't embarrass herself further by groaning with the realization, even if she wanted to. But what should she tell him? He seemed sincere. And Jay would talk about the experience for ages. Just thinking of his smile brought out one of her own. That was it, then.

She nodded. "That sounds wonderful, Mr., uh, Blane."

Another full smile was her reward. What was it, again, that she'd found so intimidating?

"Great. Do you want to tell your son or should I?"

"You should do it. You're the one inviting us, and I don't want to take away from your generosity."

As if flustered by her praise, he looked away with a silent nod. Strange. She'd done every embarrassing thing one could think of since he approached them. Yet here he was refusing eye contact, and, if she wasn't mistaken, sporting a little color on his cheeks. How could someone with such a high-profile profession that flourished or fell with the adoration of fans be uncomfortable with a simple compliment?

Jay looked up from his spot on the floor as they approached. He swiped across the phone screen and handed it back to her as he stood. Once again, Blane crouched in front of him.

"How would you like to go visit the stadium with me today? You can see how it's set up, and you might even get to see some of the other wrestlers."

Jay sucked in a deep breath. "Maverick? Would I get to see Maverick?"

The possibility alone put a sparkle in his eyes. A chuckle rumbled from Blane's chest. He reached out to ruffle her son's hair. Jay didn't flinch. He simply stood there smiling like it was Christmas morning with a room full of presents waiting for him.

Blane shrugged one shoulder. "I can't promise Maverick will be there, but even if he's not, I can make sure you get to spend some time in the ring. How about that?"

Jay pulled his gaze away from Blane to look up at her. The expectancy on his face was enough to bring the sting of tears. Would she ever regain control of her emotions?

"Can we, Mom? Can we come back? Please? Pleeeeaaase? I promise I'll be super good."

The waiting tears evaporated with her laugh. Nothing could beat the joy of seeing her son so excited. There was no way she'd even consider saying no. "Of course, we can. We'll go eat lunch and be back in two hours."

As Jay jumped up and down, venting his excitement, Trinity turned to Blane. The exuberance of a small child could be daunting to people who weren't used to it. She didn't know Blane's background, but she doubted he'd had much up-close-and-personal experience with children. A warning might be in order.

"He's definitely excited. You've just given him a gift I'll never be able to top. I'd like to say he'll be more reserved when we come back, but I can't make any promises. You sure you want to do this?"

He smiled, watching Jay. "Absolutely."

# 2

Trinity checked her watch as she sat beside Jay. Ten more minutes before Blane's meet-and-greet time was done. Surely, she could entertain her son for that length of time. He'd flown through lunch, barely touching his kid's meal in favor of chattering non-stop about every scenario he could dream up for what the afternoon would be like.

Wrestling had been Tucker's favorite way to spend father-son time with Jay. Every week they had watched Maverick and a host of others she obviously couldn't name, much less picture, fight it out in pre-determined matches. And the monthly pay per view shows? Those were like the Super Bowl to them. It had taken everything in her not to interfere with their dramatized play during and after the matches.

Now, she was thankful for every dive off the couch and ineffective chokehold Jay had tucked away in his memories. Picturing them together left her regretting the lack of photos of their roughhousing. They would have meant so much to Jay. But she'd been less than interested in their hobby.

"Who do you think we'll get to meet?" His barrage of chatter continued.

Who? Besides Blane Sterling and Maverick, she'd be hard pressed to name anyone. "I don't know who you'll meet. It could be just you and Mr. Sterling."

"I don't think so," Jay countered. "There's got to be lots of wrestlers there."

"Maybe."

An impatient huff escaped his little lips.

"Jay, honey," she began, "I know you want to meet a lot of wrestlers. But remember what Mr. Sterling said. They might be there. He can't guarantee it. But you can be thankful even if Mr. Sterling is the only one you see because you still get to be in the ring. Lots of people don't get that chance."

"It's so cool that I get to be in the ring."

"Yes, it is." She smiled. Message sent and message received.

"But who do you really think I'll get to meet?"

A little of the wind was sucked from her parenting sails. So maybe the message wasn't fully received. She couldn't blame him, though. This trip was a way for Jay to connect with his dad once more. It was a priceless gift, even if Jay was too young to fully understand it. And Blane was stepping in to make it even better for him. It wasn't required, and it was the last thing Trinity expected from the world of wrestling that held no interest for her.

But Blane, from their brief meeting, seemed different than she imagined. Or maybe she simply didn't know what it meant to be a professional wrestler after all. She'd scanned each poster of the current champion as she and Jay walked down the hall to the conference room. Shots of him in the ring were enough to trigger the intimidation she'd experienced when he approached them.

Between his height and muscular build, he made most of

his opponents look like average-sized men, when they were far from it. And his face. He sported the same blue eyes and even the dimples in some of the shots, but it looked completely different. His eyes telegraphed an intensity she could feel through the photos. He was fierce, and he was on a mission to annihilate his opposition.

The man in question was across the room. Even wearing a dress shirt and slacks, he could never be confused with a businessman. But paired with the smile he turned on the camera while posing with his fan, the warrior stepped aside to reveal the man who'd offered her son the afternoon of his dreams.

She placed an arm around Jay's shoulders. He was watching the action at the front of the room. When his hand lifted in a quick wave, she looked back to Blane. He returned the wave with a wink in Jay's direction before turning his attention to the fan standing beside him.

"Mr. Sterling," She couldn't make herself call him Blane in conversation with her son, "should be done in a few minutes. Do you need a trip to the restroom before we leave?"

Jay's gaze darted around to make sure no one heard her question. He shook his head.

"Are you sure?"

Slender shoulders rose and fell. His lips were a tight straight line as he nodded.

"Yes, you do?"

His exasperation was barely contained. "No. Yes, I'm sure I don't. Can we talk about something else?'

"Sure." Trinity smiled and ruffled his hair. "What do you want to talk about?"

He shrugged and turned his attention back to Blane at the front of the room.

*And while I'm at it, when did he stop being my little boy?*

Though his voice held no disrespect when he answered, his message was clear. He could take care of things like remembering to use the restroom without her aid. This new territory that mixed her child who craved cuddles when scared by a nightmare with the boy who clearly thought he could get along fine without his mother's help, was unfamiliar and uncomfortable.

With her focus on her son, Trinity knew when Blane drew near. The shadow that fell across them as he blocked the path of the room's overhead lights would have alerted her even if her son's bright smile hadn't.

She turned and stood in one move. Jay followed her example.

Blane nodded to her before looking down at Jay. "Looks like I'm done here. Are you ready to head over to the stadium with me? "

"Yes, sir!"

Excitement oozed from every pore of her son's body. With this kind of stimulus, he might never sleep again.

"And what about you, Trinity? Everything set to go?"

"Yes, just let me get my keys." She opened her purse and dug through the contents.

"Why don't we take your car back to your hotel, and you two can ride with me. The company SUV has enough room for us to be comfortable, and it will be easier than you trying to follow me on unfamiliar roads. Besides, parking at the stadium is a nightmare."

Trinity paused with her hand on her keys in the bottom of her bag. Following him to the venue was one thing. Riding alone with him, company car or not, was another.

"Oh, no. I couldn't ask you to do that. It's too much already."

Blane looked her in the eyes, and she nearly forgot what

they were talking about. When he added a pleading smile, all hope of remembering was lost. She forced herself to listen.

"You're not asking. I'm offering. It's not any trouble. I'll be able to get you in and out of the venue quicker and without the parking charge." He paused in his plea to wave a well-dressed businesswoman over. "Besides, Pamela, will be with us for the duration since we're technically going to share her vehicle. Isn't that right, Pamela?"

The woman scanned back and forth between them. Trinity knew she could be wrong, but she had the distinct impression Pamela had agreed to no such thing.

"Pamela, I wanted to introduce you to Trinity Knight and her son Jay. They came to see Maverick today but missed him. They're the ones who are riding with us over to the stadium for dress rehearsals."

Though she smiled, the woman still seemed a little confused. Trinity accepted the hand she offered for a brief shake.

"Yes, of course. Give me fifteen minutes to wrap things up here, and I'll be ready to leave. It is so good to meet you, Trinity." She glanced down. "And you, too, Jay. Now, if you'll excuse me, I'll get everything taken care of here so we can go."

With introductions out of the way, the woman nodded politely and left their little trio to join a couple of men in discussion across the room. Trinity opened her mouth to point blank ask if Pamela's afternoon had just been hijacked, but Blane beat her to the punch.

"Please, let me do this for you."

With that disarming smile still doing its duty and the prospect of going with him alone handled, how could she say no? She grabbed a scrap of paper from her purse and scribbled her phone number and the motel address on it before handing it to him.

"Okay. Jay and I will drop off our car, and you can pick us up there. We'll head out and wait for you."

The wattage of his smile would have shattered light bulbs. "Great. I'll get my stuff. And when Pamala finishes whatever it is she's working on, we'll meet you there."

―――――

"Are you going to tell me what's going on?"

Blane shrugged in response to Pamela's question. "Nothing's going on."

The look she shot him as she pushed her glasses up farther on her nose told him she didn't believe him. When he realized the idea of riding alone with him to the venue made Trinity uncomfortable, he'd seen Pamela's presence as a blessing. She could be the buffer, and she'd played the part perfectly even though he'd surprised her.

Did she deserve to know what was going on? Probably. But he hated to divulge Trinity's situation without her knowledge. He was sure it wasn't a secret. However, Pamela was part of the PR department at Universal Wrestling Organization. She was also a sister in Christ. As a believer, she worked within a different code of ethics than some of the other PR people he'd met through the years.

She still watched him. Waiting. She knew, but she wasn't going to push.

"To be honest, I'm not sure what it is about those two. They came to see Maverick, but I guess she got lost or something. They missed him. Trinity was close to tears as she apologized, and instead of whining about it, Jay comforted her. He was the one who missed his big chance to meet his wrestling hero, but he didn't want his mom upset.

"It wasn't until I stuck my foot in my mouth that I found

out he was there with his mom because his dad passed away. I don't know why. I just felt I had to do something."

Pamela smiled and shook her head. "I know why. It's because you're a good man with a heart of gold, Blane Sterling. You may look big and tough on the outside, but inside you're all squishy and soft."

Blane forced a scowl. "You can't be letting that out, Pamela. I've got a reputation to protect."

"Don't I know it. The company makes enough off you and that intimidating scowl to keep us all in jobs. But seriously, you felt a nudge from the Spirit, and you took it. I wouldn't have expected anything else. Next time, though, try to give me a little warning."

Blane smiled and considered her words. Had it been a nudge of the Spirit? He hadn't even considered it at the time. The ideas came quickly, and he acted on them without giving it much thought. But he had prayed that morning, as he did each morning, for God to bring the right people to him and to use him to make a difference for Him. It seemed God had done exactly that.

The SUV turned into a parking lot, and Blane frowned. He leaned forward so the driver of the modified SUV would hear him. "Are you sure this is the place?"

"Yes, sir. 2210 West Bridge Street, the Sunset Motel. Not the Ritz, huh?"

In his early years wrestling, Blane stayed in some shady places. There wasn't a lot of money or notoriety as he worked his way up to the big leagues. As bad as some of those places had been, they looked like the Taj Mahal compared to the dilapidated building in front of him. Peeling paint, outdoor entrances, and gutters barely hanging on the roof's edge were only the start of the problems.

If he wasn't mistaken, there appeared to be a drug deal

going on in a remote corner by the graffiti-covered dumpster. He and Pamela looked at each other. He didn't know for sure what his expression held, but Pamela's shock and discomfort were written all over her face. There was no way a single mother and her son should be in a place like this.

And over at the front entrance, apparently oblivious to all the things currently sending shockwaves of unease through his system, Trinity waited, with Jay holding her hand. He couldn't in good conscience let them stay in the sketchy neighborhood, much less this motel, another night. It simply wasn't safe. But could he arrange a move without offending?

Pamela read his thoughts. "This is not good. Don't worry, Blane. We'll figure a way to get them into a safer place."

There was only enough time for him to nod and push down his unease. He had to make everything seem normal. Blane exited the back of the car and waved. Trinity and Jay waved. Jay started to take off in a run, but one word from Trinity had him walking by her side. The kid had enough energy to take out the entire UWO roster. Blane moved to the side to let Jay in first. He stuck his head in but immediately popped back out and turned to Trinity.

"Wow, Mom! Look at this. It's like a limo!"

Trinity shook her head. "How do you know what a limo looks like inside?"

"I've seen movies, Mom."

Blane hid a smile. The kid had a point. With the seats customized in a U shape and the extended length, the vehicle was enormous. Maybe it wasn't a traditional limo, but it was an SUV version. He was glad he'd been able to arrange this one. It would help make the trip memorable for Jay.

"Well, get in here, and let's get you buckled up," Pamela called.

Jay scrambled into the vehicle, and Blane waved Trinity in

next. He pulled the door shut behind him and took his seat next to Jay, who chattered on excitedly.

"David and Spencer aren't going to believe this! A real limo! David's always bragging that his dad has a sports car, but riding in a limo is so much cooler! Don't you think a limo is cooler than a sports car, Mom?"

Trinity looked unfazed by the onslaught of words and smiled at her son. "I think both a limo and a sports car are pretty cool. They're a different kind of cool. We can be happy for ourselves riding in a limo and happy for what David has too."

"Sure, Mom. I'm happy for him. But this is *so* cool. Mr. Sterling, do you get to ride in this one all the time? I bet you do. I bet you never have to drive yourself anywhere. You're the champion, and the champion shouldn't have to drive everywhere. Do you? Do you have to drive everywhere?"

"Jay." The single word from his mother stopped the boy in his tracks. "It was very nice of Mr. Sterling to ask us to join him today, and I know you're really excited about everything. But others can't answer if you don't stop long enough to take a breath. Remember to be polite."

Jay sucked in a deep breath. "Yes, ma'am." He looked up at Blane. "But do you get to ride in the limo all the time?"

A laugh rumbled in his chest, but Blane fought it back. Laughter would not earn him any favor with Trinity. Jay's excitement and energy oozed from every pore, lighting up his eyes. He was doing an admirable job trying to follow his mother's instructions to contain it, but it bubbled just below the surface.

What she didn't realize was that wrestlers fed off that kind of energy from their fans. Coming out to the music and the cheering, even the jeering in the case of the current company heels, pumped up each one of them to put on the best shows possible.

He leaned over to Jay as if he was sharing a big secret. "I don't get to ride in the limo all the time. But I think it's pretty cool too."

As Jay sat back in his seat with a satisfied look on his face, Blane glanced across the space to the bench seats where Pamela and Trinity sat. Pamela tried to look busy with some papers in her lap, but he could see her smile even with her head down. Trinity, however, sent him a look that he believed translated into "*Et tu*, Brute."

Maybe his comments did border on traitorous, but at least he hadn't fueled Jay's fire with how he really felt. Riding in a limo was way cooler than a sports car, no matter what David might think.

# 3

B lane wasn't kidding about the parking situation at the stadium. The lot wasn't filled nearly to capacity, but fans littered the sidewalks around the building, all hoping for a chance to see their favorites up close on their way in.

The SUV pulled to an entrance at the back of the building. The hoards were kept to the outer perimeters by security personnel. Trinity nearly shuddered, thinking about how hard it would have been to enter through the front with Jay in tow. *Thank you, Jesus, that I decided to ride with him.*

"There he is!"

"Blane! Blane!"

"Over here!"

Excited shouts for attention met them as soon as the object of the crowd's interest stepped out of the SUV. Blane waved and moved toward the chants. When he was away from the vehicle, Pamela stepped out before ushering Trinity and Jay to follow.

"Their attention is diverted. Let's get inside quickly. The less people notice you, the fewer questions we'll have to field."

Understanding the urgency, Jay jumped to the ground without hesitation. Trinity followed. She could tell he wanted to stay with Blane. Jay watched as the champ signed autographs and posed for selfies, but she nudged her son from behind. Thankfully, he followed Pamela without further hesitation, and they reached the venue without anyone taking notice.

"Blane will be along in a minute." Pamela stopped just inside the door. "But I have to run. I've got a meeting with the head honcho, and you don't keep him waiting. Will you two be all right hanging out here until Blane comes in?"

Trinity nodded. "We'll be fine. And thank you for allowing us to ride with you. I got the feeling it wasn't on your list of things to do today, but we appreciate it."

Pamela smiled without confirming or denying Trinity's observation. "I really enjoyed meeting you and Jay. I hope we get a chance to talk again soon. Have a great time this afternoon!"

"Thank you." Trinity let the omission slide. "We will."

With that, Pamela strode down the hall as quickly as her patent leather heels would allow. A woman on a mission. But she'd taken time to put a complete stranger at ease just because Blane asked her to. Was she that nice, or was there something more than a working relationship between them? Not that it was any of her business.

"Mom, can I play a game on your phone while we wait?"

Trinity handed the phone over. Sounds of activity throughout the stadium reverberated through various corridors. An occasional passerby gave Trinity and Jay a questioning glance, but no one approached them.

Trinity's thoughts circled back to Pamela and Blane. They would make a cute enough couple, she supposed. Pamela definitely didn't sport the same harried momma look that

Trinity had made her signature style. And she was nice, at least as far as Trinity could ascertain from their brief interactions. There was good rapport between Pamela and Blane too.

Trinity considered the man in question. Pamela could do much worse. The man was huge, and she wouldn't want to see him truly angry. His wrestling face was intimidating, and she couldn't imagine it directed at her. Tucker had always been clean shaven and kept his hair short. Trinity liked the look, but she couldn't deny that Blane's look with the ponytail and full but shorter trimmed facial hair worked well for him.

And that didn't even take into account the muscles on top of muscles that no dress shirt could hope to hide. Or the way his eyes lit when he laughed. Those blue eyes …

She realized those blue eyes were looking at her, and she was off in her own world like she'd taken leave of her senses. She could feel the heat in her cheeks.

"Sorry. I guess I was wool-gathering."

"No problem." He excused her with a one-sided smirk. "I was only apologizing for taking so long. I didn't mean to leave you guys by yourselves. I thought Pamela was still with you."

Trinity shook her head. "She had a meeting, but we're fine. It's not a big deal. You have to give back to the fans, right?"

"More than you know, especially for the champion. Once popularity slips, well, it makes the road a little tougher and a lot more unsure."

"What road is that, Mr. Sterling?"

As Blane's attention shifted to Jay beside her, Trinity felt the last vestiges of embarrassment drain away. She'd never been more thankful that her son seemed to hear everything that went on around him and didn't possess the ability to rein in his insatiable curiosity.

"Every person has goals," Blane explained as his large hand engulfed Jay's thin shoulder. "And the road I mentioned is the things that happen to get them to their dream. For a wrestler, the goal is the championship belt. And the road he takes to get there is made up of all the matches he must compete in to reach the championship match."

Jay's features scrunched into what Trinity called his thinking face as his head dipped in a slow nod. She appreciated Blane offering an explanation instead of pushing Jay's question to the side, but she wasn't sure how much of the answer went over his eight-year-old head.

"Sorta like when I wanted to get Mrs. Tate's All Star Reader Award. I had to practice my sight words every night, even when I wanted to play video games instead."

"Did you get the award?"

"I sure did." Jay's chest pushed out as he stood straighter. "And I was first in class to get it."

Brows rising high, Blane let out an appreciative whistle. "That must have been one hard road, but I bet your mom was super proud of you."

Jay looked from Blane to her. She smiled and nodded before Jay returned his attention to the man in front of him.

"She was. She even took me out for pizza to celebrate. And she put my certificate in a frame on my bedroom door. Was your mom proud of you when you won the belt?"

"She called me to tell me how proud she was before anyone else had a chance. And speaking of my belt, I need to head into the dressing room and make sure my clothes are ready for tonight. You want to come with me? You can see my belt, maybe even try it on for size, if you promise not to try to beat me for it."

Jay rolled his eyes. "I couldn't beat you yet. You're bigger than me. I beat my dad a few times, but I think he let me win."

"And why would he do that?"

His face scrunched as he thought about how to answer.

"I'm not real sure. Maybe cuz he thought everyone should get to win sometimes."

Blane nodded as if he was seriously contemplating the validity of Jay's answer. "You know what I think?"

"What?"

"I think you're right. I think maybe he wanted you to win sometimes because he loved you a lot and knew you'd enjoy winning."

The expectancy in Jay's face as he looked at her for confirmation took Trinity's breath away. Jay knew his daddy loved him, but how hard would it be to remember that when he'd been taken away from him at such an early age? She opened her mouth to speak but decided on a nod instead. Talking was out of the question with the lump lodged in her throat.

———

Blane fastened the heavy belt around Jay's waist and watched him preen and pose in the dressing room mirror. Stopping suddenly, Jay frowned into the glass before turning to Trinity.

"I need to take off my shirt," he announced.

"And why is that?" Trinity looked skeptical.

"Mom," he said with a roll of his eyes. "You know why. This is wrestling."

"I don't know, Jay," she reasoned. "I may not have watched with you and your dad, but I think I've seen wrestlers with their shirts on."

"They may start the match with a shirt, but they always come off by the end. Especially the champion. He doesn't ever wear a shirt. You can ask Blane. He'll tell you. Please, Mom."

"Don't drag me into this." Blane threw up his hands in surrender.

A momentary look of disappointment was aimed at him before Jay's attention returned to Trinity. "Please. Can I? I've got to look like a pro."

Trinity rubbed her lips together, and Blane had the sneaking suspicion it was intended to stifle a laugh. But would Jay's persistence pay off?

"Fine. Hand it here."

With his shirt removed, Jay once more began to strut in front of the mirror. The child's powers of persuasion were impressive. As Blane watched her using her phone to take pictures of Jay looking like a real wrestler, Blane doubted that if Jay asked for the moon, she wouldn't make it happen.

He watched their reflections from the corner of his eye as he checked out the rest of his gear for the night. He'd thought about letting Jay try on the long black leather sleeveless duster that was a key element of his costume each time he entered the ring but decided it might topple the petite boy. Even if it didn't, the ankle length garment would look more like a robe with a train fit for a wedding dress on the boy than the attitude announcing piece it was intended to be.

Blane didn't offer, and it didn't seem to bother Jay. He was perfectly happy to flex his non-existent muscles while his mom took pictures.

"I'm coming for you, Maverick." Jay's little boy voice dropped comically low as he threatened his imaginary opponent.

This time Trinity couldn't suppress her laugh. The contented sound brought out Blane's smile. He loved being able to do something that brought enjoyment to others, especially those he thought needed an extra dose of joy in their lives.

The carefree sound was almost enough to free the image stuck in his head since he'd talked with Jay about his father in the hallway. He'd sensed her eyes on him and momentarily looked up from Jay. That's all it took to set an invisible weight on his chest. Her wide, clear blue eyes held pain that was unmistakable. He could almost feel her loss as if it were his own.

Maybe he should apologize. It was possible they didn't talk about Jay's dad that much. Grief was a tricky subject, and he honestly didn't even know how long ago their world had been shaken. While he meant it as reassuring and could tell from what little they'd shared that his words were true, they may have been too much too soon for still healing hearts.

A knock on the door drew the attention of everyone in the room. The door opened, and one of the backstage crewmembers stuck his head in. His gaze paused briefly on Trinity and Jay before settling on Blane.

"Ready for a run through of your entrance? Make sure everything is timed right?"

"Yeah. We'll be right there." He turned to Jay. "Ready to go learn how to make an entrance?"

# 4

Trinity watched from the outside edge of the ring that Blane had called the apron. His entrance music blared once more through the empty stadium. Without people filling the seats, there was nothing to impede the sound's progress through the building, leaving it to echo back. The cacophony didn't appear to faze Blane or Jay in the slightest.

Jay waited beside her as Blane ran through the entrance twice. The first time was done without music. The man who'd apparently choreographed it led Blane through each step. Then, he'd stepped to the side and allowed Blane to run through it with his music.

As soon as he got the nod of approval from the choreographer, he motioned for Jay to join him at the top of the ramp. Trinity moved behind a nearby audience barricade so she could see the scene playing out in front of her as completely as possible.

As the music reached its crescendo, Blane thrust his arms from where they were crossed at his chest out to the side and above his head as if celebrating his victory before the match

27

even began. Trinity smiled as Jay, right beside him, mirrored his every move. In tandem they strutted down the ramp to the rhythm of the music.

"It'll look even better tomorrow night."

Trinity startled.

Pamela spoke from beside her. "With the pyrotechnics and light show, not to mention thousands of screaming fans."

"I don't know." Trinity watched Blane lift Jay to stand on the second rope in the corner of the ring posed like a warrior, though this particular one was small and thin. "I'm not sure I'll ever see an entrance that tops this one."

Pamela rested her forearms on the barricade in front of them. "You may be right. And actually, that brings me to the reason I came to find you."

Trinity frowned and pulled her attention from the pair now wrestling in the newly constructed ring to face the woman beside her. "You came looking for me?"

"Yes, I did," Pamela assured her with a nod. She shifted her focus to the ring momentarily then back to Trinity. "I'm not sure you realize how unusual all of this is in the wrestling world."

"I'm not sure I do either. But I have a feeling you're about to fill me in."

Pamela's smile was all business. "Wrestlers see fans all the time. We even have special meet-and-greets for fans who come to us as part of wish programs. Supporting sick kids and their families has always been part of the UWO's way to give back to fans. All the wrestlers participate, especially when they're the hero the sick kid wants to meet."

"But Jay isn't sick, and he isn't part of any program."

"My point exactly. Fans, kids included, miss seeing their heroes all the time. It's disappointing, but it happens. The wrestlers can't make every fan's dream come true, and they know better than to try. But you and Jay got Blane's attention."

"No." Trinity interrupted with a shake of her head. "We weren't trying to get anyone's attention. Jay and I were having a talk, just between us. It wasn't meant for anyone or to accomplish anything other than letting him know I was sorry I messed up. Blane approached us, and we never asked for a thing."

Pamela placed a hand on her arm. "I know you didn't. I wasn't accusing you of anything. It's an observation. Through no attempt of his own, Jay got Blane's attention. Blane is currently the face, the ultimate good guy of the UWO, and we think letting others see this side of him could only boost his popularity."

Air left her lungs, and Trinity had to force them to take more in. Tears stung her eyes. She tried not to stammer. "You mean, Blane, he asked us here as a publicity stunt? He's using Jay to make himself look better?"

Pamela's eyes went wide. "Oh, no. No, Blane would never do something like that. I know you don't know him, but he is a good guy. He would never use a child in that way, pretending to be nice just for a photo op. And we don't want to use Jay or you either. That's why I'm here. I want to ask your permission to take this story a step further. It would benefit the UWO and Blane, but it would also benefit you and Jay."

"I'm not following. What would benefit us?"

"We want to call it, Champs in Training. It will expand on what Blane is doing right now, only with the cameras rolling. It would include front row seats for you and Jay at the championship event tomorrow night. Seats like that are hard to come by for Ring Wars. And to get the full effect of what it means to be a champion, Jay would get to pick one wrestler and walk down the ramp with him as his entourage for the night."

"He could enter with Maverick?"

Pamela nodded. Her smile brightened. "If that's who he chose, yes, of course. But that's not all. Our wrestlers all stay at the Brightmore Hotel, and you would too. We have a room reserved for you and Jay for tonight and even tomorrow night. So, what do you say? Can Jay be the first UWO Champ in Training?"

It sounded like a dream come true for Jay. But what about the crowds and cameras? "What if it comes time for him to walk out with his wrestler, and it's just too much?"

"We'd still have plenty of footage to use. No one wants to force a scared child to do something they're not ready to do. Kids are going to be kids, after all."

"Can I ask him? I don't want to make him do this if he isn't up for it."

"We wouldn't have it any other way." Pamela got Blane's attention in the ring and waved him and Jay over.

Trinity led Jay to the first row of seats and explained everything just as Pamela had, careful not to push the more exciting details or leave out the more nerve-wracking items like thousands of screaming fans. His eyes grew with each part of the plan until he couldn't sit still anymore. He stood in front of his seat, but the gentle hold Trinity had on his arms kept him from jumping up and down. As it was, he danced around like he hadn't been allowed to take a potty break for days.

"Are you sure? Coming down the ramp with Blane was a lot of fun, but the building is empty. It won't be empty tomorrow night. There will be lots of people ..."

"I know."

"And lights."

More dancing. "I know."

"Plus, it will be really noisy."

"I know. I know. I know. Can I go tell him now?"

Freeing his arm from her grip, Trinity smiled. She didn't think she'd ever seen him this excited. "Yes. But be sure to tell Miss Pamela who you're going to walk down the ramp with tomorrow night. You may have to practice with him first."

Jay flew back to where Blane and Pamela stood by the barricade. She didn't doubt Pamela had already filled him in, but Blane knelt and listened to the tidal wave of words crashing on him from her son. Hopefully, his excitement wouldn't wane in the face of a thousand screaming fans and television cameras pointed straight at him. She walked over to them just in time to hear Pamela question him.

"And do you know who you'd like to walk with down the ramp? Should I call Maverick now and tell him the good news?"

Jay thought for a moment. "No. Don't call Maverick. I'm going to be on Blane's team."

Shock. It was the first emotion reflected in Blane's face, followed by a humbled expression. He scooped up Jay and sat him on the barricade. "Are you sure about that Jay? I know Maverick is your favorite. You sure you don't want to walk out with him?"

*Uh oh.* With Jay's bottom lip tucked between his teeth, the warning couldn't be clearer. In moments, his eyes would fill with tears. Trinity recognized the signs but was unsure how to extricate him from the situation without causing him embarrassment. *Lord, let Blane know what to say.*

"You don't want me to be your team?" Jay's voice was barely a whisper.

Blane dropped his head back and sucked in a breath before looking Jay straight in the eyes. "Nothing would make me happier than having you on my team. I just know you've been waiting to meet Maverick. If you want to walk out with your favorite, I won't be mad or upset. You know that right?"

Though he nodded, Jay still looked unsure. "Maverick's my favorite, but I want to stay with you. Can I be your team?"

When Blane stepped closer and wrapped Jay in a hug, her son nearly disappeared in the muscular arms. "Always. You can always be on my team."

Trinity wiped a trickle of stray moisture from her cheek, glad Blane's back was to her, and Pamela's attention was trained on him and Jay. This day was nothing like she'd expected. Blane surprised her from his first words, and it didn't seem like he would stop any time soon. What wrestlers must be like had never entered her thoughts, but even if it had, she doubted she'd have come up with the man hugging her son.

"Well, that's settled then." Pamela's practicality broke the moment's spell. "Blane? Why don't you and Jay run through your entrance again, with the cameras, to make sure it's perfect for tomorrow. I'm going to see if the costume creators can whip up a miniature version of your entrance outfit for Jay. When you're all set, the SUV will take all of us back to Trinity and Jay's motel. Then, they can gather their things and head over to the Brightmore."

After getting some of Jay's sizes from Trinity, she hurried off to settle all the details. Blane and Jay headed back to the ramp where a small camera crew was waiting. Trinity sat back in the seat she'd just vacated. So many changes happening so quickly. She forced herself to take a deep, calming breath.

She'd only wanted to honor Tucker's wish and bring Jay to the event in his place. It was supposed to be a simple trip. Come meet Maverick, watch the show, sightsee for a few days, and then return to their normal lives. Now, she could give Jay the trip of a lifetime. Tucker would have loved it. She was happy for Jay and thankful for the unexpected blessings. So, what was it that left her feeling off-kilter and a little overwhelmed?

She didn't have time to sort through her tangled emotions before the song ended and the entrance was deemed perfect. Jay skipped over to her with Blane and cameras close behind. He ushered her and Jay through the building and into the SUV before climbing in with one of the camera men. It didn't take long for Jay's enthusiasm to fill the silence with comments and questions.

"Why is the camera guy with us?"

"He needs to get some footage of the Champ in Training," Blane explained.

"Do they follow you around all the time?"

"No. Not usually."

"But you're the champion," he stated like it made all the difference.

"Yes, but cameras only follow me when I cut a promo or go to special events."

"What's a promo?"

Blane smiled. "When wrestlers talk to the backstage reporters, that's called a promo. It lets the wrestlers tell more of their story to go along with what happens in the ring."

"You mean like when Maverick was mad at Damon because Damon pinned him, but he said it didn't really count because Maverick pinned him first but the official didn't see it because he was trying to get Damon's friend to go away from the outside of the ring and then after it was all done the lady with the microphone talked to Maverick backstage and asked him what happened and Maverick started talking about how it wasn't fair?"

"Uh," Blane stammered, caught off guard by the onslaught of words. "Yep. That would be a promo."

Brows furrowed, Jay's attention went from Blane to the

camera man and back again. "I still think they should follow you around. You're the champion."

The vehicle pulled into their motel parking lot before anyone could formulate a reply. Grabbing her purse from the seat beside her, Trinity stepped out of the car with a smile. How could she have worried Jay would clam up in front of the cameras? Not her son. In the spotlight and center stage worked perfectly for him.

After helping Jay out of the car, Trinity turned back to Blane. "We'll pack up and meet you at the hotel."

"You have the address, right? Do you need me to stay and help? Entertain Jay while you get everything packed?"

"Yes. No, and no," she answered. "Jay is going to help me with the packing. We'll be fine."

"Let me get your number. I'll text you mine, and you can let me know when you get settled." Blane pulled his phone from his pocket as he spoke.

While it sounded like a valid reason, Trinity couldn't help wondering if it was an attempt to give her his number in case they ran into trouble. He'd not said anything, but she'd seen the look on his face when they'd picked her and Jay up. It declared her accommodations unfit and revealed his concern for them. Considering it mirrored her own misgivings, Trinity wasn't about to argue. She rattled off her number and in seconds her phone dinged with his incoming message.

"Got it. We'll let you know when we get to the hotel." She assured him with a wave before taking Jay's hand and heading for their room.

Before she'd cleared out the first drawer of their things, a knock caused her to pause.

"I'll get it," Jay announced, jumping from the bed and skipping across the small room.

"Oh, no, you don't," Trinity responded, snagging him by

the arm as he went by her. His innocence was a hazard in this area. "Adults get the door, remember?"

"Fine," he agreed before trudging back to his place on the bed.

Trinity peeked out the peephole. *What on earth was Blane still doing at the motel?*

"You're still here," she announced the obvious as she opened the door.

"Pamela and I were just about to leave," he began, "when we realized how hard it has to be packing with an energetic boy underfoot. We couldn't leave knowing we could do something to help."

It was an excuse. She was a single parent. It wasn't a secret that alone was how she did most tasks in life at this point. But it was sweet of them to offer to watch out for her safety, which is what she was certain they were doing, without insulting her pride.

"What did you have in mind?" she asked.

"How about he," he said tilting his head in Jay's direction, "comes out here with us, and we play while you pack? We might even be able to run off some of that energy boys come equipped with."

She snorted. "Not likely. Jay doesn't wear out easily. But I will take you up on the offer to play while I pack." She glanced at Jay on the bed, practically salivating at the idea of more time with Blane. "Jay, would you like—"

"Yeah! Come on, Blane. Let's go play." He hopped from the bed, ran across the room and out the door in record time.

Trinity laughed. "It won't take me long."

"Take all the time you need."

Without Jay clamoring for her attention, Trinity had their belongings packed and loaded into her car within a few minutes. After turning in their room key, she met Blane and

Pamela playing tag with Jay in a grassy area beside the building.

"I've got everything loaded," she announced, when Blane turned his attention from the game to her arrival. "If you and Pamela want to head out, we'll be right behind you. I have to make one stop, but it shouldn't take long."

"Will you still call and let me know when you get settled in your room?"

"Sure," she agreed before nodding to Pamela. "And thank you both for staying. It made things go a lot easier. I know it wasn't in your plans for the day, but I appreciate it."

Pamela's smile was warm. "We were happy to do it. We'll see you later."

———

A quick round of goodbyes later, Pamela and Blane pulled out of the parking lot while Trinity made sure Jay was securely buckled in. Happy to leave the dingy motel room for something in a nicer neighborhood, Trinity didn't attempt to stifle Jay's excited chatter as she took them through a drive-through for some hamburgers.

"Mom! Mom! There it is!"

Trinity tapped the brakes at Jay's abrupt announcement. Blowing out a breath to calm her nerves, she glanced in the rearview mirror. Jay was practically wiggling out of the confines of the seatbelt. She could correct him later about startling a driver. Right now, she was going to pull over, retighten his seat belt, and give him his meal to distract him the rest of the way to the hotel.

"What is it?" Trinity turned off the car and twisted herself over the seat to ensure her son was safely buckled.

"It's the Batman Building!"

She followed his pointing finger. In the distance, a giant building shaped like the superhero's cowl was illuminated against the darkening sky.

"I think you might be right." Confident the belt was secure again, Trinity handed Jay his meal.

"When Blane and I were outside playing, he asked me if I knew where the Batman Building was." Jay took a french fry from the bag and stuffed it in his mouth. "I told him Batman lived in Gotham, but he said he had a building right here. He told me I should look for it on the drive to the hotel. When I said I didn't know where it was, Blane told me I'd know it if I saw it. He said it looks just like Batman. That has to be it, doesn't it, Mom? That's got to be Batman's building."

"Maybe. Let me check."

Trinity glanced that way again. There was no denying the tall building with antennas piercing the evening sky on either side looked remarkably like the superhero. She grabbed her cellphone as she sat back in the driver's seat. A quick Internet search confirmed it. The towering building overlooking the city like the fabled protector it resembled was indeed nicknamed the Batman Building.

"You've got a good eye, kiddo."

"Do you think he's there?"

"Didn't you say he lives in Gotham?" Trinity shrugged. The last thing she wanted to do was spoil his fun with the truth that the building housed a company's offices. How boring would that be to an eight-year-old? She smiled at him in the mirror.

Jay's lips twisted to one side. "Maybe he just visits sometimes."

"I think you're a very smart kid." Trinity avoided a direct answer as she pulled away from the curb.

Jay continued chattering about all things superhero for the

remainder of the drive. Trinity threw in an 'mm hmm' or 'you may be right' when appropriate, but her heart was thanking God for the unique way He was redeeming this trip for Jay after her blunder. Blane was a surprise, but he was going out of his way to give Jay an amazing trip. Telling him to find the Batman Building was a small thing, but it was one more fun memory for him to take home in this unexpected stage of their Nashville adventure.

# 5

"Thank you for working this out, Pamela," Blane said, not for the first time during their conversation.

Pamela waved away his gratitude before getting up from the sofa in his suite's sitting area. "I told you, it's good for the company. I'm a PR person, after all."

Following her lead, he stood as well. They both headed toward the door. Blane opened it, holding it for her. "We both know it's about more than that."

She shrugged. "Maybe, but you're not going to give away my secret. How did that go again? 'I've got a reputation to protect.'"

"Good night, Pamela. See you tomorrow."

"Yes, you will. Good night."

He shut the door behind her before moving restlessly through the hotel room. Being alone never bothered him. He relished time spent on his own when he was on the road. There was only one difference this time, and it happened to be in the room next to his.

As much as he wanted to, he wouldn't seek her, or rather,

them, out. They'd called to say they were settled. When he'd asked if they wanted to get dinner, Trinity declined, telling him the stop she'd had to make was at a drive-through to get Jay a kid's meal. He'd experienced more in the last twelve hours than he usually did in a month. An early bedtime was a necessity. Another day of adventure waited for them tomorrow.

Spending more time with them sounded perfect, and he didn't realize how much he looked forward to it until it was no longer an option. But Trinity was right. He'd been around kids enough to understand their need to replenish the seemingly inexhaustible stores of energy they used up in the course of an exciting day. So, instead of enjoying their company, he paced his room like an animal at the zoo.

He collapsed onto the sofa and snatched the remote from the table beside it. After scrolling through the cable offerings at least twice and finding nothing close to grabbing his attention, he shut off the television and tossed the remote back onto the table. He laid back against the cushions and stared at the ceiling.

What was he doing? He had a big match in less than twenty-four hours, but was he even thinking about that? No. He was focused on a woman he barely knew and her son. Maybe it was time for a change of scenery.

Making his way to the sliding door, he opened it and stepped out onto the tenth-floor balcony. As he sucked in a deep breath, a woman's voice in one-sided conversation made its way to him from the adjoining balcony. He paused before passing the end of the brick wall separating their landings and into her line of sight.

"I know I should be happy, counting my blessings and all that. But it's hard, you know?"

Trinity's voice was unmistakable. She must be speaking

with someone on the phone. But her voice was off. It was quieter, huskier than he'd heard in their previous conversations. Was she crying or about to start?

"Tucker should be here. Not me. This was their thing, and I didn't realize how much it would hurt to try to step into his place. I feel like that's all I've been doing for the last eighteen months, and I don't know how much longer I can do it."

Her voice broke completely at that point, and Blane knew he either had to make his presence known or step back inside. Neither appealed to him. Trinity seemed like a strong, self-assured woman. In his limited experience, women like that didn't like to have the façade ripped away. It embarrassed them, and humiliation led to anger. He wasn't sure where he stood with her at the moment, but he knew he didn't want to be the focus of her ire.

Besides, she was speaking with someone she obviously trusted. She needed that outlet, and he didn't want to take that from her with a surprise appearance. He stepped back through the door and quietly closed it. Not that he felt great about that choice either. He was a protector by nature, always had been. Stepping away from someone who was in pain grated on him. Knowing it was for Trinity's best didn't erase his desire to help.

His feet seemed weighted as he walked back to the sofa he'd vacated and plopped down on the cushions. Hearing Trinity cry left a weight in his chest. He'd have to intercede for her in the only way he knew how. And if it happened to be the best way, so much the better.

"Lord Jesus, I can't imagine what Trinity must be facing. I've never been so deep in love that I've wanted to commit to forever, and I've never had forever ripped away from me. I don't know what happened, but You do. You see her. You see her pain. You see her desire to be the best mom she can be, and her pain over having to do it alone. Lord Jesus, be her strength, her peace, and her joy. And if she doesn't know You, let me be Your light in her life while she and Jay are here."

He continued praying scriptures over her and Jay. And, as it always did, pouring his heart out to his Savior lifted the heaviness, giving his heart room to move from petition to praise. He said his amen and looked toward the balcony. The sky behind the glass had moved from the shades of twilight to a dark expanse, artificially illuminated by the city's lights. He had no idea how long he'd spent petitioning on their behalf, but he was sure it had been long enough to safely make his way outside once more.

Trinity's laugh greeted him as he slid the door open. The light sound worked to dispel any doubts he had about joining her outside. She must still be speaking with whomever was on the other end of the call, but at least he wasn't interrupting at an emotionally charged moment. He cleared his throat in warning before he stepped past the brick onto the front half of the balcony where a small table and chair waited for him.

Instead of following his urge to find Trinity, he looked out over the city, needing to let her set the tone. She didn't disappoint.

"Hi neighbor. This is a pleasant surprise."

He smiled but before he could answer back, she turned her attention back to the phone.

"No, not you, Autumn. Apparently, Blane, the wrestler I was telling you about, is my neighbor for the night. He just came out on the balcony."

He transferred his gaze back to the horizon so she could finish her call with as much privacy as their close quarters would allow. They'd talked about him? Of course, they would talk about him. He'd been with her and Jay for most of the day. Trinity would have to talk about him to relay the events of the day. It didn't mean anything. And neither did the satisfied feeling spreading through him with the thought.

"Thank you."

He glanced over to find Trinity setting her phone on a table identical to the one on his balcony. "For what?"

"Everything. You didn't have to come speak to us at the meet and greet. You didn't have to invite Jay to come to the stadium or arrange a ride so we wouldn't have to go alone or let Jay try on your belt or practice his entrance when you did. And having him look for the Batman Building on his way here, that just added to the fun. True, I nearly ran off the road when he shouted that he'd found it, but he talked about nothing else the rest of the way home. It was totally worth the heart attack he gave me."

"I'm glad he enjoyed it. I figured what boy doesn't enjoy a good superhero."

"Superheroes and wrestling. Two things Jay's always loved." Trinity smiled at him. "Seriously. I know everything that happens after today is a requirement of the Champ in Training thing, but today? Today—that was all you. Thank you."

"You're wrong."

"About?"

"Today was my choice, but tomorrow is too. I know it's part of the whole Champs in Training promotion, but I'm thrilled Jay wants to be by my side tomorrow. I've had a blast, and I'm so thankful I came over and spoke with you and Jay at the event today."

She fiddled with her phone, spinning it in lazy circles on the table. "Why did you?"

"Talk to you?"

A nod.

He ran a hand through the hair he'd freed from its band

when he'd arrived at his hotel room. How did he explain something he wasn't sure he fully understood? "I may not have a clear answer. I went into the day thinking it was going to be more of the same. Fawning fans, bright smiles, and a million camera flashes.

"Then, before my part even started, I hear you apologizing to Jay about missing Maverick. At first, it got my attention because I can count on one hand the number of times a mother and son have come alone to events like this. Then, I saw Jay put aside how he was feeling to make you feel better. His ability to do that touched me, and I felt like I had to reach out."

"You caught him on a good day."

Blane shook his head. "I don't think so. I'm sure there are days he's a handful. I remember what it's like to be a precocious little boy with energy to spare. But what I saw today is deeper than that. It's who he is, or more specifically, who you're raising him to be."

She looked away from him, out over the balcony railing. "It's who his father raised him to be."

If only there wasn't a foot of space between their balconies and another three covering the distance to where she sat. He longed to reach out, touch her arm, let the contact add weight to his words. "I'm sure it is, but don't sell yourself short. I watched you with Jay today, and if what I saw was indicative of how you are every day, you're doing an awesome job building on the foundation you and Jay's dad laid together when he was still here."

A hand brushed her cheek removing the tears trailing down her face. The last thing he wanted was to make her cry. The laughter he'd heard from her earlier worked in him like a cold glass of lemonade on a hot summer day, waking his senses and leaving him refreshed. He'd much rather soak in that sound. But she needed to hear the truth.

"Thank you."

"You don't have to keep doing that. I'm only calling it like I see it."

"Still, it means a lot."

Blane licked his lips and leaned back against the balcony railing, crossing his arms over his chest. "Feel free to say no, but can I ask what happened?"

She stood and made her way to the corner of the balcony. As she looked anywhere but at him, the scant feet between them felt like a canyon. He wasn't sure if she was going to say anything, and he was just as conflicted about whether he should break the silence. She sucked in a deep breath and released it just as slowly.

"It was cancer. Pancreatic."

Blane's own life hadn't been touched by the dreaded disease, but he knew enough to understand pancreatic cancer was not a good diagnosis even by cancer's standards. "I'm sorry."

She sniffed. "Tucker and I'd been married since we were in our early twenties. Kids really. And Jay came along when I was twenty-seven. The diagnosis came five years later. Tucker fought hard, and he kept everything positive for Jay, maybe even for me and himself. When things got really bad near the end, their weekly wrestling watching time became even more important to Tuck."

A wistful smile graced her lips. "Curling up on the couch, sometimes the bed, and watching the shows together was the one thing he could always do with Jay. They kept the routine right up until the end. Early on, when he still thought remission was a possibility, they spoke of coming to a championship together. When he died eighteen months ago, I determined I'd make it happen. I'd give Jay the experience

Tuck had wanted for them. You're making it better than they even dreamed. Thank you."

Her gratitude was barely a whispered thought at the end of her story. Love, loss, fear, and determination reflected in her face as she spoke, leaving Blane's throat tight. Still leaning against the cool metal, he edged as close as the balcony railings allowed before reaching across the dark space between them and letting his hand glide down her arm. He hoped the gentle contact would bring some measure of peace. He'd said it before, but he had nothing else to offer.

"I'm sorry."

Her mouth was a tight line as she rubbed her lips together and nodded.

"Thank you for telling me. I didn't mean to pry or make things harder for you."

Her laugh was a short, harsh bark, void of joy. "Telling it is the easy part. It's living it that's hard. But I wanted you to know how much this trip means to Jay, to me. It's why I chose to let him be part of the Champs in Training when Pamela suggested it."

"Trinity." He waited until he had her complete attention. "I promise you, I will do everything in my power to make sure this is a trip Jay will never forget."

Melancholy tinted her smile. "You already have. I don't think you understand what it means that Jay chose to be part of your team instead of holding out for Maverick. Tucker always said he was the best, and his daddy's word was gospel to Jay. No offense."

"None taken." He hoped his good humor was evident in the dim lighting

"Whenever they played wrestling after watching a match, Jay was Maverick taking down whichever bad guy got in his way. You've made an impression."

The thought was humbling. He'd only done what he felt God would have him do. He'd listened to a prompting he hadn't understood, and God used it to give a little boy memories to last his lifetime and remind him of what he shared with a father he no longer had. And it even managed to bless his mother in the process.

"I don't know what to say."

"You don't have to say anything. I just wanted you to know."

Standing together in silence, Blane reclined against the balcony railing studying the ground beneath his feet. A mixture of emotions tumbled through him, and he attempted to sort through them in the silence. Out of the corner of his eye, he saw Trinity resting her palms on the protective ledge as she looked out at the city blanketed by the night.

Where should a conversation go after topics as life-changing as the ones they'd shared? He had no idea, but the silence between them wasn't heavy, so he was content to let it be.

Trinity turned to him. "I guess I'd better head inside. We've got a long day tomorrow, and I didn't get a lot of sleep last night."

He frowned but didn't question. He didn't have to.

"Let's just say, I think I might be able to get a little more rest in our new accommodations than I did in our former ones."

He grinned and nodded. He'd have to remember to thank Pamela again for the brilliant PR idea that got Trinity and Jay out of the wreck of a motel they'd stayed in the night before. "I should probably turn in too. Big night tomorrow night. But if you want, I'd be happy to have you and Jay join me for breakfast in the morning. There's a few of us that get together in the hotel restaurant while we're in town. I could introduce you and Jay."

She yawned and walked toward her door. "Sounds great. Just knock on the door when you're ready. Jay's superpower is being up with the sun no matter where we're at or how late he stayed up. Good night, Blane."

"Good night. Pleasant dreams."

# 6

True to her word from the previous night, Jay jumped onto Trinity's mattress long before she was ready to start the day. She groaned and rolled over to her side. She could feel him crawling over the top of the comforter toward her but tried to ignore it. Sleep hadn't come easy once she returned to her room.

Every time she'd shut her eyes, the day's events played across the black canvas in her mind like a movie in her own private theater. And while most of the scenes were amazing, they were also overwhelming to process. But that's exactly what her brain tried to force on her while all she craved was restful sleep.

"Ten minutes. Just give me ten minutes. Then I'll get up, okay?"

"But I'm hungry. Can I have one of the candy bars from that little fridge in the corner for breakfast?"

Would a five-dollar candy bar and a sugar rush be worth ten more precious minutes of sleep? Could she say yes and still be a responsible mom? She rolled onto her back and opened one eye. Jay's puppy dog eyes pleaded with her to agree.

"A candy bar for breakfast? I don't think so."

"I'm so hungry. I think I'm going to die." His voice was a growling mix of drama and desperation.

"You're not going to die," Trinity countered with a laugh. "Maybe win an Emmy for best morning performance by an eight-year-old, but definitely no starvation."

He frowned. "But I'm still really, really hungry."

Closing her eyes for one more tiny moment, she released a soul deep sigh. Rest would run from her once more. Maybe one of these days she'd catch up to it. But today she had a boy ready for breakfast.

Her eyes flew open as her conversation with Blane came back to her. Breakfast. She looked at the bedside clock. Red numbers glared at her chastising her for daring to stay in bed until six forty-five. She pushed back the covers and instructed Jay in one move.

"Go jump in the shower while I get our clothes ready. Make it quick, but wash everything, including your hair. Blane invited us to breakfast this morning, and I'm not sure what time he'll be here. We need to get ready so when he gets here, he doesn't have to wait."

"Blane's coming? Yes!" He pumped his fist in the air and ran for his shower without the usual complaints.

Trinity set out their clothes for the day and made the bed while Jay took his turn. Turning on the television, she found a channel with cartoons to entertain him before leaving him to dress while she quickly took care of getting herself ready.

She ran a brush through her hair with one hand while she used the hair dryer on it with the other. The gentle waves falling down to the bottom of her shoulder blades were one of her favorite physical qualities, but rushed mornings made her question whether it might be better to chop it all off. Shorter hair would save drying time. One last pass with the dryer would have to do.

"Do you like superheroes? Superheroes are my favorite. Some are just really strong, and that's good too, I guess. But I like the ones with powers. Do you like the ones with powers? My favorite powers are the ones who can move things without picking them up. They just think it and things go shooting around the room. I'd like to be able to do that. Or maybe be invisible. Or fly. What about you? What superpower do you like best?"

Blane had already arrived. She made a mental note to remind Jay not to open the door without her permission. Trinity grabbed her makeup bag for a quick addition of lip gloss and mascara while half listening to the conversation in the adjoining room.

"Hmm. I think I'd like telekinesis too."

"What?"

"That's the one you were talking about where people move things with their minds. I think that one would be cool. Or maybe I could have a whole new superpower where if someone has a need, I can make it appear. If they're hungry I could make a sandwich appear. Or if they were cold, I could make a jacket appear. I could help a lot of people with a superpower like that."

"I think I still want tele ... to move things with my mind."

Trinity chuckled as Blane laughed. Apparently, the idea of moving objects around a room was more exciting to her son than creating food and clothing out of nothing, even if it did help people. But Blane didn't need that superpower. Or rather, he already had it. After all, he'd seen her and Jay and made the impossible happen to help them.

Granted, what he'd done for them was more frivolous than

feeding the hungry, but it meant the world to her. Maybe she should let him know she knew his secret identity. Blane Sterling, superhero.

Her cheeks heated at the idea, and she knew telltale color filled them better than the blush in her makeup bag. Maybe she would keep her thoughts to herself instead. She flipped off the light switch and stepped into the living room area.

"Sorry to keep you guys waiting."

Jay popped up from the couch and turned the TV off with a click of the remote. A quick once over from Blane as he stood left Trinity glad she'd forgone the blush in her morning routine. It seemed nature would supply enough of that on its own.

"Don't worry about it. I got here early. The guys will just be getting started."

"Well, then—" she grabbed her purse "—lead the way."

Trinity was thankful for Jay's chatter as they took the elevator down to the hotel restaurant. She'd only had to remind him to use his indoor voice in the hallway one time, giving her opportunity to work through the reason for these reactions she seemed to have every time Blane came near.

Her peaches and cream complexion had always shown her blushes quite easily, but it had been ages since she'd found her cheeks coloring up so often. The last time had been, well, it must have been right when she and Tucker started dating. One look from him was all it took. Over time, as they got more familiar with each other, it didn't happen as often. But Tuck had the ability to make her feel like a schoolgirl right up until she lost him.

Why was she suddenly blushing so easily again? Yes, Blane was a good-looking man. His build and coloring were Tuck's opposite, but that didn't matter. She'd never had a single type that garnered her attention. And she had to admit, Blane seemed genuine in his care for people. That was always attractive. But she was a single mother. Her loss was fairly recent, and she had the sole responsibility of raising her son. There was no way she was falling for a near stranger, and a wrestler at that. It wasn't possible.

Blane led them through the tables scattered about the dining room to one in the far corner. As they approached, the men stood from their spots around the table.

"Morning everyone. This is Trinity and her son, Jay. He's been chosen as the Champ in Training for the company's new promotion." Blane went one by one around the table introducing the men by their ring personas and the name she should use to address each one. She nodded a greeting while Jay stood by her side, awestruck. When they were done, Blane pulled out a chair for her before taking his own seat beside her with Jay on her other side.

After everyone placed their orders, a man she believed Blane introduced as Damon Prince slapped his palms down on the table getting the attention, not only of everyone at their table, but also that of some of the other restaurant patrons.

"Before our food gets here, I think we should say grace. Preacher, want to do the honors?"

"Sure."

As every head bowed, Trinity sat in stunned silence looking at the man beside her as he began to pray. As he petitioned God for their day, her mind tripped over the fact that Damon had called him Preacher. Was this another wrestling name? Was it a persona from his early wrestling days?

"Are you feeling all right?"

Trinity nodded. She'd been so lost in her thoughts, she hadn't heard a word of Blane's prayer or realized it had ended. She was staring at him like she'd never seen him before and felt the telltale heat in her cheeks yet again.

"I'm fine. I was just thinking is all."

He leaned close and spoke for her alone. "Care to share?"

No. Yes. Maybe. She wasn't even sure what she could ask that wouldn't seem offensive. "You're just different."

A single brow raised high, and his sideways smirk uncovered the dimple on one side. "Not sure if I've been insulted or complimented, but I think I'm going to have to wait to find out. This isn't the place or time for that kind of discussion."

"So, Trinity." Damon saved her from having to formulate an answer. "Is being Mom to our Champ in Training your full-time job, or is there something else that demands your time?"

Trinity guffawed. "Whether I have another job or not, being mom to a precious but precocious little boy is always a full-time job. But it pays in hugs and kisses, and since the electric company does not take that form of payment, I work as a freelance children's book illustrator."

Damon's brows rose. "Wow. And what does Jay's dad do?"

"My daddy is in heaven."

Said as matter-of-factly as if he'd just announced the sky was blue, those words shouldn't open a pit in her stomach. But they did. Every time. She collected the uncomfortable glances from the men around the table like unwanted but fully earned badges on a Girl Scout sash.

"I'm so sorry." Damon's volume dropped to a respectful level. "I didn't know."

Trinity smiled tightly and nodded her acknowledgment. With the familiar sting behind her eyelids, she didn't trust herself to answer. Why was dealing with the same thing she'd dealt with for the last year and a half so difficult all of a sudden? At home, she'd moved past the tearfulness for the most part. Here she seemed to fight it every time someone spoke. True, back home everyone already knew, and there were relatively few questions. Here it seemed like all she did was explain.

Before the situation got any more awkward, the waitress arrived with their food. When everyone's attention was diverted, she felt the warm strength of Blane's hand over hers. Instead of the sympathy she expected radiating from his eyes, she was surprised to find strength in their blue depths.

His touch was gone as quickly as it had come. The waitress passed Blane his plate and then proceeded to do the same for her and Jay. Trinity dug into her food like everyone else, but thoughts raced through her mind. She could admit that a part of her wanted to dig deep and find out all she could about Blane Sterling. And that part was growing with each interaction.

But to satisfy her curiosity, she'd have to try explaining what set Blane apart from what she expected without offending him. In her experience, people didn't like to be classified as different or to have their livelihood questioned.

Conversation flowed freely around the table. Trinity had to pause her eating a few times to answer questions, but for the most part, the wrestlers included Jay in their talk. He was the Champ in Training, after all. Quiet reminders to chew and swallow each bite before speaking were given when needed, but Jay handled himself well considering he'd never been in a situation like this. As she encouraged him to use his napkin to wipe his hands, his eyes went wide at someone coming up behind her.

"You're Maverick! Mom, look. It's Maverick. He's here."

The awe in his voice was unmistakable. She turned to find a man, much smaller than Blane but solidly built, swaggering up to the table. His gaze rested on Jay, but something in his expression seemed less than engaged.

"Last I checked I was. But the real question is, who are

you?" His voice was louder than necessary, and his cheerful tone was a little over the top.

"I'm Jay. I'm the Champ in Training. And you're my favorite. I came to see you yesterday, but you were already gone. I was a little sad, but Blane took me to the stadium. I thought I might see you, but you weren't there either. I'm Blane's partner tonight, but I really wanted to see you too. Are you going to eat breakfast with us?"

The grin he gave Jay didn't reach his eyes. It barely reached his lips. Hopefully her son was unaware of the man's disinterest. He started to speak but snagged a passing waitress. "Coffee. Black. To go." He turned back to Jay. "It's really great to meet you, but I'm not really hungry this morning."

The waitress returned with a steaming to-go cup. Maverick took a sip before handing her some bills. "Perfect. Keep the change." He acknowledged each of his fellow wrestlers with a glance before addressing Jay with a wink. "I've gotta go, but maybe we'll see each other tonight."

Trinity watched the man's retreating back before turning to her son. The hope in his eyes as he watched his hero walk away caused a pain in her chest. Couldn't the man spare a moment for a little boy who idolized him? Though Jay didn't frown, the smile that had shown with the strength of a thousand suns when Maverick entered faded completely. Time for damage control.

Mustering up excitement she didn't feel, Trinity tried to soften the blow. "Wow. You finally got to meet Maverick. That is so cool."

His eyes flicked up toward her before returning to the doorway Maverick exited through. "Yeah. David isn't going to believe I got to meet him, but I did."

"Will you excuse me for a minute? I'll be right back." Blane tried to sound like nothing was wrong, but there was an edge to his voice. Without waiting for a reply, he followed Maverick's path out the door.

Trinity shifted in her seat. She only wanted Jay to have a memorable trip. Their presence causing trouble was the furthest thing from her mind. Yet here she and Jay were, surrounded by perfect strangers, while the one man she felt semi-comfortable with was chasing after her son's hero to do— who knew what Blane was going to say or do.

The empty plate in front of her suddenly became the most interesting thing in the world as she refused to make eye contact with the others gathered around the table. What could she say to ease the tense situation? Was an apology called for? Before she could formulate a plan, Damon broke the silence.

"So, you're Blane's partner tonight, huh?"

"Yes, sir." Jay's voice sounded unsure.

"Well, what are you going to do when I win his championship belt tonight?"

Slender shoulders drew back as Jay sat up straight and stared the man down. David and Goliath flashed through Trinity's mind. She hid a smile behind the napkin she lifted to her mouth under the false pretense of wiping it.

"You're not going to win it."

"I'm not, huh? What makes you so sure?"

Jay's chin lifted. Defiance at its best. "You're not going to win, because Blane is the biggest and the strongest. Besides, I'm on his team tonight, and I always beat my daddy. You won't be so tough."

Trinity's mouth dropped open in horror at the brazen trash talk coming from her son, but the men around the table didn't seem to mind. If their chuckles and outright laughter were any indication, they actually enjoyed the banter.

"I guess you've been told, Damon. That championship belt is staying right where it belongs, right there around my waist."

Blane mimed the shape of the belt around his middle as he rejoined the table. He didn't look upset. Maybe the confrontation she was concerned about was a figment of her imagination. She settled back to listen to the back-and-forth bravado occurring around the table. With his partner back, Jay fully engaged in the antics.

As breakfast wound down, the wrestlers said their good-byes and left to go do whatever it was that wrestlers did on the day of a big match. It sounded like several were going to work out, but that made no sense.

"They're going to the gym? Isn't that like training on the day of the big race or something?"

"Sure, they are. I will too, in a bit. It won't be a big workout, but it will be enough to get the muscles warmed up and the blood pumping. Early this afternoon, I'll meet with Damon down at the stadium to go over the match and make sure we're on the same page with everything that's supposed to happen."

"But you know who's going to ..." she paused and motioned toward Jay with her head. "You know what, in advance. What is there to go over?"

"What we do may be scripted, but it still takes quite a bit of athleticism and coordination. While a lot of injuries are more for dramatic effect, what we do is complex. One wrong move, one time of not being able to trust your competitor, or some other unavoidable issue and a wrestler can end up sidelined for weeks. Some can take them out of wrestling forever. It can happen in a moment." His voice softened as he spoke.

He stilled and clasped his hands together on the table in front of him.

"Have you ever made one of those mistakes?" Her own voice was quiet. "The ones that end a wrestler's career?"

He stared at his hands. "No. I've never made that kind of mistake."

There was more to the story. No one could convince her otherwise. But Trinity couldn't push him for more details. She didn't know him well enough for that. An Internet search might yield answers. With his popularity, there was sure to be plenty of information on the web for public consumption. However, she pushed the idea aside as quickly as it formed.

If she'd only heard of Blane Sterling, that might be a feasible option. But she was getting to know him, and searching out the information, even if it was common knowledge to wrestling fans, seemed like an invasion of privacy. She'd wait. Blane would either tell her or he wouldn't, but her curiosity wouldn't get the better of her.

"Mom, I have to use the bathroom."

The interruption was just what they needed.

"Come on then. I think I saw the ladies' room out in the lobby."

"But I don't want to go in your bathroom. It's for girls. I'm big. I can go in the one for boys."

Trinity shook her head. "Nope. It's either that or we go back up to our room. Can you wait that long?"

"No, but ..."

"I'll take him."

"You don't have to do that. It's not that I'm worried about the hotel. But I can't set a precedent for when we get back home. It's just me and him there, and we have to do what we have to do."

"I get it. But you're not on your own here. Let me take him for you this time. Then, we can all head to the gym for a workout. My partner needs to get his muscles warmed up before his big debut."

Without waiting for an objection, he sauntered down the hall with her son's hand clasped in his. She couldn't have responded if she wanted to. *You're not on your own here.* That's what he'd said, and even though she knew it wasn't a deep and meaningful declaration, the thought that someone was in her corner, even for a time, brought a sense of relief that overwhelmed her.

Grabbing her purse, Trinity headed after them to the lobby. The restroom break would only take a couple minutes, and she wanted to be ready to leave when they were. Blane was already rearranging his day to accommodate them, and she wasn't going to be responsible for running him late to his workout.

# 7

"He was so excited, Autumn. You should have seen him. When Blane got one of the up-and-coming wrestlers who won't have a match tonight to teach him real wrestling moves, I thought Jay was going to explode with excitement."

Autumn laughed, fully aware of what an overly energetic Jay looked like. Being an honorary aunt meant she'd spent a lot of time with their family before Tucker died. After Trinity lost him, Autumn was a daily fixture in their home, even moving in with them for the first few months to help them adjust.

"I wasn't sure I'd get him to go to sleep. He was so wound up. But as soon as his head hit the pillow, he was out. He's had quite an exciting weekend so far, and tonight won't change that. Blane will have to tame a tornado tonight when they walk in together. You did order the pay per view, didn't you?"

Autumn's huff came over the line with clarity. "Did you really have to ask? This is my nephew we're talking about. I may not be a wrestling fan, but I'm not going to miss his big night. Besides, I want to get a look at this new wrestler friend of yours."

"I'm rolling my eyes at you."

"I know."

"It's not like that."

"Like what? All I did was call him your new friend. Would you prefer acquaintance?"

"You know what I mean. I can hear it in your voice. Friend does not mean friend when it comes from your mouth with that tone."

"I'm sure I don't know what you mean."

Trinity knew the exact expression Autumn wore without seeing it. Big eyes, fluttery lashes, and an insincere shot of 'I'm innocent' mixed in to complete the look. She'd seen it often, and thanks to her best friend's influence, she'd even begun seeing it mirrored in her son.

"You know exactly what I mean."

"You two sounded awfully chummy on the balcony last night. And I'm pretty sure you also said he was good looking. Does Eric have reason to be jealous?"

A groan escaped before she could stop it.

"The date was that memorable, huh?" Autumn pounced on the obvious issue.

"Memorable? Maybe. But not in a way resembling anything good. If Theresa Cavins wants to find her nephew a girl, she needs to look elsewhere. It isn't happening with me."

"Ouch."

"He was late and requested I go ahead to the restaurant and save our reservation until he arrived."

"Not the best start."

"Oh, it gets better. When he arrived, half an hour later I might add, he immediately told the waitress he expected good service if she wanted a good tip. Then, while she was still in earshot, he told me 'You have to let them know up front what's expected of them.'"

"Wow."

"The meal was filled with wonderful conversation, all about his accomplishments, his likes, and what he expects of the women he dates."

"I thought the guy was, how did Theresa put it, 'A nice, handsome, Christian guy.'"

Trinity shrugged, though Autumn couldn't see it. "That's what she said. He is very clean cut, and she's not wrong about his attractiveness. He does go to church. He made sure to tell me exactly how often and all the things he does to help ensure his church is a 'pillar of morality and respectability to the world.'"

Did that last bit sound like she was playing judge and jury with his soul? She hoped not, but damage control might be in order.

"I'm not saying he isn't a believer. Maybe he went overboard trying to impress me. Or he could have been nervous or had a bad day or something. Whatever it was, Eric won't get a second chance to make a new impression."

"So, this wrestler guy, Blane, was it? I guess he doesn't have any reason to be jealous then." Autumn's devious smile was apparent in her tone.

"That isn't what I meant. I was only telling you about my awful blind date. It wasn't a statement on hidden feelings for Blane Sterling."

"Let's test this theory. What did you talk about after I got off the phone?"

She was tempted to lie, but even if it wasn't wrong, Autumn would see through it. She would also make too big a deal of the truth. "I started out thanking him for everything he's done to make the trip special for Jay. I asked him why he did it, and we ended up talking about my parenting, how Jay's turning out, and how we lost Tuck."

The inhale of breath through the phone was immediate. "You talked with Blane about Tucker?"

"I've talked with a lot of people about Tucker."

"You really haven't. You've answered questions about how you're doing. You've come to a lot of us for help and encouragement in dealing with being a single parent. But to dive into your experience with Tucker with someone who wasn't there in the first place? That's uncharted territory for you."

"I talk about it. Remember when Miss Gertie tried to set me up on a blind date with her brother's wife's nephew or whatever he was? I talked with him about Tucker."

"No. You told him you'd lost Tucker to cancer and moved the conversation on. Is that what happened last night? A brief synopsis of that single fact and then on to better topics?"

"Not exactly. Still, I only shared because Blane did so much for us. It doesn't mean anything. He's a nice guy who's easy to talk to." Trinity stood and paced around the room. "That's all. Really."

Silence pushed her to attempt a redirection of the conversation. "Now if we can move on, there were a couple strange things that happened this morning. I wanted to speak with him about them, but he was busy working out and teaching Jay. I only brought Jay back to the hotel so he could rest before tonight's event. Otherwise, I'm sure he'd have taken us to the stadium where he and Damon are doing a run through of tonight's match."

"First, I'm glad you didn't go with him for that. Jay thinks these guys are super-heroes. It would kill him to know it's choreographed. Second, when you say strange, do you mean the disturbing kind of strange?"

Trinity stopped in front of the sliding door and looked over the balcony to the city beyond. She could just make out the stadium in the distance. "No. It wasn't disturbing. In fact, I think Blane may be a believer."

"He definitely seems like a great guy and all, but what makes you think he's a Christian?"

"When we went to breakfast today, one of the guys called him Preacher and asked him to pray. I know it's not much, but it made me wonder."

"And the other thing?"

"Jay got to meet his favorite wrestler today."

"That's awesome!"

"It really wasn't. I mean, Maverick wasn't mean or anything. He was simply disinterested and rushed. After everyone has been so nice to him, Jay seemed confused by it. The other guys covered it well and made Jay feel better. But after Maverick left, Blane went out after him. When he came back, he just sat down and acted like nothing happened."

"Maybe nothing did happen?"

Trinity flopped back onto the couch. "I don't know. It seemed a little too coincidental. I hope Jay and me being here isn't causing a problem with the group. They seem pretty tightknit."

"I wouldn't worry about it. What is it Miss Gertie always tells us? Don't borrow trouble. Ask him about it if you want to, but I wouldn't let it bother you any. Even if they did have words, it's not on you."

"Maybe." The sound of soft footsteps caught Trinity's attention. "Hey, I think Jay's waking up. I'd probably better go and get us ready for tonight."

"No problem. Have fun watching both your guys tonight."

Trinity disconnected the call to her friend's teasing laughter. Autumn was proud of herself for sneaking that last bit in. But Blane was not her guy. It didn't matter that he was sweet and kind and good-looking. There was nothing between them.

A glance at the clock told her it was time to get ready. She headed to the bedroom to get Jay set up for a quick shower. She still had to pick out the perfect outfit, and it wouldn't hurt to touch up her hair and makeup. With Jay so prominent in the evening's event, she might end up with a camera aimed in her direction. Her desire to look her best definitely *did not* have anything to do with Blane Sterling.

———

*Just breathe.* Trinity stood behind the barricade in front of her first-row seat. The lights, people, and noise were more than overwhelming for someone whose idea of a full stadium was nowhere near the close to seventy-thousand fans currently chanting for their favorite wrestling stars.

The most-known stadium in Cape Girardeau, Missouri where she lived only held around seven thousand. Once Tuck talked her into a Cardinals' game at Busch Stadium. Even with the venue sold out, the crowd hadn't quite reached forty-six thousand, and then it seemed like everyone in the world must have been present.

The enormity of the masses around her was beyond comprehension. The energy of the crowd tore through the room like a midwestern twister, full of power and unable to be tamed. At least, unlike a tornado, the fans weren't bent on destruction. Still, how would Jay react coming through the curtain to a mob like this? His experience with crowds of any size was limited to a movie theater on discount Tuesday.

She watched the matches progress to the main event, knowing Pamela had Jay in her charge behind the scenes. There, he watched the same competitors fight it out on a screen surrounded by those waiting to enter the ring and those who'd already left it. Even if he couldn't be out front, she knew he was having the time of his life.

The show kept her interest, though her enthusiasm never reached the frenzy of the fans surrounding her. The level of athleticism the performers exhibited couldn't be denied. As amazing as it was to see the average-sized wrestler fly from the top ropes and bounce all over the ring with gymnastic style moves, some of the men made the normal-sized guys seem like children.

When they leaped over opponents and dove through the ropes without grazing them, Trinity could only watch in awe. She couldn't even make it past the first round in limbo without touching the stick!

Engrossed in the action around her, Trinity didn't realize how much time passed until the lights went dim for the main event and the first pulses of Damon's music filled the air along with the boos expected from the audience when a bad guy made his way to the ring. Damon posed on the ropes for the crowd before the lights dimmed once more.

The music for Blane's entrance and the accompanying laser show began. Blane, with Jay at his side, stepped onto the top of the ramp, their heads down and their arms crossed. The crescendo brought their heads up and their arms spread wide to each side and Blane gave Jay a nod for them to stride to the ring.

Watching Jay with his eyes glued on the scene in front of him, Trinity doubted he even saw the cue. Trinity's pulse raced quicker than Blane's intro music. Her son was not going to make it down the ramp.

Staying in position, Blane spoke to Jay. The words were lost in the chaos to all except the one meant to hear their message. Jay looked up, making eye contact with Blane. A few more words and Blane nodded. Jay answered with a decisive nod of his own. Together they made their way to the ring.

In the corner of the ring, Blane hoisted himself onto the second rope, posing like a warrior. After basking in the roar of the audience, he stepped down and lifted Jay to strike the same pose. Trinity's cheer blended with the crowd.

Blane set Jay back on the mats, and they stood face-to-face with Damon. Jay's slight back was to Blane, but his arms were crossed across his chest in the same pose Blane struck. They even sported the same defiant look as they faced the opponent.

Glaring at Jay, Damon demonstrated his lack of intimidation for the crowd. The stare down continued until Damon finally broke eye contact. When he looked back, Blane's lips twisted in a knowing smirk. The unspoken first battle had been won. Blane lowered a palm to Jay who promptly slapped five across it. Together, the pair entered their corner, where Jay was handed off to an official. They moved to stand beside the barricade as the real match began.

As soon as the bell rung, Damon came out fighting hard. Would Blane lose his title in the match? Damon grabbed him from behind, lifting him high.

How could he lift someone as big as Blane with such power? Trinity sucked in a breath her lungs refused to release as Damon bent backward to essentially throw Blane over his own bridged body and onto the mat. With Blane now on his back, Damon pinned his shoulders to the ground. Trinity's pulse pounded as the official counted.

"One." The official called out.

"No," Trinity breathed. He couldn't lose. Not tonight.

"Two."

Blane kicked out of the hold, throwing Damon halfway across the ring as he did.

"Yes!" Trinity's cheers joined the chorus of those around her.

Blane shook his head, his uncontained hair wild from the match's activity. Jumping to his feet, he approached Damon who used the ropes to slingshot himself toward Blane in a charge. A heavy forearm across the top of his chest clotheslined Damon, stopping him in his tracks. Blane left him on his back and climbed to the top rope. He jumped from his perch doing what Trinity could only describe as a belly flop onto Damon. Pressing his opponent's shoulders into the mat, Blane waited for the official to offer the count.

"One."

Damon kicked out. Back and forth the match continued. First Damon, then Blane took the upper hand. Both men moved with skill and speed. The impact of the mat against bare, sweaty skin caused friction burns to both their torsos.

A knee to Blane's head opened a small gash next to his right eyebrow. He continued as if nothing happened. Finally, Damon went down to the mat. While he struggled until he was on all fours, Blane crouched in the corner egging him on to get up.

Finally, Damon stood on shaking legs. Blane ran toward him, gave an almost imperceptible hop, and threw one leg up in front of him as soon as he was close enough to strike. The sole of his boot connected to Damon's face with enough force to knock him flat on his back. Blane covered him and the official counted.

"One."

"Two."

"Three."

Trinity cheered as loudly as anyone in the audience. The fact that the winner was pre-determined did nothing to dampen her enthusiasm. A pride she didn't understand considering the circumstances filled her chest at the knowledge that Blane would retain his title.

Blane turned to Jay and waved him over to the ring. The official watching him led him to the stairs and helped him through the ropes. Jay marched over to Blane, who handed him the championship belt. With Jay holding it high above his head, Blane picked him up, put him on his shoulder, and turned to face her. Balancing Jay with one hand, Blane pointed at her in the audience, then back at Jay

A smile that bright hadn't graced her son's face in a long time. It was enough to bring tears to her eyes, but she wouldn't give in to them. Jay had reached the age of easy embarrassment and having his mom crying about him on national television would most assuredly put her on the worst mom in the world list. Instead, she clapped and cheered until her voice went hoarse.

The referee who'd been in charge of Jay moved in front of Trinity on the other side of the barricade. He spoke, but with all the noise, it was impossible to hear him. Trinity leaned in close.

"What did you say?"

"I'm supposed to take you backstage now. I need you to meet me at the end of the barricade. I'll get you through security there."

The man pointed out exactly where Trinity was to go. She nodded her understanding before checking the area to make sure she had all her belongings. Working her way through the crowd, even though it was dispersing, was slow. More than once, other fans jostled her. The tension in her shoulders released as she reached the wall of muscle providing security for the event. The official must have told the guards to watch for her, because they waved her through without hesitation.

She looked for the telltale black and white of the referee's shirt and considered her options when she didn't see it. Approaching the trio of security men who'd let her through was a possibility, but none of them seemed like talkative, or even friendly, types. Taking the initiative and walking herself backstage was another option.

Would that be allowed? Following rules was important, especially when not doing so could result in public embarrassment. Knowing her luck, she would make her way behind the curtain only to have some over-zealous wrestler take her down quicker than a kick from Blane. And the debacle would end with security escorting her from the premises.

Trinity headed back to the rows of seating. Before she could reach the security guards, she heard her name. She turned and saw Pamela waving at her from the edge of the entrance stage. She met her halfway up the ramp.

"I'm so glad I caught you. Even with most of the fans leaving, I thought finding you would be a nightmare. Joe, the official who directed you this way, apologizes. He got pulled backstage before you made it over here."

"I think he was taking me to find Jay."

Pamela nodded. "And that's exactly what I'm going to do. Last I saw him, Blane was taking him back to his dressing room. But they may not have arrived there yet."

"Isn't it the room he took us to yesterday to check on his costume?"

"That's the one."

Trinity frowned. "Why wouldn't they be there yet? It wasn't far from the stage."

Pamela grinned, her perfectly filled brows raised high over her expertly highlighted eyes. "Have you met your son? Every time they passed a wrestler in the halls, Jay had to stop and talk to them. He's chatted up a storm from the moment he stepped behind the curtain."

"I am so sorry." She groaned. "I'd like to say he's not usually like this, but he's a motormouth on a normal day."

"Don't worry about it. The guys were amused, and the girls thought he was adorable. They were eating it up. But if his future as a Champ in Training doesn't work out, he might have a future in deep sea diving. He's got the lungs for it. I don't think he stopped once to take a breath."

Trinity laughed. "I've always thought he had a future as an auctioneer, but your idea has potential too. Jay loves to swim."

When they reached the end of the hall, Pamela knocked on the dressing room door. "Blane? Are you boys decent?"

"Door's open." His deep voice sounded from inside. "Come on in."

Trinity bit her lips to keep from laughing at the scene before her. Blane perched on a table with his foot propped on a chair, his arm resting across his thick thigh. As he'd done all evening, Jay recreated the pose, his little foot stretched as far as it could go to reach the chair from where he sat on the table's edge. His whole body wobbled as he tried to keep his balance with his arm resting across his bony leg.

"Hey, Mom. Me and Blane are just talkin' about our win tonight. Damon gave a good fight, but he didn't stand a chance against us. That lady tried to say he almost beat us, but he didn't. Did he Blane?" Offense clung to Jay's words.

What lady dissed their win in front of Jay? And how much of an earful did she get in return? Trinity looked from Blane to Pamela and back again.

Blane smiled and ruffled Jay's hair. "But what did I teach you about the interviewers?"

"They only want to get us riled up. It makes their story better." Jay emphasized the point with a curt nod.

Pamela touched her shoulder. "Don't worry. We will make you and Jay a copy of his whole night, including the interviews, to take home. It will be a souvenir to help him remember his time as the Champ in Training."

Jay beamed next to Blane.

"Thank you. He'll love it. But truth be told, I don't think there's a chance he will ever forget this trip. Now, however, I think it's time we head back to the hotel. It's past your bedtime."

"Mo-o-om! Do we have to?"

Before she could speak, Blane inserted himself in the conversation with a shake of his head. "I'm thinking your mom is right, Jay. We were pretty tough on our muscles tonight. We all need to head back to the hotel and get some rest so our bodies stay healthy. Pamela, I know it's not your job, but would you do me a favor and have them get the car ready since we'll all be riding back together?"

As Pamela left to do Blane's bidding, Trinity had to remind herself to keep her expression bland as Jay nodded his approval, his brows drawn down in the serious look he reserved for dire situations. Mom apparently held no sway over knowing what was best, but if Blane breathed it, so be it.

"Can Blane come with us?"

"Honey, you heard him. Blane said we're riding back to the hotel together."

"No. I mean, can Blane come with us and read my Bible story with me and say prayers with me? Can he, please?"

*Oh mercy!* What prompted that idea? Trinity knew it was innocent, but Jay had no concept of the reality that not everyone prayed or read Bible stories on a regular basis. She scrambled to come up with an answer to let Blane out of the potentially awkward situation.

"Sure, I can do that, if it's okay with your mom."

Her gaze flew to Blane's. She had to admit he appeared decidedly less disturbed by her son's comments than she was.

In fact, he seemed completely at ease with the request, watching her, waiting for a response to a question she knew for a fact he *was not* asked every day. Anything coming from a child probably fell on the unusual end of the spectrum for wrestlers. How many spent extended time with their youngest fans, much less chauffeured them around town?

"It's okay. Isn't it, Mom?"

She hoped her smile didn't look as unsure as she felt. Blane's subtle nod confirmed his offer.

"Mom? It's okay, right?"

"Sure. Blane is welcome to join us for stories and prayers."

Pamela's return drew everyone's attention. "Well, Champs, the car is ready. Let's get back to the hotel."

# 8

Blane sensed Trinity watching him from the doorway as he sat beside the bed where Jay was tucked in under the covers. He'd felt her silent presence through his retelling of David and Goliath, prayers from both him and Jay, and through the 'one more story, pleeeease' that Jay requested. Too bad the boy's fatigue got the better of him before Jesus called Lazarus from his tomb.

Tugging the covers a little higher on Jay's chest, he tucked them around the child before facing Trinity. The thoughtful expression on her face couldn't be described as either a smile or a frown. If only they were familiar enough with each other for him to understand what it meant. They weren't even close enough for him to ask outright.

When she turned from the doorway, Blane followed, stopping only long enough to partially close the bedroom door. Trinity seemed like the type of parent who would want her child to have that comforting sliver of light if he woke in the night, also a way to hear him if he got restless.

Trinity stared out the patio door when he entered the suite's living room area.

"I thought I might sit outside for a while." Her voice lacked any animation. "You're welcome to join me."

It couldn't be confused with a warm welcome, but maybe she was ready to talk about whatever was distracting her. He grabbed a couple bottles of water from the minifridge, knowing it was the company and not Trinity paying for the room, before following her out the door.

With legs pulled up and tucked in beside her, Trinity was already seated in her chair from the previous night. He handed her a bottle and claimed the only other chair. Twisting the cap off the water, he waited for her to speak. It wouldn't take long. She'd been preoccupied all evening.

Or he could be wrong. He'd drained his bottle of water, and she still hadn't spoken. She'd hardly moved, except to set her unopened bottle on the little table between the chairs. Blane couldn't say for sure if she saw the city laid out before them, but he doubted it, trapped as she seemed to be by her thoughts.

"Want to tell me what's on your mind?" She'd invited him to join her when she could have asked him to leave. He could take the chance of seeming rude and open the door to possible answers.

She looked at him as if he were a puzzle with too many pieces and no picture on the box. Maybe he'd have to be content with silence.

"You're different than I imagined you'd be."

Her voice didn't sound insulting, and he had no reason to believe she was saying it in a negative way. But, even if she meant it as a positive, it begged the question of what she'd previously thought of him. It left him with the impression that her views of him had been less than savory.

"I'm not sure what you mean."

"You're a wrestler."

Did he really have to comment on that one? Seemed obvious enough.

"I saw posters lining the hallways. A lot of them were you in the ring. And I saw you in the ring for myself tonight. You're frightening."

Blane frowned. "Frightening? Like I scared you?"

Her lips twisted to the side as she bit the inside of her cheek. She shook her head. "Not really, no. Maybe frightening is the wrong word. But you definitely looked, I don't know ... intimidating? Fierce and angry and ready to take out anyone who threatened your title."

"And you didn't expect that?"

"No. That's exactly how I imagined professional wrestlers."

"I'm not sure I follow."

"You're not like that at all. You're this huge guy, taller than the average tall guy, and you're bigger built than them too. And it's all muscle. And you've got a darker complexion with the nearly black hair and the whole beard and mustache."

She took a sip of water before continuing. "And really the only things on the lighter side are your eyes, which are this incredible bluish-green color that provides a striking contrast. I mean, they really grab your attention. Not that it's that hard to get with your height and build and everything else working along with them. You'd get anyone's attention."

Blane could tell the moment she realized she was side-tracked. Her own, almost gray-blue eyes were wide to begin with, but as she caught the direction of her thoughts, they became huge. Her cheeks immediately showed her embarrassment.

While part of him found the whole situation comical, especially the mortified look on her face that made her completely adorable, he knew what it was to find oneself in a socially awkward situation. He'd been humbled publicly, and it wasn't a good feeling. He had no desire to increase that feeling, no matter how innocently, in Trinity. Feigning ignorance of her declaration seemed the best way to free her to continue.

"I'm not like that, but everything about me is like that?"

Combing the waves of hair away from her face with both hands, Trinity released a deep, unsettled sigh. "I'm not explaining this well. Your look perfectly fits who you are on the posters and in the ring. They match your tough talk when you pick up the mic to challenge your opponent. But then, everything else is different. You see an upset little boy at an event, and you step in to make his day better."

She steepled her hands and rested them against her lips. "But you don't stop at the minimum. You go above and beyond to see that he has an amazing time, even knowing you're not that boy's favorite wrestler. And, after being with him all day long and having him right beside you in the ring, when you've worked hard and are tired, you still find it in yourself to honor his request to tell him bedtime stories and pray with him. Why?"

The answer she needed would clarify things for Trinity and give her insight into who he was as a man. Until that moment, he didn't realize how much he wanted that for her. "Because who I am in the ring is just that, who I am in the ring. It's a persona, a character like an actor in a television show. The reason I reached out to you guys is because I saw a hurting little boy, and I knew, or at least I hoped, I could help take away some of that disappointment.

Blane ran his hand over his mustache and down his beard as he considered his next words. "As professional wrestlers in the public eye, we have the ability to do some good for some people. We're where we're at because of the fans. It gets to me when we take the fans' appreciation for granted, when all they want is a small acknowledgement of their existence and we blow them off because we think we have something better to do. It's especially not right when it's a child."

"Like at breakfast this morning? You went after Maverick. Was that the reason?"

He shrugged. "Partly. Maverick's young and impulsive. He's holding onto the party boy image the company used to love showing off. The company has since learned that bad behavior is one thing when it's part of the show. Real life bad behavior becomes a liability for all of us."

"I can see why it would be," she agreed.

"It's a lesson Maverick has yet to learn. I've been there. I didn't see how others were trying to help me grow beyond the attitude, but I have hope that Maverick will learn the lesson a little easier than I did. I'm just glad Jay doesn't seem any worse for wear after the way Maverick treated him."

As Trinity reached across the space between them and laid her hand on top of his, warmth traveled from his fingertips up his arm. Her hand against his looked small and delicate releasing an urge in him to care for and protect her. The sweet smile on her face filled her eyes with its light.

"Jay couldn't have asked for a better experience. I can assure you, he's not missing Maverick at all. And if everything else hadn't done it, coming here tonight sealed it. I really hope you didn't feel like you had to come, because everything you've done for us has been more than enough."

Why did explaining his reasoning suddenly make him nervous? He was proud of his faith, and from everything he'd seen, Trinity was raising her son with a knowledge of God. It shouldn't pose a problem, but experience told him it still could. Others had questioned the genuineness of his faith in the past. Though he didn't fully understand why, the idea Trinity might be one of those people caused his heart to beat a little faster. Still, he had to be true to himself.

He stood, moving to the balcony railing. It was easier to order his thoughts without taking the chance of seeing doubt in her eyes. "I didn't feel like I had to come. I wanted to. I want to take every opportunity I'm presented with to tell others about my faith and to encourage others in their faith. This was one small way I could do that for Jay, and I've learned how important it is for boys to have men model faith for them."

Her chair scraped against the concrete as she stood. Warmth moved down his arm as she laid a hand on his shoulder, and he turned at her gentle nudge to do so. Her eyes glistened with unshed tears. His relief at her acceptance turned to shock as her arms came around him.

"Thank you. Thank you for sharing your faith with me and for caring about one little disappointed boy in the crowd."

Hers was a friendly embrace of gratitude, not a desperate embrace of desire. He knew that and responded in kind wrapping his arms loosely around her shoulders. Still, her head rested right in the center of his chest, and he couldn't deny the urge to tighten his arms around her.

She fit perfectly against him, and he briefly entertained the thought that she was where she belonged. Dipping his head slightly, he could breathe in the citrusy scent of her shampoo. The silky strands trapped under his hands on her shoulders created an overwhelming want to lower his head onto hers and allow the softness to rest against his cheek.

Instead, he stepped out of the hug, crossing his arms across his chest.

"I'm glad God gave me the opportunity to help out." He

cleared his throat and grasped for a new topic to steer him away from thoughts of pulling her back into his arms. "What are your plans for the rest of your time in Tennessee? Going to see what all Nashville has to enjoy?"

She took the space he offered and returned to her chair. "We haven't enjoyed time away since before Tuck got sick. I planned on spending the next five days just being in the area with Jay, letting him be a carefree kid for a while before going home."

"What does that look like, exactly?"

"Tomorrow, I'd like to find a church to visit. I hate to miss services, even if we are away from home. After that, I'll need to scout out a new place for us to stay. Tonight's our last night on the company's dime, and I definitely don't have the funds to continue staying here."

An idea popped into his head, but there were details to work out. He'd make a couple calls first thing in the morning, and hopefully, he would have a fix for her accommodations before breakfast. As for church, that he could take care of immediately.

"I'd be honored if you and Jay would join me for church tomorrow. I live in Mountain Springs, about an hour and a half from here. It's close enough for work, but a little more in the rolling hills and away from the big city. It's still a good-sized church, but nowhere near the mega-churches here in Nashville."

"I don't know. I'm not sure Jay can handle getting up early enough to attend a service over an hour away."

"It would depend on how late he usually sleeps in, but we wouldn't have to leave until about eight fifteen. Small groups meet early, but the main service doesn't start until ten. And while I'd usually go for both if I was home, I'm used to only going for the worship service and preaching when I stay in Nashville on a Saturday night."

"Are you sure we wouldn't be any trouble?"

"I promise you, it's no trouble. And that way you'll at least know one person when you walk through the doors. I'll meet you in the lobby with coffee and doughnuts tomorrow morning at eight fifteen. You and Jay can eat while I drive. Sound okay?"

Trinity covered her mouth as a huge yawn escaped. "I'm so sorry. I promise you're not boring me. Tomorrow sounds great. I'll have us downstairs and ready to check out a few minutes early so I can stow our stuff in our car while we're gone. I'd hate to miss checkout and end up owing another night."

A look at his watch confirmed it wasn't terribly late for him, but for a single mom, eleven might be a bit later than she usually stayed up. He headed toward the door. Trinity followed.

"Great. I'll be ready. But for now, I should let you get some sleep. Good night."

She held the door open as he stepped into the hallway. "Night. And, Blane?"

"Yeah?"

"Thanks again, for everything."

He raised a hand to wave off her thanks before thinking better of it. He let his hand drop as he smiled at her. "You're welcome." He was still smiling when he heard the door close behind him and the locks slide into place.

———

Trinity swept her hand across the nightstand until she hit her phone. She flipped it face up and squinted as the display lit up. One. It was nearly one o'clock in the morning, and she was still tossing and turning in a bed so luxurious, she should have fallen asleep the second she crawled under the covers.

When Blane left, she'd been exhausted but decided to take the time to pack their suitcases. It made more sense than rushing around the next morning. Luckily, Jay was a heavy sleeper and hadn't been disturbed when scant light from the hallway made shuffling around a necessity in accomplishing the task. When she laid down in the bed next to his, it was already an hour and a half later than she usually sought sleep.

But with sleep eluding her, Trinity unplugged her cell phone from the charger and padded into the living area. Trying to distract herself with games would only make matters worse. Social media wasn't much better, but that's where she found herself, scrolling through pointless memes and endless rants, trying to bore her brain into a fog.

Opening the message portion to see if there were any clients she needed to respond to, Trinity noticed the green dot next to Autumn's name. Not so unusual. Autumn waitressed until close at a restaurant. On weekends that meant late nights and the need to unwind before seeking her bed when she got home.

Still up?

Trinity hit send on the message.
The ding came through in seconds.

Yes. But I'm surprised you are.

Can I call?

Sure.

Trinity punched in the number. Only half a ring sounded before Autumn answered.

"What are you doing up?" Autumn questioned.

"I need your help," Trinity began without preamble. "I know it's late, but my mind is racing, and I know I'll only be able to sleep if I can talk this out with someone."

"Give me a minute." Her groggy voice almost covered the rustle of sheets. A yawn mixed with her footsteps as she walked into another room. "Is this a glass of water to wake me up type conversation? Or do I need something stronger?"

Trinity considered the options. "Stronger. Definitely, stronger."

The clink of glass as a cup was removed from a cabinet and the grind of an ice maker filled the silence. The pop of a soda can tab, followed by the sound of liquid filling a cup, came right before Autumn's sigh.

"There. That's better," she announced. "Now, what's going on?"

"It's Blane."

"Did he do something? Do you need help?" All fatigue dropped from her friend's voice as she slipped into protective mode.

Trinity ran a hand through her hair. "No. It's nothing like that. It's just."

"Just what?"

"He's ... I don't know how to explain it." Trinity rubbed the back of her neck as she sought the right words. "In the ring, Blane is this incredibly intimidating guy. He's huge, and he gets this fierce look. It's a look I wouldn't want directed at me."

"So, now that you've seen him in action, he scares you a bit?"

"That's just it. In the ring, he's completely daunting, but he's not like that at all. He's been amazing for Jay. Really gone above and beyond what the company asked. And not just for Jay."

"This guy sounds great. Treating you and Jay like the incredible people you are. Enjoy it. You and Jay deserve a little bit of spoiling."

Trinity sighed. "He's generous and kind to a fault. Jay roped him into coming back to our room with us to tuck him in. Not even a hesitation, Autumn. And ..." Trinity cleared her throat and started again. "And you should have seen him reading a Bible story to Jay. Praying with him. In one evening, Blane showed Jay what it means to be a man of faith. To a little boy he barely knows and who no longer has a daddy to do it for him. It fills my heart with gratitude."

"And maybe your heart's not only being filled up?" Autumn questioned. "Maybe you're losing it a little too?"

A groan escaped as Trinity considered the appreciation that prompted her spontaneous hug. Was Autumn right? Was there more to it than a platonic hug born of being grateful?

"What does that groan mean?" Autumn's focus lasered in on Trinity's internal struggle.

Holding back would serve no purpose. Autumn could tell when she was being less than truthful. But did she have to tell her about the confusion-inducing hug? No. She could work around that point.

"I hugged him," she blurted out.

*Great.* Her tired mind worked against her common sense.

"And?"

She should clam up just out of spite for the expectation she heard in Autumn's voice. A best friend didn't need to know everything. Some things were private.

"And it was nothing like I expected." Trinity considered his build. With the muscles on top of well-defined muscles she'd seen in the wrestling ring, she would've imagined hugging Blane would be like holding onto a brick wall, cold and hard. But, of course, her embrace hadn't been premeditated. It left her surprised.

Oh, he had muscles. That much couldn't be denied. She felt them where her cheek rested on his chest. His back muscles stretched under her fingers as he put his arms around her. But his strength didn't translate into taut, hard muscles.

"It felt safe and warm." She could at least acknowledge that detail if nothing else. The desire to stand in his embrace listening to his heartbeat would remain her secret. It didn't matter anyway.

"But I made him uncomfortable," Trinity admitted quietly. "He stepped away almost as soon as the hug started."

"Maybe that's not what happened," Autumn suggested. "It could be something else entirely."

"No," Trinity said shaking her head. "He did the right thing. I can't fault him for that or wish it was different. Blane's been a gentleman this entire time, and I let my tendency to be physically demonstrative and impulsive make things awkward."

When Tuck had been there, his level-headed outlook on life reined in that side of her. She thought his influence had tamed it for life. What a way to find out she'd been wrong!

"He probably wonders what kind of clingy, emotional freak he's gotten mixed up with."

She could hear Autumn's nails click against a hard surface. "I don't believe that for a minute. And, I don't think you do either."

"Maybe you're right," Trinity placated her. There was zero chance he wasn't doing exactly that. More than likely, he was sequestered in his room at that very moment trying to figure out how to put distance between himself and the cute little boy with the needy mother.

Sequestered? Did she really think the word sequestered at one in the morning? She was exhausted. Too exhausted for ten-dollar words or more thoughts about Blane and his never-ending supply of muscles. Which she shouldn't be thinking about whether it was one in the morning or one in the afternoon. He was proving himself a good, temporary friend. A friend that would be gone after tomorrow's, no today's, church service.

"Did I lose you?" Autumn questioned.

"No," Trinity answered. "I'm still here."

And still thinking about the only man who'd made her consider how good it might be to move beyond the solitude she'd become comfortable with since Tuck died. He'd been her first love, and she assumed after he was gone, he would be her only love. How could a couple days with a man who was going to walk right back out of her life open her up to the possibility there could be more?

But none of that mattered. She was supposed to be going to sleep. It was time for tough love.

"I should try to get some sleep though." A yawn punctuated her words. "We're supposed to go to church with Blane tomorrow. And I know Jay won't let me sleep in. Thanks for the pep talk. You get some sleep too."

"Anytime. Good night, and sweet dreams filled with a certain hunky wrestler." Autumn's giggle continued until Trinity hit end.

Nope. There wasn't a chance Trinity would take that last piece of advice. Blane was not thinking about her or their hug. And neither would she.

He was, like any sane person, sleeping. Blane was taking them to church, but he was not a permanent fixture in her life. He would be gone tomorrow, and it would be her and Jay again. Besides, it was too soon. Tuck had only been gone for a year and a half. What would everyone think?

Talking was good. It would allow her some control over her thoughts so she could sleep. She crawled into bed and under the covers. Breathe in. Breathe out. Breath in. Breathe out. Rhythmic. Like a heartbeat. Like Blane's heartbeat ...

# 9

"Where is he, Mom? Where's Blane. You said he'd be here, but I don't see him anywhere. Do you think he forgot us?"

The slam of the car trunk banging shut made Trinity wince. She hadn't intended to close it so forcefully. Shutting her eyes, she sucked in a deep breath. Calm. Smile. And go.

She looked into her son's sweet face, lit up in anticipation of another day with Blane. "I'm sure he didn't forget us, sweetie. We're a little early, and he said he would meet us in the lobby. Why don't we head that way now and see if he's waiting for us?"

With his hand tucked into her own, they crossed the parking lot and entered the lobby. As soon as he caught sight of Blane across the room, he tugged free and took off before Trinity could recapture his hand.

"Blane! Blane!"

It wasn't quite a yell, but it most certainly was not an indoor voice, especially for a hotel as nice as this one. Trinity gritted her teeth and forced a steady pace to join them.

"And then Mom said ..."

"Jeremiah Tucker Knight, would you like to tell me why I'm upset right now?"

His chagrinned face and puppy dog eyes wouldn't influence her. Her son was a smart boy and capable, but he had a streak of impulsiveness that reminded her too much of herself at his age. Training him to control it now was preferred to helping him out of the messes it could create later. For the millionth time in his short lifetime, she prayed that some of his father's steady, thoughtful temperament was hiding somewhere in his DNA.

Hoping to find an ally, Jay looked up at Blane. Trinity kept her gaze on her son. From the corner of her eye, she could see Blane watching the action without speaking. Even his expression remained noncommittal. Wise man.

A slight shake of his head. "Sorry, buddy, but this isn't something you tag team. You made a choice to act a certain way, and all our actions have consequences. Your job now is to listen to what your mom has to say and learn from it for the future. It's tough, but every man must do it."

Jay's face puckered in thought. His solemn nod at Blane's words took some of the heat from Trinity's displeasure. She forced herself to remain open, almost neutral as Jay turned back to her.

"So? Do you know why I'm upset, or do I need to tell you?"

He sucked in a deep breath and squared his shoulders. "I ran away from you. And I used my outdoor voice inside."

Her smile was gentle. "Yes. And I'm glad you recognize that. Running in a busy hotel lobby could hurt someone, and it's not polite to be overly loud indoors. It interrupts people's conversations."

"I'm sorry, Mom."

"I know you are. And because I also know you didn't mean

to disobey and are super excited about seeing Blane again, you won't have any consequences this time. But remember this for next time, okay?"

"Okay."

She took his hand and looked to Blane. "I think we're ready to head out now, if you are."

———

A powdered sugar-framed smile from back seat's occupant greeted Blane as he looked in the rearview mirror. Maybe the bag of mini doughnuts hadn't been his best idea. Jay's red polo shirt was in danger of becoming pink from the sweet dust sprinkled all over it. Next time, he would think it through a little better.

*Next time?* There wouldn't be a next time. An uncomfortable weight settled in Blane's chest. Trinity and Jay would go home in a few days. For one who travelled as much as he did, a four-hour drive should be an easy trip. So why did it feel like they might as well be across the country? And when did keeping them close start to matter?

"I think I'm going to have to hose him off when we get to the church." Trinity's voice was light, and Blane knew without looking there would be a smile to go along with her observation.

"Yeah, I'm sorry about that. Seems I didn't think through my choice of breakfast foods."

Warmth spread through his forearm under her touch. He focused on the road and her words.

"Rookie mistake, but I won't hold it against you. I'm pretty sure if I were thrown into your world, I wouldn't make it down the ramp and to the ring without mishap."

No imagination was creative enough to conjure an image of

Trinity active in the wrestling world–his world. She definitely didn't fit inside the ring, but was there a place for her in the periphery? If not, where did that leave them? He shook his head trying to dislodge his wayward thoughts. Leave them? There was no *them* to leave.

"Are you okay?"

He faced her with a brief smile before returning his attention to the road. "Yeah. Just trying to picture you in the squared circle."

"The what?"

"The squared circle. The wrestling ring. You really aren't a fan, are you?"

"Sorry," Trinity laughed. "No. I left all that to Tucker and Jay. I guess that means I fail the test, and I'm not fit for the, uh, squared circle."

Blane grinned at her attempt to use the unfamiliar phrase. "I'm not sure you're main roster material."

"You sure?"

"Yeah. There's no way you'd land on the main roster. Not even sure you'd make it to the independent circuit, and some of those people take anyone."

Trying to ignore the fact that he'd taken her original question in a safer direction, Blane laughed at his meager joke. He could answer without hesitation when it came to his opinion of her in-ring ability. But she'd asked him if he was okay. Considering the path his thoughts tried to go down, that was a completely different question. Would she broach the bigger subject or let it go?

He could feel her eyes on him. The seconds passed like days. He refused to look anywhere but the road and forced a smile.

"You're absolutely right. I barely belong in the audience, much less the ring."

Turning toward her, he raised an eyebrow. "Really? I thought you looked pretty good out in the audience, cheering right alongside the best of them."

Rose filled her cheeks. Maybe there was hope she could belong in his world after all.

She waved a hand through the air and rolled her eyes. "I was cheering for my son and his partner. A mother's love will do that to a person."

Never mind.

"Mom? Are we almost to Blane's church?"

She glanced at her watch and shrugged behind her seatbelt. "I'm not really sure."

"It'll be about five minutes."

"You heard Blane. We'll be there in just a few minutes. Are you finished with your doughnuts?"

"Yep. I ate the whole thing and my chocolate milk."

She fished a package of wet wipes out of her purse and handed one back to Jay. "Brush yourself off as best you can, and then wipe your mouth and hands. But be careful to only brush the crumbs onto the towel under you and not on Blane's car seat."

Blane had told her the towel was not necessary when Jay climbed into the car with his bag of doughnuts. Another rookie mistake. He and the upholstery owed her a thank-you for her foresight.

"I think you'll really like my church. They have a special class time for kids your age, and they always seem to have a blast."

"Can I go to the kids' church, Mom? Blane says it's going to be fun. You wouldn't want me to miss the fun stuff, would you? So, can I go? Pleeeaaase."

———

93

Trinity swallowed the tightness in her throat. Maybe doughnuts hadn't been a great breakfast idea. Easy? Yes. But their sweetness soured when an unexpected case of nerves, that coincided with pulling into the church parking lot, hit her hard. If only she could muster up some of Jay's enthusiasm.

No, that wasn't right. She was excited to worship with Blane at his home church. Maybe it was Jay's complete lack of concern over having to make a good impression that she wished she could commandeer for herself.

With Jay successfully dropped off in the children's church rooms and Blane's barely-there touch right above the small of her back, propelling her in the direction of the sanctuary, she didn't have time to analyze the missing element that would allow her to navigate this unknown without the added embarrassment of losing her breakfast on some unlucky parishioner.

"Blane! Hey, Blane! Where've you been?"

The enthusiastic voice echoing through the large entryway caught Trinity's attention. She turned to find a gangly teen boy rushing down the hall toward them with a trio of boys about his age following closely behind. They stopped in front of Blane, each sporting an expectant look. It must be hard to worship freely in a congregation filled with adoring teenage fans.

Blane looked anything but put out. In fact, his stance was as loose and relaxed as the boys. And, though she couldn't quite name the difference, his smile was night-and-day different from the ones he showered on the fans at the photo op and outside the event when he signed autographs. It wasn't that one was fake and the other real. Blane seemed to genuinely enjoy interacting with his fans. Maybe this one seemed more personal. Yeah, that was a good way to describe it.

"Where are your manners, Troy?" His tone was joking, and the boy took it in stride. "Can't you see I have a guest with me today?"

Four pairs of eyes swung her direction. The one christened Troy held out his hand. "Hi. I'm Troy. Welcome to Four Pines Church. So, are you Blane's date or something?"

Beneath his beard, Trinity could see the muscles in Blane's cheek tighten, but at least he didn't groan. Leave it to teens to make things awkward.

Heat crept up Trinity's neck, even as she chuckled at Troy's forwardness. "No. We're just friends." Were they friends? Maybe she should amend that. "My son was the one chosen to go in the ring with him last night as the Champ in Training."

Troy shifted his focus to Blane. "You had a match last night?"

Images of bouncers she'd seen in television and movies flashed through her mind as Blane crossed his arms in front of his chest. One brow raised as he shook his head.

"Of course, I had a match last night. I have a match nearly every Saturday night. Thanks for caring."

"You're not Blane's fans?" Trinity's confusion got the better of her as she blurted out her question in the middle of their conversation.

Blane laughed. "These guys? No way. I'm trying to make fans out of them, but they'd rather watch baseball and have me school them in video games."

Troy rolled his eyes. "Yeah, right. You can school us in video games like I can be the next UWO champion."

"Fine. You humor me when playing video games and refuse to trounce me completely. But you guys wanted something, what was it?"

Troy had an expectant, almost pleading look, that was

mirrored on the other boys' faces even though they seemed content to let him be their spokesperson.

"My mom said you might not be going on the camping trip next weekend. She's wrong, isn't she? You are going, aren't you?"

"I wasn't sure last time I spoke with your mom, but yes, I've been cleared to have the weekend off. I may be a little late if I can't tape my promos ahead of time, but I'll be there."

Energy buzzed through the group, but the boys kept it contained to approving nods and a quick, "That's cool."

Trinity didn't have much experience with teenage boys, but it didn't take a genius to know they'd be as offended as Jay if she let on that their attempts at reining in their excitement was cute. She opened her purse and rifled through it with her head down.

"We should get in there. Service is starting soon. We'll see you at the campout."

Blane cleared his throat.

"It was nice meeting you. I hope you enjoy the service."

Trinity looked up from her purse. "Thank you. It was good meeting you too."

The trio waited only for Troy's first move before following him down the hall and into the sanctuary. Blane watched them go.

"I would've sworn they were fans when they first walked up as excited as they were to see you."

Blane smiled down at her. "Nope. Just some boys that need a little attention from believing men in their lives."

"And you give them that attention?"

"It's a ministry the pastor and I started together. We have several boys with absent fathers and several young fathers with no idea how to grow their boys into godly young men. We try to fill in the gaps, giving both groups what they need with special events, game nights, camping trips, and things like that. It gives the boys skills they can use later and a faith foundation. It also gives the ones without fathers in the picture someone they can come to for advice and just to make memories with."

"That's wonderful. The way you pour yourself into those who need it. Do the fathers ever get resentful taking advice from someone who isn't a dad?"

"Since I don't have kids, I can't really say. I let the pastor head up that part. But I can be an uncle or big brother to kids like Troy who don't have a dad in the picture at all. The ministry allows the teens and the fathers to make great memories, and it supports the dads in their parenting. Everyone wins."

Blane's love for the ministry and the boys in it was obvious in his tone. If Trinity hadn't already been half-infatuated with the man, this new revelation would have pushed her past the line. As it was, her respect for him and the way he lived out his faith seemed to grow with each new experience with him.

"You're a pretty amazing guy, Blane Sterling. Has anyone outside the wrestling ring ever told you that?"

A quick shrug preceded Blane's uncomfortable glance toward the sanctuary. "We better go find our seats. Service is about to start."

Trinity could only shake her head at his embarrassment as she followed him through the doors and down the aisle to a pair of empty seats.

# 10

Blane fought the urge to fidget like a child during the opening announcements. Trinity's compliment buoyed his mood. Her words felt even better than retaining his belt had the previous night. Attention in the ring was normal. Trinity's praise tied his insides in knots. He couldn't deny the time he spent with her left him wanting more. It would be great if her assessment of him meant he had a chance with her.

But a compliment could be a compliment and nothing more. Would he want to lose their growing friendship to pursue the unsure path to a relationship? And did she even consider him a friend? She seemed to distance herself from the word when speaking with Troy. Maybe all their time together was simply a mom doing what it took to give her son a memorable time. It didn't feel that way, but could he trust his feelings?

A sense of being watched came over him. Blane glanced across the aisle to where his parents sat. If she was chagrined at being caught watching him, his mother's face didn't show it. The time spent with Troy and the guys had kept him and

Trinity out of the sanctuary until the announcements started. While he'd called his parents to explain the situation before he left the hotel, he hadn't had the opportunity to formally introduce them to Trinity before service.

That was a mistake. Curiosity may have killed the cat, but it was a main source of sustenance with his mother, at least where he was concerned. He could almost see the direction of her thoughts as she glanced past him to Trinity before returning to him with the raise of her eyebrows, a tiny, pursed smile, and a lift of her shoulders. Like a child awaiting a surprise.

Oh, this could be bad. He should have made the time for introductions before she had an entire service to let the wheels in her mind run in the wrong direction. But there was nothing he could do about it now. Anyway, that wasn't his purpose in attending services. He turned his attention back to the stage where the praise team had taken their positions and prepared his heart and mind to leave everything else behind and simply focus on worshiping God.

———

Trinity, with Jay's hand safely tucked in hers, made her way through the crowd of parishioners eager to get to their Sunday dinners. Finding Blane in the crowd was easy considering he was at least a few inches taller than most of the men. His back was to her as she stepped away from the crowd to meet him, but he turned immediately when the couple he was speaking with nodded in her direction.

"Blane, you'll never guess what we did at kids' church. It was so much fun. They let me tell everybody about me. And I told them how I got to be your partner and be in the ring with you and help you keep your title. And all the girls thought it was silly, but they don't really count because girls are the silly ones."

The dramatic eye roll and tilt of his head accompanying his announcement brought a chuckle from her and Blane. Both tried to hide it. Jay was so excited.

"But the boys," he continued. "The boys all asked me questions and stuff until the teacher finally made us sit down and have our Bible lesson. But as soon as it was over, we got to play, and they all wanted to play with me. Then I got to tell them everything."

"Sounds like you made some friends. That's great, buddy." Blane ruffled Jay's hair.

The older woman he'd been speaking with when Trinity and Jay walked up placed a hand on Blane's arm. "Aren't you going to introduce us to your partner, Blane?" Eyes too similar to Blane's to allow for her to be a non-relation took in Trinity before she added with a sweet smile, "And the woman, I assume, is his mother?"

"Mom, Dad, this is Jay Knight, my partner from last night's match. And, yes, this is his mother, Trinity. Trinity and Jay, these are my parents, Gordon and Aileen Sterling."

Trinity extended her hand to Blane's mother before also shaking his father's hand. "Mr. and Mrs. Sterling, I'm so pleased to meet you. I have no doubt you know this already, but you've raised a talented and thoughtful son. He's been wonderful to my son and me, and we can't tell you how much that means to us."

Motherly pride lit up Mrs. Sterling's face. "Please, dear, it's Gordon and Aileen."

Gordon slapped a hand across his son's shoulder. "Yes. We don't stand on formality around here, especially when our son brings home a lovely woman for the first time in ages."

The urge to gape like a fish was overwhelming. Surely he

didn't mean? But there was nothing else he could mean. What if Blane assumed she thought what his father obviously believed true? Oh, this wasn't good.

"We're not ... He's not ... We're friends. That's it. I don't have designs on your son or anything. I mean, not that Blane isn't wonderful. Any woman would be blessed to have him in her life. He's a man whose faith seems to encompass everything he does, who he is, really. And he's a good-looking guy and all, but we're not together."

A tug on her hand reminded Trinity that little ears were listening to every word being said. "But we are together. We came here together. And last night, we were together at wrestling and in our room too."

Could this conversation get any more embarrassing? Jay just announced to Blane's parents, in a church no less, that they were together in their hotel room. And she couldn't brush off his concern. It was her own doing getting into this conversation while he was present.

She sucked in a deep breath and smiled down at him. "Yes, sweetheart. You're right. We are together right now, and Blane did come read you a bedtime story last night. I'm sorry if what I said confused you."

She couldn't look at the trio standing around them. She needed a moment to compose herself. "How about you and I head to the restrooms before we leave."

Without waiting for a response, she allowed her gaze to flit toward Blane and his parents without lingering on one long enough to see them. "If you'll excuse us for a second."

———

Blane kept his focus trained on the short hall Trinity had fled down. He wanted to chase after her, assure her. Of what, he wasn't sure. That it wasn't like what his father implied? It wasn't, but that didn't mean a small part of him wouldn't welcome it. More than a small part, if he was honest with himself.

The innocent comments from Jay thoroughly embarrassed her. They didn't have to be lifelong friends for him to see that. Coupled with his dad's comments, horrified might be closer to the truth. It had only taken his father's insinuation to bring fire to his own face. But was it more than an uncomfortable misunderstanding that heightened her own embarrassment?

"I'm sorry, son. I didn't mean to cause her discomfort. I just assumed when you called this morning and explained what you wanted, Trinity was becoming more than a work project or even a friend. What can I do to fix this?"

Blane shrugged and shook his head. "I wish I could tell you. We've gotten to know each other quite a bit over the last few days, but I have no idea how to make this better."

He was convinced his mother perceived more than she saw.

"You're not together, but you're interested. Am I right?" Her words confirmed his suspicions.

Licking his lips, he considered how to phrase his answer. He didn't want to lead his parents to believe something that wasn't true, but he wasn't even sure in himself what truth was in this situation. Maybe that's where he should start.

"I don't know, Mom. I wish I did. Trinity is a beautiful, strong, interesting woman. Yes. Yes, I'd be crazy if I wasn't interested in her. But we're friends, and even that hasn't been solidified, not really. She and Jay have been through a lot. They've lost a lot in the last couple of years. I'm not sure she's ready to try again."

He paused. How far should he venture into the topic? "Even if she is, there's Jay to think about. She's not going to let just anyone in her life, not with Jay in the mix. She won't risk him getting hurt, not even for the chance at a relationship. It's going to take a special kind of man to overcome all that."

His mom's hand was soft against his cheek. "Good thing, you're a special kind of man then. Let me go fix this." She turned to his father. "Gordon, you go get the car pulled around. I'll only be a minute."

# 11

Blane watched Trinity's eyes light up as she laughed beside him at his parents' kitchen table. He owed his mom for working her magic in the situation. Not only had Trinity and Jay re-emerged from the restroom in record time, she'd agreed to join him for lunch at his parents' house. Now, she sat beside him laughing at stories from his childhood.

"No one told me I'd need a rule about not dragging the mattresses from the beds into the backyard so he could jump off the garage roof," his dad relayed the latest story. "But at least that time, one of his friends wasn't waiting below to take the brunt of the fall."

"Was that a regular occurrence?" Trinity wiped a joy-filled tear from her eye. "Using his friends as crash pads, I mean."

His mom and dad rolled their eyes in tandem.

"If only that was the worst of it." His mother laid a hand on Trinity's arm. "You know you have a wrestler in the making when your backyard becomes a makeshift ring for all the neighborhood kids. It was never a shock that the kids all congregated here after school and on the weekends. What was surprising was that their parents continued letting them come after they started returning home covered in bumps and bruises."

Jay's eyes grew large as he looked at Blane from where he sat across the table. "You had a wrestling ring in your backyard?"

"Not a ring like the one we wrestled in last night. This was made out of mattresses after I convinced my mom not to throw out our old ones when we bought new."

"Can we get new mattresses at home too, Mom? You won't even have to throw away the old ones. I can put them in the yard. You don't even have to help. I can do it. I'm strong enough."

"And what would you do with those mattresses in the back yard?" Trinity asked playing innocent. "You wouldn't be thinking of making your own wrestling ring, would you?"

Eyes wide, Jay's palms landed against the table on either side of his plate. "It'll be great, Mom. You'll see. David and Spencer can come over. Oh, and Tim. Then we can do tag teams. I bet me and Spencer could beat David and Tim, no problem. And I can be safe. Blane taught me everything. You'll see, Mom. We should really do it."

Blane gave Trinity a sheepish smile as she shot him a look that declared him the mastermind behind her son's plan. He could stay in hot water, or he could rectify the situation. While seeing how she would dismantle Jay's idea could be interesting, he still needed to stay on her good side to enact the second half of his plan. Lunch was only the start.

"Mattress rings can be a lot of fun." Blane saw Trinity's eyes narrow. Maybe it wasn't the best thought to lead off with. "But they need a lot of care to keep them in good condition. It's not just about getting them outside. You have to have a place to store them out of the weather when you're not using them."

"I could do that. I could. Really."

"And you have to move them in and out of that spot every time you use them," Blane continued. "My mom wouldn't even think of letting me have a mattress ring when I was your age. I had to wait until I was at least ten."

Wide green puppy dog eyes only enhanced Jay's frown. He looked more heartbroken than he had when he realized he'd missed Maverick at the meet and greet event. Without thinking, he responded to the disappointment.

"Hey, it's fine though. You'll be there soon enough. And until then, well, I've got to train with my partner sometimes, right? You and me, every chance we get."

Though Jay beamed, Trinity stiffened beside him. Maybe he hadn't thought through the offer, but he would figure it out. Maybe he could visit on weekends off. Or Trinity and Jay could possibly come back for a visit every now and then. Whatever happened, Blane knew he didn't want them to finish this weekend and walk out of his life for good. Now if he could get Trinity on board with that plan, he'd be set.

Two hours later, the excitement of the weekend caught up with Jay. He fell asleep on the sofa while watching a movie, and Blane saw his chance. "Want to take a walk outside with me?"

Trinity's smile was tight, forced. "I'd better stay inside in case Jay wakes up."

"Gordon and I will watch him. You two run along and enjoy the fresh air."

*Bless you, Mom.* "What do you say?"

"Sure."

Too bad she didn't look or sound convinced. Blane would

take what he could get. Together they made their way outside. He was content with the silence only until the front door had shut behind them.

"Do you want to tell me what's bothering you?"

"Do you really not know?"

He licked his lips. "I'm guessing it has to do with telling Jay he needs to get a bit older to have a mattress ring and balancing that disappointing news with the reminder we're partners."

She huffed as her balled fists found her waist. "You didn't simply remind him that you're partners. You pretty much promised Jay you'd get together to practice. You can't tell a kid his age things like that. Empty promises only lead to more hurt than any disappointment from not getting to have a mattress ring. What am I supposed to do when he asks when his partner is coming to train?"

Palms up, he flung his arms out to his sides. "You call me. We work out a time to get together. It may not be every other weekend, but I'll find a way. Do you think I'd make empty promises to Jay after all he's been through, or to any child for that matter? Is that who you think I am?"

Her shoulders drooped as she looked at the ground between their feet. Her voice was quiet. "I just don't want Jay to get hurt. I don't think I could handle that coming from you."

Nearly toe to toe with her, he drew closer. She refused to look up. Blane tucked his fingers under her chin and gently applied pressure, lifting her face. Tears brimmed in her blue eyes.

"I'd never hurt Jay."

A noncommittal nod. He dropped his head so close to hers, their foreheads almost touched. He waited until she looked him in the eyes.

"And I'd never hurt you. You know that, right?"

His free hand lifted to wipe a stray tear from her cheek. "It's not about this weekend for me. I want you and Jay to stay in my life. I don't want to lose our friendship after you go home. It's crazy, but after only a few days, I feel closer to you than I have to anyone for a long time. And I think you've felt it too. Am I wrong?"

A slight shake of her head. Good they were on the same page. When she tucked her bottom lip between her teeth, Blane's attention dropped there. He hadn't realized how close they were standing or how easy it would be to draw her the rest of the way into his arms and kiss her doubts away.

But friends don't do that. Friends offer reassuring smiles. Hopefully, his was. He forced his gaze from the temptation of her lips. Big mistake. He could easily lose himself in her eyes. Where were these thoughts coming from?

Their relationship was firmly planted in the friend zone. She'd given him no indication she wanted anything more. Taking her into his arms, he forced himself to bypass the romantic kiss idea in favor of resting his cheek against the silk of her hair. A guilty pleasure for sure, but it didn't entice him into thoughts of the more romantic gestures he'd previously entertained.

A gentle cough cleared the gravel from his throat. "Good. We understand each other. Like it or not, you and Jay are stuck with me for the foreseeable future."

Her deep intake of breath pressed her further into his chest before she stepped away from his hold. His arms had never been so empty. The urge to draw her back in was strong, but he gave her space. She looked back at his parents' house and changed the subject.

"I think I should probably get Jay. We've got a little bit of a drive to get back to the car, and I still have to find a place to stay."

"About that. What would you think of staying here for the rest of your stay?"

She frowned. "Here? With your parents?"

"Here." He pointed to the garage next to the house. "In the apartment above the garage. It's fully functioning with a kitchenette and a bathroom. I used it before I had my own place and when I needed the accountability to stay on the straight and narrow while still living as an adult."

Her head tilted to one side, draping her strawberry blonde waves over her shoulder. She didn't ask, but he saw the question clearly.

"I told you I understand Maverick and others like him. It's not something I'm proud of, but I let the lights, the fans, the fame go to my head. I wasn't walking with God back then, and I've done more than my share of things I wish I could take back. I embraced the party lifestyle wholeheartedly. But we have a God that not only forgives, He uses those things to help us reach others if we let Him."

"You've hinted at the rest of your story before. Can I hear it now?"

She waited, not pushing. He'd given his testimony dozens of times. It had even been recorded and shared on the church's social media pages. Blane wanted Trinity to know who he was, all of who he was. But they needed to finish their current conversation first.

"I have no problem sharing it. But Jay will be waking up soon. Right this minute might not be the wisest choice. How about first, you tell me if you want to stay in the apartment? You can save your motel money to do extra fun stuff with Jay. I've already asked Mom and Dad, and they're fine with it. In fact, I think they'll enjoy having Jay to spoil a bit more."

He turned her toward the backyard and pointed past it and beyond an open field to a log cabin nestled in the tree line.

"And I'll be close by. That's my place over there. When I'm not working, I'd like to show you and Jay some of my favorite places around here, if you'll let me."

"Are you sure your parents are okay with this?"

"Positive. How about it? Will you stay?"

# 12

Trinity smiled as the scenery passed by the car window in a blur. Jay opted to stay with Blane's parents instead of enduring another long car ride. Besides, he'd been practically giddy when he found out that not only was he going to be with his partner a little longer, but he was also going to be staying where Blane used to live. He was happily jumping on Blane's old bed in the apartment with Gordon and Aileen looking on like carefree grandparents when she and Blane decided it was time to retrieve her car.

Honestly, she was pretty happy too. The Sterling family's generosity would keep her from having to pay for a hotel, and that meant she and Jay could be a little less careful and a little more carefree for the rest of their trip.

She turned from the window. Blane focused on the road ahead. In their lives that had been turned topsy-turvy in the last couple years, he was such a pleasant surprise. After losing Tuck, friends and family blessed her beyond measure as they came alongside her, helping her and Jay adjust to their new way of life. Now, Blane, who was a complete stranger only three days ago, was quickly taking a place in both the list of her blessings and her friends.

A half-smile showcasing one of his dimples appeared as he shifted his attention briefly from the road and then back. "What's that look for?"

"I was thinking about how I planned out this weekend only to have it turn out completely different from what I thought."

"Is that a good or bad thing?" He asked without looking away from the road.

"Definitely a good thing." She smiled. "I know I've said it before, but thank you for doing all this for Jay. I know he doesn't realize how unusual all of this has been. He will someday. But I see it now, and I want to thank you."

"You're welcome, but you don't need to thank me. This weekend hasn't gone the way I expected either. I've done these events a hundred times, and I've never come out of them with guests for the weekend."

Her chuckle matched his. "It is a little crazy, isn't it?"

"A good crazy, maybe. Whatever it is, I'll take it."

"Did you mean what you said?"

He paused to turn off the interstate before answering. "About what?"

"Outside your parent's house. You said you didn't want your time with Jay to end. You said you want to stay in touch with him after we go back home and hinted you might even come to see him sometimes."

"That isn't what I said."

Her heart plummeted. She should've left well enough alone, should've kept her mouth shut and been content to enjoy the next few days without considering what the future might hold. "Oh."

Blane pulled his car into the hotel parking lot next to hers and put it in park before facing her. "What I said was that I didn't want my time with *you* and Jay to end. I want to stay in touch with *you* and Jay after you go home. And I want to come see *you* and Jay as often as I can.

"When I said this weekend hasn't gone as I thought it would, it was about more than Jay. That kid made me love him the minute he told you not to be sad, and the more time I spend with him, the more I want to be part of his life."

"Sure," she agreed quietly. "I get that."

"But he wasn't my only surprise this weekend. You came right along with him, and you've worked your way into my life without even trying. Watching how you are with Jay, allowing me to be part of your time with him, allowing this wild Champ in Training idea to take place, seeing your strength but also having you trust me enough to share your struggles. I feel like God blessed me this weekend with a special friendship that I don't want to end when you leave."

The sting of tears left Trinity blinking. Hearing Blane voice her own thoughts about their relationship brought her hope going forward. Blane wouldn't forget them after they returned home. She didn't have to worry for Jay. Of course, he proved more resilient than she did most of the time. He'd bounce back without a problem.

It was herself she was really concerned about. Knowing she could move forward in their friendship without fearing the pain of having it snatched away meant she didn't have to be guarded during the rest of their time together.

"I don't want it to end either."

"Good." His smile turned mischievous, his tone playful. "Now get out of my car. We have a long drive home."

———

The more Trinity thought about their conversation, the more she felt butterflies set free in her middle. Sure, Blane had used the L word when referencing Jay, but it didn't matter. She didn't want him to love her anyway. It made her giddy just knowing he saw their friendship for what it was and valued it as much as she did. Blane listened. It made her want to tell him every detail of her day. She felt protected and cared for in ways she hadn't experienced since Tuck was alive.

Wait. That couldn't be right. Tuck was her husband. Blane was a friend. Admittedly, he was becoming a close friend in record time, but it was because their time together was short. Wasn't it?

She paced the small living area of the garage apartment while Jay was taking his bath. The whole evening had been restful and enjoyable, though it was nothing out of the ordinary, except for the company. Jay had been helping Aileen make homemade pizza for dinner.

When it was done, Gordon spread out a large quilt on the living room floor and all five of them enjoyed the cheesy goodness while watching one of Jay's favorite animated movies. It was the perfect family night, and it wasn't even spent with her family. It was so natural and comfortable, Trinity hated to see it come to an end, but Jay needed his sleep. Blane planned to stop by before going home and hash out a plan for the next day.

Blane. He was so sweet. The way he joked around with Jay, pretending to steal pizza off his plate. Not to mention the way he'd refilled her glass without her asking and split the last brownie with her, giving her the much larger half. And he was going to help her plan fun activities for her and Jay to enjoy together while he was working out. It was one more instance of his heart to help others, and it reminded her of what a

Christian man should be. Why did that cause her pulse to quicken?

She grabbed her cell phone off the end table and punched in the familiar number.

"Hey, girl. What's up?" Autumn's voice came through after only one ring.

"I need your help."

A slight pause. "Is something wrong? Did something happen to you? Is Jay all right?"

Trinity ran her fingers through her hair. "Jay's fine. Nothing happened. I just need you to tell me I'm not crazy."

Autumn's laugh rang through the speaker. "I can't tell you that. My mama taught me never to lie."

"Ha. Ha. Very funny. I'm serious here."

All humor fell from Autumn's voice. "What's going on, Trin?"

She shook her head though no one was there to witness it. "I need you to tell me. It's Blane."

"Has he come on to you or something? Did the prince routine finally wear off and leave an ugly toad in its place?"

"Not at all. Blane is exactly what he has appeared to be from the time we met him at the meet-and-greet."

Autumn didn't speak on the other side of the call as Trinity filled her in on every aspect of their time in Tennessee. Only the occasional "oh", "mhm," and audible sucking her breath in confirmed to Trinity her friend remained on the line.

"We're friends, closer than I ever imagined I could be this quickly. But there are times it feels like more than that. Is it crazy to think I might be falling for this guy?"

"Oh, girl."

"I'm serious. Tuck's only been gone a year and a half."

"That's more than enough time for a heart to start healing and open up to new possibilities."

"But he's completely different than Tuck. I mean, I know that's fine. As much as I loved my husband, I wouldn't want another Tucker. I've caught myself comparing the two at different times, but one never comes out better, just different. You know?"

"Sounds like there isn't an issue with that then. So, what is it?"

"It's only been a few days. Am I crazy for thinking something's happening that quickly?"

Autumn chuckled.

Trinity grimaced. "I don't see what's so funny."

"Trin, it's not like either of you is considering marriage. You like the guy. You can admit it. Attraction can be instantaneous. Add in the fact that he's proven himself a caring, Christian man, and yes, you better believe it's okay for things to happen quickly. But you've told me how you feel about Blane. How does Blane feel about you?"

Trinity was positive Autumn heard her sigh. "I have no idea. He admits we're close, but it's in friendship terms. There are times I've thought I saw more in a look he gave me, but I don't know. I never had to guess with Tucker, and I've been away from this part of relationships for too long. I'm not sure I can trust my instincts."

"I think your instincts are just fine. Maybe you should start listening to them more."

A knock on the door rushed Trinity's answer. "I guess we'll find out one way or the other. But listen, I think Blane's here. We're supposed to discuss plans for tomorrow after Jay gets in bed. I need to go."

"Call me and let me know how things go?"

"Definitely. And thank you. I don't say it enough, but you're the best."

"I know. Just don't forget it. Bye."

Trinity hung up the phone and opened the door. In a few minutes, Jay would be done with his bath and tucked into bed for the night. Then, she and Blane could talk. She forced down jitteriness as Autumn's words about trusting her instincts ran through her mind. Their talk convinced her. As much as she appreciated their friendship, she'd be open to more. But would Blane?

# 13

"But why can't Blane spend the night? We could watch movies and play games and stuff."

Innocent as Jay's post-story and prayers request was, there was no way she could give in to this one. But how did one explain situations like this to an eight-year-old when that child only wanted to have his new friend stay over? His mother didn't even figure into the equation in his mind.

"How about you give me and your mom a minute to talk about it, okay?" Blane spoke up from the doorway. "I think we can come up with something even better. How's that sound?"

The stars in the midnight sky didn't sparkle as much as Jay's eyes as he flopped back against the pillows on his bed. He looked to where they stood in the doorway. "What are you waiting for? I've got to get some sleep. We're going to have a big day tomorrow. Go. Talk. Love you, Mom." He shut his eyes and lay still under the covers.

Trinity flipped off the light and smiled at his antics. "Love you, too, Little Mister."

"Love you, too, Blane."

Trinity's eyes flew to the man in question. The expression on his face was unclear. It wasn't a frown, but he didn't sport a smile either. His mouth was slightly slack as he silently questioned her. A nod and smile gave him the assurance he needed. He shifted his attention back to Jay who continued to lay still under the covers with his eyes shut.

"Love you, too, partner."

Trinity smiled as she followed Blane into the small living room. Blane better have a stellar idea in mind. If not, they were going to have a seriously disappointed little boy on their hands. In his defense, every idea Blane came up with had been a winner with her son. As quickly as her own relationship with the man was developing, Jay was already fully attached.

The expression on Blane's face as she dropped onto one end of the sofa stopped all questions about whatever plan he had in mind as an alternative to a sleep over. Shock. If there'd been an accident or some life-changing news she would've reassured him and offered him a comforting blanket.

"It's pretty amazing, huh?" She simply spoke in a calming voice.

Though he looked at her, Trinity wasn't entirely sure he saw her. When their gazes finally connected, a frown creased his brow.

"You don't think I'd say something like that if I didn't mean it, do you?"

Snippets of their earlier conversation ran through her mind. She shook her head. "No. Jay surprised you. That was evident. But you weren't placating him. You told me earlier that you love my son, and I believe you. But I do think you're coming to realize it's a big deal."

"Definitely. In my business, I hear that people love me all the time. They shout it from the stands. But it's fickle. It's superficial. They love me like they love Taco Tuesday or a good cup of coffee. This is real. I've not had that happen before."

"I think you're more loved than you realize." She frowned. "What about the youth at the church? They love you."

He waved her words away. "No. They enjoy their time with me. They may even look up to and respect me. But that's different."

How could he say that? She tried to keep shock from showing on her face. "You don't see it. You really don't? Blane, those boys, the one that did all the talking?"

"Troy?"

"Yes, Troy. You said he didn't have an adult role model in his life. That you're that person for him, like an uncle or big brother?"

"Yeah. So?"

She laid back and shook her head at the ceiling before facing him. How could he not see it?

"So, he's a teen boy. They don't profess their love for anyone except the cute girl in biology class, and even then, it's hit or miss. Moms don't even rate an 'I love you' unless it's pulled from them like a wisdom tooth. Troy does more than enjoy guy time with you, and he feels more than respect for you. You're the father figure in his life. You give him your time and attention and care freely. He loves you, and I'm sure some of the others do too."

Blane rubbed his hand over his beard, considering her words, weighing the truth in them. She got the impression he took his role seriously, but knowing the teens held the same love for him that her son expressed would add an extra element of responsibility to the work he did with them.

"I think you're a pretty wise woman, Trinity Knight."

She rolled her eyes. "I know. I'm just glad you realize it."

"There's just one question left."

"What's that?"

———

He smirked and noticed the wariness that immediately entered Trinity's expression as he did. "You were the cute girl in biology all the boys professed their undying love to, weren't you?"

The rose flooding her cheeks only added to his attraction. She was beautiful in a cute way. Girl next door. Wasn't that what they called it? He had no doubts any boy in his right mind would have professed his undying love for her in biology class. Or sitting next to her on a sofa.

Well, maybe he'd suffered one too many concussions in the ring, because that was not a thought he planned to entertain. It was hard enough to focus on friendship when every minute he spent with Trinity showed him one more reason to take another step closer to being a completely lost cause. But friendship is what she wanted, and he was determined to honor that.

"Not really."

He raised his eyebrows. "What? I don't believe it for a second."

She shrugged. "They didn't have a chance. Tucker and I met my freshman year in drama class. We started dating and never stopped. He's the only one who had the chance to confess his love for me."

"Does it bother you to talk about him?"

She licked her lips. "Sometimes. At home, everyone knows what happened. So, beyond the initial comforting words and checking in on me, there weren't a lot of questions. As his death became my new normal, it's like no one wanted to bring him up at all. But he's part of everything in my life, all my memories. And I see him each time I look at Jay. My best friend, Autumn, and I still talk about him."

"That must be difficult."

"It is," she agreed. "There's also this really great elderly lady named Miss Gertie. She's a hoot, but she's also one of the wisest people I know. She and I have spoken of Tucker a few times. There are days and situations when it's hard, but for the most part, it's been nice to talk about him with someone who didn't know him or us together. Does that make sense?"

"I think so. I've never experienced the death of a loved one or even a love like that"

"Does it bother you to talk about him? It tends to make people uncomfortable." Her voice was soft and unsure.

Blane shook his head. "Not really. He's part of who you are. I can't get to know you without also getting to know you and Tucker. I know I may have seemed uncomfortable, but it's less about my own discomfort and more about causing you more pain than you've already experienced."

Trinity cleared her throat and fidgeted with the ruffle on a throw pillow resting on the couch. The smile she gave him seemed a little forced. "You didn't come over tonight to talk about all this. You're supposed to be helping me plan out tomorrow's adventures. And you have yet to explain this alternative idea for tomorrow night that's even better than a sleepover."

"Camping."

"Camping?"

"Camping."

The frown causing her lips to pucker assured him of her internal struggle as much as her sigh. When she began chewing on her bottom lip, he knew she needed more of an explanation.

He offered a lopsided smile. "I'm not asking you to let Jay

spend the night camping with me, at least not like you're thinking. You've shown a huge amount of trust in me this weekend by even agreeing to come back here to stay in my parents' apartment for the rest of your trip."

"You've done nothing to make me not trust you. And the way the boys and the other people at services this morning react to you only helps confirm my trust is well-placed."

He put up a hand to stop her. "But it doesn't matter. Jay is your world and your responsibility. No matter what the circumstances have told you to this point, I'd never put you in a position like that. I hope one day we'll know each other well enough that experience will prove what you want to believe right now, but that day isn't today."

Her smile seemed easy. Maybe his pre-emptive strike had taken some of the pressure off her.

"So, tell me. How does this camping thing work then?"

"Tomorrow, Jay and I will do all the normal camping things. We'll roast hot dogs, play catch, and maybe even fish in the pond. You can have the evening to yourself, and…" He pointed to the window over the kitchen table. "We will be right outside that window the whole time. I'll set up two tents. One for you and Jay. One for me."

"I'm not sure I do sleeping bags on the hard ground."

"Don't worry," he laughed. "I'll set up an air mattress for you. When it's time for Jay to go to sleep, you can come put him to bed. Then, you can go back to your evening by yourself, hang out by the fire, whatever you want."

"You know what? You're better at this kid stuff than you think. Jay is going to love it. Now, how about you help me with my plans for the rest of the week."

"What do you have in mind?"

Trinity handed him a pile of brochures from the end table

beside the sofa. "I got these at the hotel, but I'm not sure which ones will be the best options for us."

He moved from the recliner to sit on the opposite side of the couch so they could browse through them together. An hour later, Trinity had a plan for the week that included some of his favorite area attractions. She and Jay would spend the time when he was working exploring. He would join them when he could, and they would join him for an outreach opportunity with UWO.

A glance at the clock on the wall told him he needed to leave or risk overstaying his welcome. He stood and headed to the door. "I should probably head home. You need to get to sleep so you and Jay can both enjoy your day tomorrow."

She stood and led the way to the door. The hand she playfully placed in the center of his chest to stop his retreat set off fireworks inside him. He raised his eyebrows in question, forcing his mind away from what her nearness did to him.

"Oh, no you don't. You promised you'd share the rest of your story with me. We've traipsed through every page of mine this weekend, including tonight. It's your turn."

A knot lodged in his throat. Blane swallowed. She remembered the promise he'd nearly forgotten he'd made. Her story was painful, tragic even, but beautiful. High school sweethearts meet and stay together until death parts them. His was nothing like that. He hadn't considered the stark contrast that existed between what she shared and the ugliness of his own tale.

While he knew God used the less than attractive parts of his life to reach others, Trinity was already a strong believer. The only thing his story might succeed in doing was to shock her or worse. Would the truth of who he was repulse her?

Unable to look her in the eyes, he spoke to the floor. "It's been a pretty heavy night, already. Don't you think? Maybe we should save my story for another night."

Her hand dropped to her side along with the playfulness he'd seen. There was no misinterpreting the disappointment in the tiny smile she forced.

"Sure. You're right. Maybe tomorrow?"

"We could do that." He nodded. "See you tomorrow?"

She stepped away from the door. "Tomorrow."

"Good night, Trinity."

"Good night," she murmured. "Pleasant dreams."

He looked over his shoulder as he stepped out onto the small landing. "You too."

As he made his way down the steps, Blane ran a hand through his hair, pulling the band out and freeing it from his usual ponytail in the process. The confusion in Trinity's eyes remained with him as he walked across the field to his cabin. Why couldn't he just tell her? His story wouldn't have taken that long to tell.

Time wasn't the issue. The hesitancy was about the woman. She saw him as he wanted to be seen, the dedicated Christian and successful wrestler who knew who he was and what he was after in life. He'd hinted at his past, but hearing about her own storybook past, she wouldn't understand his less than savory one.

He'd never hesitated to share his testimony. God redeemed messes, even the ones Blane had created. Others found encouragement to live their faith through what God did in him. He'd seen it. But it wasn't all happy endings. There were times his story proved too much for some people.

What if she couldn't accept it? Accept him? It was a lot to handle. Others hadn't proven up to the challenge. What if Trinity decided he wasn't good enough for her son? As much as that would hurt, the pain would pale in comparison to what it would be if she decided he wasn't worthy of being in her life.

Losing Trinity was the last thing he wanted. Blane was teetering on the edge of pursuing more than the friendship they currently shared. The whole, dirty truth had to be shared. But would he be able to live with the consequences?

# 14

Trinity closed her laptop and put away her sketch pad and pencils. She'd accomplished all she could for the evening with Blane and Jay playing outside the window next to her. Mini-golf and horse riding at a local stable before Blane met them at the local aquarium after work made the day full and wore her out. Jay had endless energy, but she'd needed a power nap while Blane and Jay spent the early evening fishing in the pond.

A knock on her door had come just as she'd awakened. Blane and Jay decided she needed a hot dog and mini bag of chips. On the way out the door to make s'mores, Blane had stopped long enough to ask Trinity if she'd like to sit by the fire after Jay went to sleep and hear his story.

She hadn't pushed. It wasn't hard to see Blane's hesitance to share, though why it had suddenly developed she couldn't say. But he'd brought it up, and she was anxious to hear his testimony in full. He'd shared bits and pieces, and she had a good sense of who Blane was at his core.

Still, he'd mentioned her past with Tucker was part of who

she was today, and the same was true for him as well. His present was shaped by who he was in the past, for good or bad. Though this time, she was certain it shaped him for the better.

A text alert buzzed its arrival. Jay was nodding off in his camping chair by the fire. She sprang from her seat and out the door. She could see Jay, head to his shoulder, in the firelight.

"I wasn't sure if I should try to move him or not." Blane spoke as she crossed the yard to stand beside him.

Trinity grinned, hearing her son's soft snores. "He's out. Nothing's going to wake him at this point. I'll just carry him into the tent and get him into bed."

"Let me." Blane scooped Jay up with ease.

Not sure which of the two family-sized tents he'd set up for her and Jay, Trinity followed Blane. As Blane tucked him into the sleeping bag, Trinity dimmed the battery-operated camping lantern that sat beside the tallest air mattress she'd ever seen. Instead of a sleeping bag, the vinyl was covered with a fitted bed sheet and topped with a light comforter. Warmth flooded her chest as she considered the extra care Blane had taken to see to her comfort.

"Night, Partner."

Blane's whisper drew her attention back to Jay. Blane moved toward the tent opening and waited as she pressed a kiss to Jay's forehead. True to her word, he'd not moved through the entire ordeal. She nodded to Blane, and he led the way to the firepit, still glowing. As he stoked the fire, she made herself comfortable on the wooden patio swing and waited for him to join her. It was a cozy area Trinity would like to replicate at home.

Each side of the open wooden pergola was bordered by a swing. Two natural wood Adirondack chairs flanked the other two sides of the structure, providing seating space. The structure framed the raised firepit in the middle. In the distance, she could see the gentle ripples of the pond in the moonlight. Blane's cabin on the other edge of the field and pond was hidden in shadow.

The swing swayed gently as she settled back against it and let her toes push against the ground. She laid her head back and sighed. The stars were plentiful where she lived, but they were positively amazing here near the mountains and away from the city lights. Peace surrounded her, and a contentment she hadn't known in ages filled her.

———

Blane smiled as her features relaxed. The fire bathed her face in a contrast of light and shadow. He was content to sit beside her watching her soak in the quiet. He hadn't thought it possible, but the change made her more beautiful. A pressure filled his chest, begging for him to draw her into his arms. He ignored it, reminding himself of the reason they were sitting in the pergola in the deepening dark. The weight sank into his gut. It was time.

"You still want to hear my story?"

She didn't lift her head or open her now closed eyes. "Yes."

"It's not like yours."

"I don't expect it to be. You're not me."

"It's not pretty."

"It doesn't have to be."

Time to dive in. He steeled his nerves with a deep breath. "I didn't grow up in church. At least, not like you. We went to church on holidays and even a few other Sundays. But it was something we did because it's what good people in town did. And what we heard in that church was really a lot of the good stuff. We heard of God's love, which isn't bad in itself, but it was twisted. God's love wouldn't leave room for hell to exist. Sin didn't need spoken of because it brought people down."

Knowing other young men were still hearing that incomplete message was heartbreaking. In times when information was readily available, believers needed to do a better job of getting the truth out to those who needed it. But this wasn't the time for that discussion.

"It was very inspirational, or maybe motivational would be a better word, but it left out our need. I grew up without a knowledge of sin and my need for a Savior. As long as I was a decent person, I felt like I was fine. God didn't enter into the equation of my day-to-day life."

The roughest part of his story hadn't arrived, but he paused considering how everything in his past was tied together, a chain of events he wished he hadn't set in motion. "I was pretty good through my teen years since I already knew I wanted to be a wrestler. So, all my free time was spent training. No time for girls. No time to get into trouble.

"The only thing that made me keep my grades up was my dad's threat of losing the one thing I loved more than anything —the ability to wrestle. I was contracted on a small independent circuit fresh out of high school. I had plenty of raw talent and determination in spades. It was the perfect combination to get noticed, quickly."

He leaned forward and clasped his hands together on his knees, glanced at Trinity. Had she fallen asleep? She rested her head against the back of the swing with her eyes closed still. The silence continued until she opened one eye to look his way, silently asking him to continue. Looking down at his hands, he obliged.

"I debuted with the UWO after less than a year in the independents. Not many can say that. The company chairman took a liking to me. I got great opportunities from the moment

I signed. I was headlining before I knew it. It's easy for that kind of success to go to your head when you're barely twenty. I wasn't prepared for it." He stood and grabbed another log to add to the fire. Sparks danced around the flames before settling back down.

Trinity shifted on the swing. "Blane?"

He turned. Patience and trust filled her features. The rest of his story was the ugliest part. Was she prepared for it? No. Could he stop it here? That wasn't a possibility either. He rubbed his lips together and closed his eyes as if doing so could shut out the past once and for all. It didn't. Still, she watched him with that innocent expression.

Tightness in his throat choked the words he needed to say until he forced them through. "I wasn't ready for the fame. We were like rock stars, and some of us got caught up in living like rock stars. Fans screamed your name and lined the sidewalks just waiting to catch a glimpse of you. Even as a heel …"

"Wait a minute," she broke into his story though he could sense her hesitation to do so. "You were a what?"

"A heel," he answered with a tiny chuckle. "The wrestlers are either the bad guys, known as heels or the good guys, known as the face or babyface. Usually, our personas swing between the two depending on our current storylines."

"Oh, that makes sense. I may even have heard the phrases a time or two from Tucker, but I never heard them in context. I'm sorry. Please go on."

"As I was saying," he continued, "I had star power, even as a heel. I played the rebel, and I didn't leave the persona in the ring. Drinking. Drugs. I wasn't a stranger to either, but drinking was my nightly way to unwind and have fun."

He paused to judge Trinity's reaction. "My behavior became erratic and destructive. I don't know how many times I got kicked out of bars. I can't count the number of times the company had to deal with me because I messed up some hotel room. I've always been amazed they put up with me as long as they did."

If anything would push her away, it would be the next part of his story. But this chapter was bad enough. Her eyes showed no judgment, but he held little hope that would continue.

"And those fans? You've heard how rock stars have groupies? Well, there's plenty of action for wrestlers, too, if they're open to it. I'd not had time for relationships in high school, and truth be told, I didn't have relationships at that point in my life either. They were more like one-night stands. I could have a different woman in every city we went to if I wanted. And most of the time, I did."

A sadness entered Trinity's eyes as shame that accompanied the sin filled him. He shook it off with the reminder that his past was forgiven. Could there still be consequences? Yes. Could one of those be losing Trinity's friendship? Definitely. And that would be a blow unlike any he'd faced before, but it didn't change the fact he was forgiven.

"The parties, the bar fights, the women. It all escalated. It started affecting my time at work. You have to be able to adjust to the unexpected in the ring. You have to be able to react to keep you and your opponent safe. It's hard to do that when you're hungover. I got sloppy. I thank God every day for keeping me from seriously injuring someone. All I did was alienate the people who wanted to help me, because I didn't need help. I was the star."

He looked up at the sky. The peace so evident as they began the evening was gone. He took in a deep breath and exhaled it slowly.

"What happened?"

He shook his head. "God got my attention. My impairment may not have hurt my opponents, but it did allow one to hurt me. It was a mistake anyone could have made, and if I'd been thinking clearly, I could've reacted in time and kept the injury from happening. I didn't. I sustained a severe concussion and a neck injury. One minute I was on top, a rising star, and the next everyone was saying I'd never be able to wrestle again."

"Oh, Blane. That must've been awful."

"At the time, I thought my life was over." He sat back down beside her. "I was angry and depressed. I begged the God I'd never had time for in the past. I tried to bargain with Him. Just give me back my career, and I'd be in church every Sunday. When it didn't happen, I got so angry."

"I remember bargaining with Him," Trinity admitted. "When Tucker was sick. It's so easy to get angry with God when things aren't going your way."

Anger was one thing. Blane had outright rebelled. "Though I'd just promised to get my life together, I grabbed a case of beer and headed to a local park. I was several deep in the case, when I realized my pity party was being interrupted by a group at a nearby shelter. It was a church picnic, complete with worship music and a short message. I seethed until the event was over."

"What happened then?"

"When the pastor was left, cleaning up the last of the mess, I stomped over and gave him a piece of my mind. Looking back, I'm glad the families were gone at that point. I've never been big on control when drinking. My language as I berated him and his God would have made a movie about it R-rated."

She grimaced. "And how did he handle that?"

Despite the seriousness of the story, Blane smiled at the memory. "He asked me, 'When was the last time you tried talking to God when you didn't want something? What makes you think God is like a genie in a bottle out there granting wishes?' He went on to explain that what God offered was more than a bandage solution to my physical problems."

Blane shook his head. "I didn't understand. If God couldn't fix my problem, what good was He? I wanted none of it. I stormed off. Got in my truck and ripped up the business card he gave me when he told me if I wanted to talk, he'd listen."

"Oh, Blane." Raw sadness filled her voice.

"But depression followed my anger. And it was bad. I needed someone to talk to, and I couldn't get that preacher out of my head. I dug around my floorboards until I found the card and pieced it back together. Not even stopping to make an appointment, I drove to the church. The pastor sat with me for hours, praying and poring over scripture."

The freedom he felt in those moments flooded through him once more. "I finally understood my need for healing that went beyond my body. I told him I was ready to accept it, and he cautioned that accepting Jesus' forgiveness and salvation didn't mean God would fix my neck and let me return to wrestling. 'Sin has natural consequences,' he said. I wanted it anyway."

The tears on Trinity's cheeks glistened in the firelight. Blane reached over and wiped one away with his thumb.

"The pastor continued to teach me, keeping me grounded in the truth of God's word. As my spirit was healing, my body was too. One day I realized I could probably be cleared to return to the ring. I'd come to peace with God that I might never return, but I still missed it."

Would he miss it today? Yes. But he could honestly say the loss would be easier now than it was back then. God was merciful and gracious.

"After much prayer together and developing a plan of accountability with the pastor, I felt God's okay to go back into wrestling. It didn't define me as a person anymore, but it was part of who God created me to be. And I wanted to get back in there and make amends, show others God through how I approached the business."

Both Trinity's hands framed her face as she wiped the tears from her eyes. "What a beautiful story of redemption."

"Beautiful? Are you sure it doesn't make you want to turn tail and run?"

She frowned. "Why would I want to do that?"

"Because I'm not the type of guy you want around your son? Because I'm not the kind of guy you want anywhere near your life? You did things the right way. For every right decision you made, I made at least three bad ones."

"And God forgave you as freely and completely as He forgave me. It's in the past, and He's used it to make you a light that shines brightly for Him everywhere you go."

"But ..."

"No buts. Your past doesn't scare me. And it makes your willingness to share it with me that much more special. Thank you."

He wasn't given to tears, but he could feel the sting threatening behind his eyelids. He rested his elbows on his knees and dropped his head into his hands. "You say that, but living with it is different. I've been close to people before, good Christian people who couldn't handle it. I've lost so many friendships."

Freely handing her the story of his life and salvation wasn't enough. She needed to understand what his past cost him. The dreams for a future he squandered before he'd figured out he wanted them.

"There was a woman I thought was ready for more than friendship with. She thought she knew me, but when the truth of my past came out, she disappeared. The woman told me she knew I was forgiven but being alone was more than likely one of the lasting consequences of my questionable past. She was a good girl, like you. Made all the right choices, like you. Faced with the sins of my past, she walked away."

A shiver passed through him as Trinity's hand came to rest on his back. She eased closer and leaned her head toward him. "I am not that woman. I am Trinity Knight, and I am honored to be your friend."

Her breath warmed his face as she spoke softly into his ear. The words she spoke sent the warmth spiraling through the rest of him.

The tears escaped their fleshly prison. One last question. One that haunted him. One that held him back. "Do you think it's true?"

"Do I think what's true?"

"Am I destined to be alone because of my past? Would any good, Christian woman want me after the mistakes I've made?"

Her forehead rested against his temple. Her hand slid from his back, and she unclenched his hands to cradle one between her own. "No. Not every good, Christian woman will be willing to deal with your past."

He swallowed the lump in his throat and nodded without moving his head from hers. Friendship might be offered, but the hope of more was dying out like the flames in the firepit. His voice was hoarse. "Okay. I get it."

"I don't think you do. There will be women who can't accept your past. But there are those who can and would consider a relationship with you as a blessing from God."

He looked at her without trying to hide the yearning her words, no she, brought to life in him. "Who? Who would see me as a gift like that?"

A shadow of a smile crossed her lips. "Me. I would see you

as a blessing for as long as you were in my life. I'd never walk away because of the past you've been forgiven for."

Until his lungs forced an inhale, Blane didn't realize he'd held his breath. He searched her face to confirm the truth of her words. It was there waiting in her eyes as she regarded him. Empty words to soothe his pain weren't her style.

A stray strand of hair fell across her cheek, and he reached out to brush it away from her face. The side of his hand trailed down the soft skin of her cheek. Her eyes slid shut, and before his hand dropped, she reached up to hold it in place. Her lips parted to free a sweet sigh. Lips that begged to be kissed.

Drawn to her, he leaned in close, stopping with only a breath between them. He whispered, lest his voice break the spell they were under. "Are you sure?"

She didn't open her eyes as she answered. "I'm sure."

Soft and gentle, her lips responded to his. The scent of her citrusy shampoo mingled with the vanilla of her body wash and the earthiness of the fire. Hope realized worked like a drug in his system. Her closeness, her response to him stoked a fire more dangerous than the one burning just feet away from them. The flames urged him to deepen the kiss, give in to the dormant desire he'd not wrestled with in years.

But he was not that man anymore. Though he could feel the accompanying ache through his whole body, he pulled himself away enough to break their contact but not far enough to lose their connection.

Her trusting smile added a temptation to take her back into his arms, while also convincing him of the need to exercise self-control. He cupped her chin with his hand and brushed his thumb across her lips.

Blane eased back against the swing and tucked her in under his arm with her head resting against his chest. "Thank you."

A giggle shattered the last of the spell.

"What's so funny?"

"I don't think I've ever been thanked for kissing someone before."

He chuckled. "Well, it was a pretty great kiss. But that's not what I was thanking you for."

"Oh?"

"Thank you for seeing the worst of me and understanding I'm no longer that person. For trusting me with you and Jay. For offering hope I'm not condemned to being alone."

She sat up and faced him but waited until he made eye contact. "I want to be clear on something. From the moment you approached us, you showed me the real Blane Sterling, not the man with the championship belt, but a man seeking God in all he does."

"You are a most unexpected surprise." She placed her hand briefly against his cheek. "I don't know where all this will lead. I don't know how long it will last. And I'm not sure how we go forward with a relationship in different states. I can't tell if I'm excited or frightened because of that. Maybe both. But, whatever happens, I do trust you, with Jay and with my heart."

He wanted to pull her back to him, cling to her like a lifeline, but one thought stopped him. Was he falling for the woman or the hope she brought? He believed it was Trinity that snagged his heart. He'd felt the attraction at their first meeting, and it only grew as he got to know her.

But his job, the distance between them, and the addition of a child were factors that affected any relationship they could have. Trust was easily lost, and she trusted him with her heart and with Jay. He needed to be sure of what he was feeling before allowing things to go too far. It was going to be a long night, full of prayer.

"You don't know how much it means to me to hear that.

Above anything else, I want the best for you and Jay. We'll take it slow. Work out the details as they come. For the rest of the week, you're here, and so am I. Tonight, I'd love nothing more than sitting out here with you, holding you, until the sun comes up, but that wouldn't be good for either of us tomorrow when Jay wakes up ready to start the day. What do you say we call it a night?"

She stood and moved in front of him. With him still sitting, their height difference was reversed, though not by much. She took his hands in her own as she smiled down at him. "I think you're going to be very good for me."

When she leaned down, the curtain of her hair tickled his neck and cheeks moments before he felt the warmth of her lips against his. They lingered only a second before the cool night air punctuated their absence. Though her eyes were shadowed, they still reflected her trust and desire. He could stare into those eyes forever.

She didn't give him the chance, dropping his hands as she softly said, "Good night."

"Good night."

With the words barely out of his mouth, she turned to join Jay in the tent across the fire from where he sat. The dim light behind the canvas faded until only darkness remained. Satisfied all was well, he doused the fire and made his way to his own tent. He didn't waste time changing and crawling into bed, but sleep didn't come until he'd placed their relationship in the hands of his Savior. Trinity might trust him, but they'd both need to trust God to work out the details if they wanted this to work.

# 15

"Are you positive Jay is up to this?" Blane's question came as soon as Trinity opened the apartment door.

"Good morning to you too." Trinity smiled and motioned him inside. He'd obviously worked himself up over the day's plans while breaking down and storing the tents. "Come on in. We're just about ready. And yes, Jay will be fine."

"But some of these kids are really sick. I don't want it to scare him or bring up bad memories."

Just when she thought he couldn't be any more caring, Blane Sterling set out to prove her wrong. "I'm touched that you want to protect him, but Jay has seen it all. Cancer has been a reality in his life for as long as he can remember. When Tuck was battling and then again after he was gone, we made it a point to visit the pediatric ward and pass out care packages. Jay loved picking out the toys and activities we put into them."

"I'm so sorry he's had to be comfortable with sickness and death." He cleared his throat and blinked a couple times. "That's something no child should have to be familiar with."

"I agree wholeheartedly, but God's already used it in Jay's life in a big way."

Blane tilted his head toward his shoulder. "What do you mean?"

"I've never seen a kid so dedicated to praying for those in need." Motherly pride coaxed a smile even as thinking about it made tears well up in her eyes. "There's this one boy who's been at the hospital when we've visited. After we pass out the Bouquets of Hope care packages, Jay and Ryan always hang out a while."

"Every Sunday at church, Jay asks for prayer for his friend. He prays for him every morning on the way to school and every night before bed. I know adults with less dedication in their prayer lives. I'm not sure I'm not one of them."

"That's amazing." His voice was quiet. "Jay really is a champ. Just two questions."

"What?"

"What's Bouquets of Hope, and why hasn't the champ crashed our conversation?"

Trinity picked up her purse from the table. "Jay is at your mom's house. Something about the kids needing some of her super-secret recipe chocolate chip cookies. We're supposed to pick him and the cookies up on our way out."

"And Bouquets of Hope?" Blane held the door for her.

"That is the ministry I began after Tuck lost his battle with cancer. I know first-hand what families go through dealing with that vicious disease. There's a huge physical, emotional, spiritual, and financial toll on the entire family unit. We provide informational resources, Christian counselors, financial and fund-raising help, babysitters. Basically, whatever a family needs that we can provide."

No longer feeling his presence on the steps behind her, Trinity turned as she reached the bottom landing. Blane was at the top staring down at her. The intensity of his gaze was unexpected.

"What's wrong?"

He shook his head. "Absolutely nothing. You're amazing is all. You've taken the worst thing you could go through and turned it into something beautiful. Do you know how rare that is?"

"Don't do that." Trinity shifted from one foot to the other and refused to look at him directly. "Don't put me on some kind of pedestal. God's the one doing the work. I'm more selfish than I'd like to admit. As blessed as I've been for God to redeem some of my loss through this, I'd trade it a hundred times to have Tucker back. Just for one more day. Even knowing he's in the presence of God and eternally away from the ravages of cancer."

Swallowing the tightness choking her throat, Trinity closed her eyes to regain the emotions rising dangerously close to the surface. She'd fought to put this battle in her past. How could it sneak up on her again so quickly?

"Look at me, please." His voice was low and nearer than she expected.

She opened her eyes but stared at the ground until his fingertips came to rest against her chin gently nudging it up from her chest.

"Please."

He waited. Blue-green eyes silently pleaded with her to hear him out. Slowly, she nodded without taking her gaze from his.

"Thank you. I'd never put you on a pedestal, and I'm sorry if it seemed like that's what I was suggesting. God does the work. Believe me, I understand that more than most. But you allow Him to create something full of hope out of your pain. Like it or not, that's rare."

He dropped his hand to his side. Without the added encouragement, keeping eye contact was more difficult. Compliments, no matter how sincere, were never easy for her to hear. Typically, she'd brush them off, but with his unwavering attention, he wasn't leaving the door open for her usual avoidance tactics. The shadow of a grin on his lips proved he knew exactly what he was doing.

"As for your selfishness, I don't buy it. I've seen how well-adjusted Jay is. That doesn't happen when a parent is holding onto resentment. I've heard you talk about your husband multiple times without a hint of bitterness in your voice. You miss him? You'd give anything to have another good day with him? How is that selfish? That's being human and loving someone. But you don't let it feed your loss. You admit it, but you don't stay a prisoner to it. You let God heal you."

"I miss him so much some days."

"I can't even imagine." His voice was hoarse.

She allowed him to pull her against his chest, wrapping his arms around her shoulders. As her tears flowed, he didn't so much as try to quiet them. He just held her tighter, letting her cry it out even as his comfort drew more from her.

———

Blane put his arm around the frail shoulders of the boy in the hospital chair and smiled for the camera. Picture taken, he moved to an empty spot near the door. Chairs and even a couple of hospital beds had been moved into the large room to allow even the less mobile patients the opportunity to meet the dozen UWO wrestlers taking part in the outreach program. It was a humbling experience. These kids were stronger than any of them, and he doubted you could find any wrestler to argue otherwise.

Across the room, Trinity stood, speaking with the parents of a boy, barely more than a baby. As she glanced Blane's way, she smiled. Jay perched at the end of the hospital bed, playing cars with the bald toddler. Though he was too far away to hear the conversation, Jay's expression was animated. Whatever he said brought laughter from the child.

Blane didn't turn from the scene even as Pamela approached.

"They're a pretty special pair, aren't they?"

"Yes." He agreed. "I think they are."

"Be careful. Okay?" The hand she rested on his bicep punctuated her concern.

Tearing his gaze from the duo in question, Blane frowned at Pamela. "Is this the organization's PR rep or my friend talking?"

Lips a straight tight line, Pamela shrugged. Maybe his tone had been a little more defensive than he'd intended. Still, she needed to explain herself.

"Don't do that to me. What's with the ominous warning?"

"You don't scare me, you know? You can scowl at me all you want, but I've seen it a million times in the ring. I know it's an act. You're as soft-hearted as they come, Blane Sterling."

He huffed, rolling his eyes at the same time. "I'm a giant teddy bear. But you still need to answer the questions."

"Fine. As the PR rep, I'm protective of the company's investment. But I can't see how they'd hurt your reputation. It's why we did the whole Champ in Training gimmick. As your friend, I think you're falling for both mother and son, hard and fast. It could be a recipe for disaster, and I don't want to see you hurt. What happens when she can't deal with your life?"

"She knows about my past. All of it. And she's still here."

Pamela carefully schooled her features, but Blane saw the surprise. She'd been one of the few in his circle of friends who knew why Diane left him, knew the fear she'd sown in his mind with her inability to accept his past. It wasn't something he shared frequently. Sometimes the feeling created by the event bordered on humiliation. He was tainted goods. The fact that he'd shared it with Trinity spoke volumes.

"It's not your past I'm worried about."

"What then?"

"A public life was yours before the ink was dry on your first contract. You agreed to it. The scrutiny, the questions, the rumors. All of it. You know the business and how it works."

He stopped her with a raised hand. "Trinity knows who I am in the ring is only a character. Give her some credit."

"But do her friends? Her family? Do they understand the difference? What about the next time you have to play a heel? How are you going to explain that to them? To Jay?"

"Wrestlers have families. I think you're making a bigger deal out of this than you need to."

A shrug. "Maybe. But Trinity doesn't strike me as the type to have experienced the public life, much less the wrestling life. And we both know there are more Dianes out there than Trinitys. Just be careful. Please."

"Trinity is not a Diane."

"From all I've seen, I would tend to agree. But you can't know for certain. She can't even know for sure until she's there in the middle of it. Then, it's too late. Hurt becomes inevitable for you and for Trinity and Jay. Please, just watch out for yourself and them."

The woman in question gave a little wave. The conversation was over.

"I know what I'm doing. I'll be careful."

Looking at Pamela's frown, Blane knew he'd been less than convincing. His parting smile was meant to put her at ease as he removed himself from the conversation and joined Trinity. Now, if he could only get rid of the sprout of doubt she'd sown.

"Blane." Jay's smile grew wider as he looked up from the toy cars to greet him.

Another pair of eyes sought him out from the hospital bed.

He smiled at the younger boy. "Are you going to introduce me to your new friend, Jay?"

"This is Alex. He's not too big on wrestling, but he sure likes to play with cars."

Blane laughed. "Hello, Alex. I'm Blane, and I think cars are pretty cool too. Are you having fun playing with my buddy, Jay?"

Ducking his head and reaching for another car, Blane barely caught the subtle nod.

"Alex is a little shy around people he doesn't know." The petite woman standing beside Trinity extended her hand. "Hi. I'm Alex's mom, Crystal."

"Blane. And it's quite all right. I'm just glad Jay is with us today. Looks like they're becoming buddies."

"He's been wonderful. All the staff and doctors have been too. And then, y'all come and spend time with these kids even though you're bound to be busy. Y'all don't know what it means to the kids and their families."

"It's the least we can do, and we're thrilled to be able to. These kids have faced things we can't even imagine. If we can put a smile on their faces for even a minute, it's worth it."

"Alex may not be a big wrestlin' fan, but his daddy is. He's gonna be real sorry he missed you. If he didn't have to work, I guarantee he'd a been here. But even with fundraising and insurance, medical bills just keep comin'."

"Do you have a smartphone?"

Her brows created a *V*. "Sure. Why?"

"Why don't you get it out, and we can make a video for him. He shouldn't have to miss out."

If someone could figure out how to harness the energy in a smile, the hospital could have run off of Crystal's for a year. Pulling her phone from her pocket, she opened the camera. "That is too sweet. Thank you."

"No problem at all. Now, what's his name?"

"Alex. We named our little one after him."

"Perfect." He waited for her to aim the camera at him. "Hi, Alex. I'm Blane Sterling."

# 16

"I don't want to."

Trinity ignored the pouting glare her son directed at her. "You love zoos. Come on. It will be fun."

"No. Blane's supposed to come with us. I don't want to do it if he can't come too."

Blane had been unavailable to accompany them on their hike and picnic the day after their trip to the cancer ward. He was on the roster for that week's show, and episodes were recorded on Wednesdays. When he'd joined them for supper that evening, he'd also let her know he wouldn't be able to go to the zoo with them because he needed to shoot some promos. It was a work week for him, after all. Too bad her son didn't seem to understand that.

A slight breeze ruffled Jay's curls as he stared up at her. With his wind-tousled hair and big eyes watching her, it was easy to see past the stubborn set of his jaw to the disappointment bringing out his iron will. She knew he wasn't trying to be difficult. He simply wanted his new friend with them.

Trinity led her son to a metal bench outside the zoo entrance and sat to put herself on his level. "It's been super cool having Blane join us on our adventures, hasn't it?"

His head bobbed in agreement.

"I wish he could be here too. It's great having someone else join us for all the fun things we're doing. But we're on vacation. At home mommy has to work illustrating books while you're at school."

"And sometimes at night while I watch TV."

She smiled. "Yes, and sometimes then too. I've even done some work while we've been here. When you were out fishing with Blane, I stayed inside to work. After you've gone to sleep, I've been sketching and getting work done. And we're on vacation."

"Vacation's for fun. Not work." His serious voice mimicked her response when they'd been packing to leave, and she'd assured him they would spend every day doing things they would enjoy.

"Yes, it is. And we're on vacation, but Blane isn't. He's part of our adventure, but this is his home. This is where he works. We're thankful Blane has been able to join us for so many things. But because he's working, we know he can't be part of all of them. So, we have a choice to make. We can refuse to have fun unless Blane is there and miss out on a lot of things, or we can do stuff even when he can't be there and tell him all about it."

Little lips twisted to the side as Jay thought about his options. "Can we take lots of pictures? I bet Blane would like to see lots of pictures. And a video. Can we make a video for Blane? If we make a video, it would be like he came with us. Can we, Mom?"

Trinity pulled Jay in close for a hug. "I think those are both great ideas. Now, what do you say we go introduce ourselves to some animals?"

———

"And Mom said you'd prob'ly like the penguins too. So, I made a video of them playing. It's right here." Jay shoved the phone into Blane's open hand and pressed play before continuing. "I liked the penguins, but I really liked watching the otters. And the sea lion show. It was a lot of fun too. People sitting up close got wet, but we got there late and couldn't sit up front. I told Mom we should get there earlier next time, but all she said was we'll see. And we both know what that means."

Blane wasn't sure whether he was supposed to be watching the screen or Jay's animated recounting of the day's events. Trying to do both, he caught a couple seconds of the penguin video and Jay's dramatic eye roll in response to his mother's lack of enthusiasm for being drenched by sea lions on their next visit. Before he could respond, Jay snatched the phone and scrolled through pictures until he found the one he wanted. He plopped down on the sofa next to Blane and held it up for inspection.

"You'll love this one. There was a petting zoo with all sorts of little animals. And I got to feed the goats, which sounds cool, but it's a little scary too. I took the bottle into the pen and all the goats wanted to drink, and nobody wanted to take turns. I held it above my head, but that wasn't right either 'cause all the goats just jumped up on me trying to get their food. Mom had to come take the bottle from me to get the goats to go away. I'm not doing that again any time soon."

A wide-mouthed yawn punctuated the end of his story. Blane looked at the clock. A glance at Trinity confirmed bedtime was just around the corner.

"It sounds like you had a great time today. And I need to thank you."

His face scrunched up. "For what?"

"I love the zoo, and I was a little sad I couldn't go with you. But you brought the zoo to me with all your pictures and videos. That was really nice of you."

"Are you coming with us tomorrow?"

Blane didn't have to force disappointment. It was all too real. "No, partner. I have to work again. But tomorrow night, we'll have an outdoor movie night. Since it's your last night before going home, you can even choose the movie. And we'll eat nachos and popcorn and cookies too. How does that sound?"

Another yawn prevented his answer.

Trinity stood from where she'd worked at the table while Jay told him about their day. "It sounds perfect. But right now, I know a boy who needs to get some sleep."

"Can Blane tuck me in?"

He nodded as Trinity looked to him for approval.

"Sure."

As talkative as Jay had been all evening, he fell asleep as soon as Blane tucked him in. Leaving the door cracked a bit, he made his way back to the living room to find Trinity sitting on the couch.

"Please don't stop working on my account. I know you have things to do, books to illustrate, and you've kept busy with Jay all day."

She shook her head. "I completed everything I needed to. I worked ahead before we ever left for the trip so I wouldn't fall behind on any deadlines."

"You sure?"

"Positive."

Blane claimed the opposite end of the couch and faced

Trinity. If she didn't have an almost pensive look on her face, he could have happily sat there memorizing each and every feature in silence.

"Want to talk about it?"

"Talk about what?"

Blane raised an eyebrow. "About whatever has given you that thoughtful, faraway look on your face."

As he waited for her answer, Trinity's shoulders straightened, and her chin came up. She turned to him with a smile that didn't quite fill her eyes with their normal light.

"Guess I was just thinking about how nice our vacation has been. You've helped make it so much better than I ever imagined it. But after tomorrow, it's back to the real world. We'll be home a couple weeks, and then Jay will go spend a month in Illinois with Tuck's parents. After that, it's back-to-school shopping time. Summer will be a distant memory."

The excuse didn't fool Blane. Trinity had more than the end of summer blues. But she obviously didn't want to talk about it, and he wasn't going to push. "But it's going to have some great ones, isn't it?"

Trinity's smile seemed less forced. "Yes. Jay and I definitely have some great memories to take home with us."

Scooting close, he draped his arm around her shoulders while wiggling his eyebrows. "And would I happen to be one of those great memories?"

Expecting a grin, even a laugh, Blane was confused with the return of her contemplative expression. His arm dropped and he eased over on the cushions to give her space.

"Talk to me. What's going on in that beautiful head of yours?"

She refused to look at him as she stood and made her way to stare out the window. Blane's stomach tightened. Nerves happened every time he waited for his entrance music to cue up. He was used to nerves. This was entirely different, and it left him with a growing sense of dread.

"Trinity?" It was all he could ask. As much as he wanted answers, he couldn't help fearing whatever was on her mind wasn't anything he actually wanted to hear.

The sheen of tears in her eyes could be seen from where Blane stood across the room. She licked her lips and opened her mouth to speak, only to shut it again. The knot in his stomach tightened. Her throat moved as she swallowed and tried again.

"I'm afraid that's all you're going to be. Part of a memory."

What? They'd talked about this. About giving them a chance. Where had this come from? He raked a hand through his hair to the band that held it. Shaking his head, he stood but stopped himself from going to her. Before he drew any closer, he had to know.

"Is that what you want?"

"No."

It was barely a squeak, but it was the answer he hoped for. There was too much unsettled for him to take her in his arms, reassure her with his closeness. But he had to be nearer. He moved to stand in front of her and took her hands in his. He waited until she looked up at him to speak.

"I don't either. You know that, though. So, where is this coming from?"

"Jay had such a good time today."

The shift in subjects caught him off-guard. Unsure what to say, he opted to stay silent. A few seconds of uneasy silence passed.

"He didn't want to go when we first got there." She continued the train of thought. "Zoos are some of his favorite places to be, and he completely refused to go in. Had a complete meltdown in the parking lot."

The point still eluded him, but at least Blane had a way to respond. "Do you think he was tired? The week has been a full one for him. The poor kid has to be worn out."

One hand fell from his grasp, but the other held as Trinity led him back to the sofa. She dropped into the place she'd previously occupied. Blane stood awkwardly above her unsure of his welcome sitting next to her. Instead, he moved to the cushion at the far end. The silence was thick, but still, he waited. He'd opened the door to continue the conversation. It was up to Trinity to step through it.

She brushed away an invisible spot on her jeans without looking up. "It's more than that. He wanted you, and you weren't there."

His lungs deflated as Trinity looked up at him with tears running down her cheeks.

"I ... I had to work. He knows I wanted to be there, right?"

A palm across her cheek wiped away the evidence of her emotions. "Yeah, he knows. But he's eight, Blane. Eight years old. He gets that people have jobs and adult stuff to do, but he can't help what he wants. And he can't help being disappointed when it doesn't happen."

"I'm sorry."

She shook her head. "There's nothing to apologize for. But we've got to understand it's the way things are. Tomorrow is our last day here, and I want it to be a great one for Jay. But what about the next day? Or the day after that? What happens when Jay wants to spend time with you, and you can't make it up for a visit? Or worse, what happens if what we have ends, and you're not there at all? What we do matters to that little boy."

Head resting on the back of the sofa, Blane stared at the empty whiteness of the ceiling. The fears she expressed were real possibilities. There was no way to argue that they couldn't happen. As close as they were, they'd only known each other a week. Neither of them was ready to pledge their life to the other. *Please, God, help me. I don't know what to say. I don't know how to make this better. Should I even try?*

The answer came suddenly and clearly. He wasn't ready to give up on what they'd just started. Peace he couldn't explain filled Blane as he considered the situation. It wasn't a guaranteed outcome, but that wasn't needed.

"What do you want?"

"Jay—"

He shook his head. "What do *you* want?"

Trinity rubbed her lips together, staring at something over his shoulder. The fixer in him wanted to push for an answer, maybe even lead her to the one he thought she'd say. Instead, he forced himself to sit still and stay silent. If the answer didn't come from inside her, it wouldn't mean as much.

"I want my son safe from being hurt beyond what he's already faced."

"I get that. I think all mothers must feel that way, and I can see where you'd feel it more than most. You and Jay have been through a lot." He paused and waited until she looked at him before continuing. "It's admirable. But we both know it's not going to happen."

Her posture stiffened. Hitting the nerve damaged by her loss was inevitable, and he had to proceed with caution. The last thing Blane wanted was to add to her pain.

"You can close yourself off to every possibility that comes your way, but it won't keep pain away. A kid at school will call him a name. At tryouts, there will be better kids, and he won't make the team. A girl he's head over heels for will turn him down flat or worse, go out with him for a while and then break up with him. Someone else will get the scholarship or the job he applies for."

"It breaks my heart to even think about things like that." Tears rimmed her eyes. "I know there will be painful things. I do. But how can I go forward with something that might add to that list?"

"Because you know that pain may be a possibility, but love and joy are also possibilities." *God, guide my words.* "You go forward knowing no matter what happens, God is right there with you and Jay. I can't promise you'll never be victims of pain or loss again, but it's your faith that will keep you from remaining victims. It may not erase the pain completely, but it's His strength that will help you both heal and keep living the life He wants for you."

"How do you know?"

"It's already happened. You and Jay have come through so much, and you're still passionate about your faith and living life and helping others. You haven't shut him off from the world. You encourage him to try new things. And his daddy isn't a forbidden subject in your home. You've walked through the fire, and you're coming through it victorious."

Her silent gaze and blank expression left Blane wondering if she was angry or considering his words. Blane kept his place as she stood and wandered from the sofa to the doorway to the bedroom where Jay was, hopefully, sleeping. Leaning toward the crack between the door and frame, she peeked inside before turning back to Blane.

Arms stiffly folded across her chest sparked the image of a shield in Blane's mind. Was she preparing herself for battle? Putting her on the defensive was far from what he'd hoped to accomplish.

She stopped at the corner of the couch. "So, because pain is inevitable, it would be wrong to stop things now, with you, before they go further?"

He rose, facing her, but making no move to draw closer.

"No. I can't tell you if you should let us continue. That's between you and God. I'll respect whatever you decide. I only wanted to ask you to please consider not making your decision out of fear."

When she continued to watch him with arms crossed and jawline tight, Blane knew the conversation was over.

"I know I've dropped a lot on you. I'm sorry. Whatever you decide, I'll respect it. You've got a lot to think about. So, I'll leave you alone."

# 17

*'ll leave you alone.* Blane's words echoed in her mind an hour after he left. Lying in bed, hoping sleep would come, was definitely the wrong decision. Not only was she failing to evict the conversation from her thoughts, she was also forced not to fidget. With Jay beside her, even in a queen-sized bed, tossing and turning would mean a miserable night's sleep for both of them. A cranky child was the last thing she wanted on their final day of vacation.

Determined at least one of them should be rested, Trinity gave up and made her way to the kitchen. A cup of chamomile tea might help calm her body and mind enough to rest. She filled the tea pot with water and plucked a cup from the cabinet. While waiting for the water to boil, she leaned back against the counter.

*God, I don't want to be alone.* The moment Blane had uttered those words, she'd known it deep inside. Of course, he hadn't intended them that way. It didn't matter. The gravity and direction of their conversation twisted the meaning in her mind. It didn't help that he'd planted images in her mind of Jay growing up. Adulthood was still far off, but everything more experienced parents told her convinced her it would happen before she knew it.

The kettle whistled. Trinity grabbed it off the burner before the sound disturbed Jay. With cup of tea in hand, she sat at the table. Her mind returned to her last thought as she dunked the tea bag in the water over and over.

One day, she would blink, and Jay would be off on his own. Where would that leave her? Alone. And what would she have accomplished? Blane was right on that too. She could coddle and protect all she wanted, but Jay would know more disappointment and hurt than he'd already faced. She couldn't keep it all at bay, but she could keep introducing him to God. The relationship she experienced with God kept her strong. He would do the same for her son.

But reaffirming that belief in her heart failed to provide answers to her current predicament. She stood, pulled the tea bag from the water, and tossed it in the trash before dropping back into her chair.

A hesitant sip from the cup left her tongue feeling a little scorched. She pushed aside the cup. Crossing her arms on the vacated spot, she lowered her head to rest on them. Her questions would not be so easily shoved to the side.

"Lord, what do I do about Blane?"

With silence answering, Trinity felt the urge to call Autumn. Even in the middle of the night, her best friend would pick up the phone. She always did. And hearing an audible answer would be comforting. But her phone was on the charger, in the room where Jay slept. Could she retrieve it without waking him? Did she even want to try? It didn't take a genius to figure out Autumn's take on the situation.

"Blane's right, you know?" She lovingly mimicked her friend's voice. "You can't make decisions out of fear. As for the rest of it, I can't tell you whether you need to end things with the man or not. That's up to you."

No, she didn't need to interrupt Autumn's sleep. Fake Autumn was right. The decision was hers alone.

She sat up and sipped her now tepid tea. Putting it off wouldn't make it easier. It was time to figure out if anything beyond that initial fear of possibly adding to Jay's pain kept her from wanting to pursue a relationship with Blane.

Faith was a non-issue. From all she'd seen, Blane's faith was strong and true. Jay loved him. And the chemistry between Blane and her was off the charts in a way not even she and Tucker had experienced. The distance between her home and his could present problems, but certainly they could find a way to overcome those.

"What about You, God? I want Your will, Your way in my life. I need to know if You approve of this relationship, or do You want me to move on?"

Trinity swallowed the last of her tea. The silence no longer torturing her mind with what-ifs, she sat waiting for the quiet nudge in her spirit that often came when she sought God's leading. Peace came with her answer.

After rinsing her cup in the sink, Trinity returned to the bedroom. She was finally ready to sleep.

———

"Mom, can I have some more nachos?"

"Sure you can. Why don't I get them, so you don't miss as much of the movie?"

Sitting on the picnic blanket next to Jay, Blane's attention shifted from the movie projecting on the outdoor inflatable screen to Trinity heading for the folding table holding all the snacks. The lawn chairs his parents opted to use sat directly in his line of sight. As his gaze passed over them, he couldn't help noticing his mom's encouraging smile. Knowing his parents approved of Trinity was comforting.

Too bad he was still in limbo, waiting for her to decide if there was a relationship to approve.

An unexpected squawk from some character in the movie brought him back to the screen. When Jay giggled beside him, Blane determined to keep his focus on making the child's last night with them a fun one. The evening wasn't about will she or won't she. The next morning Trinity and Jay would head back to Missouri. It was Blane's job to make sure they left with great memories.

Beside him, Jay smiled up from where he sat cross-legged. "You want more nachos too? Mom can get you some."

"I think I'll stick with popcorn for now. But I'm not sure where you're putting all this food. I think you've eaten more than all of us combined."

Jay rolled his eyes. "Don't you think you're being a bit dramatic?"

A bit dramatic? Blane wasn't sure how to answer. Where did an eight-year-old kid come up with a phrase like that to begin with?

A plate of nachos appeared in front of Jay as Trinity took her place on his other side. A wry smile twisted her lips as she looked at her son. "I wonder where you've heard that before. Maybe you've heard it a few times? Hmm?"

Jay shrugged with an impish grin and turned back to the movie. Blane had no trouble believing Trinity had taught him the phrase. And even though Jay was a great kid, with his energy level and excitability, it wasn't hard to imagine there would be many opportunities for dramatics.

As the movie ended, Blane's parents helped clean up what remained of the snacks and put away the projector before

Trinity announced it was bedtime for Jay. Blane was happy to take a last opportunity to tuck Jay into bed while Trinity put away a few things in the kitchen. After helping him with his prayers, Blane listened in amusement as Jay reenacted his favorite scenes from the confines of his bed, the boy's hands never stilling as if they could act out the motions of the story.

"Can I have just one story, Blane, please?" Jay's bottom lip jutted out while his eyes took on that puppy dog look that came so easily to small children.

"Your mom said no story tonight, just prayers."

His hands clasped together in a pleading motion. "Mom doesn't have to know. You could just tell me a quick one."

One little story couldn't hurt. And it would make Jay happy. Trinity would understand. But she did say no stories. To go against her wishes, no matter how small a matter, would not be wise.

Blane shook his head. "Sorry, partner. Mom said no stories, and we need to listen to her."

"But Blane, it's my last bedtime with you. Please. Please can you tell me a story? I promise I'll be good for Mom tomorrow. I'll let her listen to the songs she likes on the radio, and I won't complain even once. And no matter how boring it is, I won't ask if we're there yet. Please, just one story."

It hurt to disappoint Jay. How did Trinity do this every day? "We can't. I'm sorry."

"But ..."

"No buts, mister." Trinity's voice joined the discussion from the doorway.

"Fine."

"Have you said your prayers?"

A curt nod was her only answer. Blane wanted to correct him but decided against saying anything. It was not his place to parent Jay in that way.

"Then, it's lights out time." She came into the room and gave Jay a hug and kiss, which he surprisingly returned. "Good night. Love you."

"Love you, Mom." Jay's voice was a little quieter than usual. Though it sounded disappointed, Blane couldn't detect any disrespect. "Love you, too, Blane."

Blane ruffled Jay's hair. "Love you, too, partner. Now get some sleep."

Movie night was set up and ready to start when he came home from cutting promos, leaving no time for him to talk to Trinity about the status of their relationship. He'd enjoyed the evening, but an unsettled feeling left him less than confident. With him on one side of Jay and Trinity on the other, it would have been easy to hold her hand during the movie.

When she'd stretched out on the blanket, resting back on her hands, he'd considered testing the waters. He chose against it. Now, he wasn't sure whether he should stay to talk or say his good-byes.

He headed toward the door, stopping short of exiting. Could he really walk out without knowing where they stood? Even if Trinity hadn't come to any decisions, knowing she was still considering her options would be something.

"I thought you might want to stay and talk." Trinity spoke quietly.

"Do you want to talk?" Blane turned toward her. The need to see her face when she answered was strong. The last thing he wanted was to leave her feeling pushed, and he was certain her face would let him know if she meant the invitation or not.

One shoulder lifted in a noncommittal shrug. "I was kind of hoping to, if you want to. I mean, I understand if you can't, or don't want to, or whatever."

The discomfort he heard in her voice broke his heart and put him on edge at the same time. It didn't sound like she was anxious for conversation, at least not in a good way. That wasn't encouraging. But it was still necessary, regardless of the outcome. Stepping away from the door, he settled into a chair near the sofa. Until he knew where things stood, he couldn't allow himself to get any closer.

Eyeing him from the far end of the sofa, Trinity couldn't stop fidgeting. Knowing her thoughts made her nervous did nothing to ease his own. His stomach tightened as it did in the ring when he steeled himself for a hard blow to the abs.

"I'm not sure how to start," she admitted, suddenly unable to make eye contact.

"Just say what you have to say."

His words at least brought her attention to him instead of the rest of the room. But the hurt on her face wasn't what he wanted. The impatience in his tone was uncalled for, and it didn't help matters at all.

"I'm sorry, Trinity," he apologized wishing he was close enough to reassure her with his touch. "That sounded way harsher than I intended. I only meant, maybe you should rip the bandage off and just say whatever is on your mind."

Wariness still reflected in her face, but she nodded. "I understand. Last night must have been difficult for you too. And then to come home and have family fun night with nothing settled. I'm sorry. And I'm sorry this conversation needs to take place at all."

Her words could mean anything. Don't rush to judgment. The reminder did nothing to ease the sick feeling growing in his gut. He tried to keep his expression passive. Not an easy feat when he was biting his tongue to keep from asking her to put him out of his misery.

"I don't know why I'm so nervous. In all the conversations we've had over the past week, I've never been uncomfortable. But it's not because I'm not settled in my decision. God and I had a long talk last night, and when I finally shut my own mouth and let Him have a say, He let me know exactly what I needed to know."

"And?"

Trinity gave a nervous giggle. "I guess I'm not ripping off the bandage, as you say. Sorry about that too. I just, I need you to know it wasn't you. You've been nothing short of wonderful this entire week. All of this is because of me. You were right. I was operating out of fears instead of faith."

If she didn't get to the point, he was going to burst. While she was moving closer, he could do without all the steps that brought her to her answer. Well, that wasn't entirely true. Knowing she recognized the truth of her defense mechanism would be worth anything under other circumstances. Still, couldn't she tell him and then go back through everything?

"And did finding that out help you make your decision?"

Her smile gave him hope. "Yes. But not like you might think. Fear wasn't a factor anymore, but I still had to work through the decision. I could look at my choices from a different perspective and decide what to do based on my wants and my faith. Ultimately, I want to be inside God's will for my life, and I was able to consider that objectively and experience His peace as I found my answer."

Was she trying to kill him? Blane gave what he hoped was a patient smile. "May I ask you to share your answer?"

Beautiful eyes grew wide. "I can't believe I did it again. I'm so sorry. While I don't know where it will lead in the future, God gave me peace in seeing where our relationship goes. That is, if you'll still have me after the wait and having to listen to me blather on."

Relief flooded through Blane. Unable to sit still any longer, he joined Trinity on the couch. Even the cushion next to hers put too much distance between them. He took her hands in his.

"I was hoping you'd say that. And while I could have done without the nervous chatter, there is nothing I want more than to still have you."

A smile shaped her perfect mouth, drawing his attention. He leaned in just enough to gauge her reaction. When she eased toward him, he took it as answer, wrapping one arm around her waist to pull her close. He kept his kiss slow and gentle. It would be too easy to stoke the fire and cross lines that wouldn't be good for either one of them.

Easing back, he shifted so she could lean back against him. He draped an arm around her shoulder, and she raised her hand to hold his. Her sigh made him smile.

"I won't want to leave tomorrow."

"I'm sure Mom and Dad wouldn't mind renting you the apartment. They've loved having you and Jay." He was only half joking, but she didn't need to know that.

"I'd be lying if I said the thought wasn't tempting. But I have a life I need to get back to in Missouri. We need to figure out how this long-distance thing between us is going to work."

Blane leaned his head back against the cushions. "In a lot of ways, any relationship would end up being kind of long-distance. I'm on the road a lot for work. I know it isn't the same, but I think phone and video calls are going to become our best friends. And any time I can, I'll visit. Travel is easier for me. I've only got myself to worry about. I do have one thought not directly related to us though."

"What's that?"

"I don't want Jay to feel left out. Our relationship is important to me, but I want to make sure he doesn't feel like extra baggage. Would it be okay for me to call and do the bedtime routine with him with a video call once a week? I can look at my calendar and see what day I could be most consistent on, and if I have to miss that night, I'll substitute in another one."

Trinity sat up and faced him in one motion. Without a word, she planted a quick kiss on his lips. "Blane Sterling, you have to be the most thoughtful, loving man I've ever met."

"So, is that a yes? I promise I don't take this lightly. As long as you allow it, I will be there for Jay. I wouldn't say I'll do it and not follow through."

She stopped his words with a hand to his chest. "I trust you. You've shown nothing but care and thoughtfulness to Jay. There's nothing he'd love more than to have his partner tuck him in each week."

Glancing over her shoulder, the clock on the wall caught his attention. He stood and looked down at Trinity. "I'm going to kick myself for doing this, but it's getting late. You have a long drive ahead of you tomorrow. You need your rest."

"Always the gentleman, watching out for me. If you're not careful, I'm going to completely fall for you, Blane Sterling." She blushed as if she hadn't intended to admit it.

He leaned down to brush a kiss across her cheek. With his lips still close to her ear he whispered. "And I'll happily join you in the fall." He stood back up. "But for now, goodnight. I'll see you and Jay off in the morning."

# 18

Trinity took a sip of lemonade as she watched Jay splash in the pool from her deck chair. "It happened so fast. I mean, I was attracted to Tuck right from the start, but the relationship built slow and steady over time. Do you think that means something?"

Autumn secured her hair into a ponytail before answering. "Considering my unbreakable single streak, I may not be the best person to ask."

"I'm serious. Besides, you've had plenty of people ask you out. You've just been wise enough to say no instead of dating just to say you have someone. There's nothing wrong with waiting for the right man."

The ponytail swung back and forth with the shake of her head. "Sometimes I'm not sure it's wisdom as much as unattainably high standards, but we're not talking about me. Does it mean something that you had an instant connection with a guy who is as sweet and thoughtful as he is gorgeous? Yeah, it means you should be counting your blessings."

"Jay, don't you dare run on the edge of the pool! We walk

on wet ground." She stared down her son to make sure he not only heard but obeyed. "Believe me, I've thanked God every day for bringing Blane into our lives. He made our trip more special than we could have hoped. He doesn't even flinch at dating with a child as part of the deal. He is so good with Jay. But is it moving too quickly?"

"I can't answer that for you. I mean, you aren't engaged yet or anything. So, that's good. Have you said those three huge, little words?"

She shook her head. "No. I can't say I'm not feeling it though. He's called every night since we've been home. You should see Jay light up when Blane video calls him to tuck him in. It's so sweet. We talk for hours, and I've nearly said those words multiple times before ending the calls."

Autumn looked out over the water and rubbed her lips together. "Is it quick? Yes. Does that mean it's not love? Absolutely not. Is it as deep a love as what it could be ten years from now? No. But you don't need me to tell you all this."

"What do you mean?"

"You had Tucker. This may be different, and that's good too. But you know what love is and what it isn't. You know how love works. And I know you've prayed about all this. Trust what God is telling you."

"But what if other people ..."

"What other people?"

Trinity sighed. "Tuck's mom and dad. I called them to see when they planned on coming to get Jay for his annual stay at grandma and grandpa's house. I told them about the trip and meeting Blane. They seemed fine with everything, until I told them Blane and I are dating."

"And?"

"And it's only been eighteen months since we lost Tucker. It's too soon. At least, that's how the conversation started.

Then they cautioned that dating Blane meant our private lives could end up being very public. They're positive Tucker wouldn't want that for his son."

Autumn leaned forward, resting her forearms on her legs. "Have you considered those concerns?"

"Yes."

"Have you asked God for wisdom in pursuing this relationship? Did you bring those concerns to Him for His leading?"

"Of course. I did before I ever spoke to them about it. And I did again after speaking with them."

"Then, and know I don't say this lightly, you need to remember they are Tucker's parents, not Tucker. It's not like when a spouse dies, the grandparents assume the vacated parental position. They are Jay's grandparents, not his parent."

"Are they right, though? Would Tucker want this?"

"I can't answer that. I do know Tucker would understand that any man coming into your life would not be him. He would know another man would do things differently than he did. If he had something to say about it, I think it would be for you to ask yourself if the man you're letting into your world, into Jay's world, loves the Lord and takes good care of you two. Beyond that, I have no doubts Tucker would trust your judgment."

Trinity reached over and playfully pushed her friend's shoulder. "You are a pretty wise woman."

"I know." The sideways smile countered any chance of arrogance in her friend's answer.

———

Trinity wanted to relieve the tension emanating from the other end of the phone call, but she knew she had to stand her ground. "I loved Tucker too. I still do, but that doesn't mean I won't ever love again. And Blane is a great guy."

"But he's a wrestler, Trinity." Her mother-in-law's impatient sigh came through loud and clear. "He's famous. A public life is not what you, and especially not Jay, need."

*Patience. Lord, give me patience.* "With all due respect, Rita, that isn't your decision to make. I've prayed about this relationship, and peace is the only thing I feel about it."

"Maybe your emotions are getting in the way? Have you considered that?"

Trinity took a deep, calming breath before saying anything. "I am not a love-sick teenager. I'm not only a mature adult, I'm also a parent who takes her God-given responsibility to raise my child very seriously."

"Be that as it may," Rita began, "if you won't listen to us on this, we may have to rethink Jay's time with us."

What? They would punish Jay for her choice? How could they even begin to convince themselves that refusing to see their grandson was good for anyone?

"Excuse me?" Certainly, Trinity misheard her.

"It's not that we don't want to see him. We do. But we don't want to condone your choice, and if you're still seeing that man, Jay will most certainly bring him up. What would we be able to say that wouldn't paint you or him in a bad light?"

"I can't believe you're considering this."

"It's not decided yet. Tate and I will discuss it tonight. We'll let you know tomorrow."

It was the best she was going to get. "Fine. Just call me when you have your answer."

The shaking started as soon as Trinity ended the call. Disappointment and anger spurred each other on inside as she replayed the conversation in her mind. Despite the direction the situation had gone, Trinity's peace over her relationship with Blane remained. But it would devastate Jay if he couldn't see his grandparents. And how could she explain the reason?

*Lord, I need a miracle to straighten this mess out. Let them give Blane a chance. Let them see I'm not forgetting or replacing their son. Help them understand I'm simply trying to continue living a life filled with love.*

As she prayed, Trinity realized she couldn't hold her in-law's feelings against them. They were wrong in trying to force her to abide by their wishes, but they were also hurting. Moving past the devastation of losing her husband had been difficult. She couldn't begin to imagine what it was like losing a son. She added an extra petition for Tucker's parents to find relief from their pain and experience healing that would allow them to accept new love in her life, whether with Blane or someone else.

# 19

Trinity took the phone from Jay's outstretched hand, kissing him on the head in the process. "Good night. Love you."

"Love you too, Mom."

When Jay snuggled deep into his covers, Trinity turned on the small monitor beside his bed. She turned off the light and headed to the patio. She always let Jay hang up when he and Blane had their weekly video call tuck in. It helped Jay understand Blane was calling for him specifically instead of feeling like an add-on to Trinity's relationship with Blane.

Lightning bugs filled the field behind their house with almost as many twinkling lights as the stars high overhead. Trinity cocooned herself into the egg-shaped patio swing her parents bought her for her birthday. It was too warm to wrap herself in a blanket, but it was cozy nonetheless.

The light from her phone shattered the darkness. She rubbed her eyes as she answered Blane's call.

"Hello again."

"Hey, sweetheart. Been waiting all day to talk to you."

"Well, Jay's down for the count. So, I'm yours for as long as you want."

"I like the sound of that. Listen, I want to get up there to see Jay before school starts. You said he visits Tucker's parents for a bit in the summer. Do you know when he's going?"

Trinity shifted in her seat. "I'm waiting to hear. Usually, it would be this Monday, but they have some things to work out first."

"What aren't you telling me?"

"What do you mean?" Even though she knew he couldn't see her over the phone, Trinity forced herself to sit still.

"It's something in your voice. There's something more to the story, isn't there?"

Trinity rubbed her neck with her hand. "They aren't sure they want to keep him this year."

"And? I know that isn't what has you sounding so stressed."

Telling the truth was hardwired into her DNA. But the last thing she wanted to do was hurt Blane. Trinity thought through her words very carefully before speaking. "They're having a hard time with me dating again. They think it's too soon."

"What does that have to do with Jay visiting?"

"They also believe a relationship with a public figure, such as yourself, isn't good for Jay. And they originally told me they didn't think they could keep him, because they knew he would talk about you, and they basically don't want to hear it."

Blane blew out a hard breath. "I'm so sorry."

"It's not a done deal. I spoke with them again today and respectfully reminded them that I get to be the judge of when to begin dating again, and I'm Jay's parent. I assured them I've prayed about this relationship and have a peace about it. I asked them to do the same and tell me tomorrow whether or not they're going to change their mind about his annual trip."

"That can't be easy."

"It's not. But it's more about Jay than myself. I don't want him to lose out because my in-laws can't deal with me moving on. And really, that's what this is about."

"You're pretty amazing. Did anyone ever tell you that?"

Trinity laughed. "I'm glad you think so. May I ask why?"

"Anger is the natural response to something like this, but you've chosen to understand where your in-laws are coming from. Instead of lashing out, you encouraged them to take the time they needed and pray about the situation."

"Oh, believe me. I was not a happy camper when they told me. I spouted off to Autumn about it. I needed my own reminders and reassurance before I handled that conversation."

"I'm glad Autumn was there for you, then. And Trinity?"

"Yes?"

"I'll be praying for your in-laws and the entire situation. And if you ever want me to call and speak with them, introduce myself, or whatever, just let me know."

Trinity smiled. That was the last thing her in-laws were ready for, but she appreciated the sentiment. Blane might think she was the amazing one, but she had to disagree. Any man who would counter the doubts of perfect strangers with an offer to reach out and smooth things over was a keeper in her book.

———

Trinity grabbed the bowl of popcorn and headed to the living room where Autumn waited to watch the UWO Summer Brawl pay-per-view. She curled her legs under her as she sat on the couch, leaving the cushion between them to hold their snack.

Autumn grabbed a handful. "Did they say anything else when they picked up Jay?"

"Not really. Though Jay asked them straight up if Blane could have their phone number so he could keep up with the weekly tuck ins. I'd told him I didn't think Blane would be able to since he didn't have the number, and I thought he was good with that. Apparently, not."

"That kid. Gotta love him." Autumn chuckled.

"And, of course with Jay asking, they didn't say no. We'll see what happens."

Trinity grabbed the remote from the coffee table and hit the volume button a couple times as the announcers for the event came on. She raised the sound enough to hear, but not too loud to prevent them talking through the matches they weren't as interested in. Between bites of popcorn, Trinity explained the moves and rules she understood, which weren't many. Neither being wrestling fans, they were more than content to chat until the headlining match.

The final commercial break ended. The challenger strutted his way to the ring. Giddy excitement pulsed through Trinity as the lights came down and Blane's music blared through the stadium. Blane made his way down the ramp with laser lights and pyrotechnics accenting each step.

"The man knows how to make an entrance. I'll say that for sure." Autumn stated as she sat transfixed to the screen.

The bell rang. The match ensued. Blane started off strong, keeping the smaller challenger on the defensive. Cheers went up from the duo on the couch with each successful move. From all he taught her about the sport, Trinity wasn't surprised when Blane charged his opponent only to have the agile man leapfrog over him and turn the tables on the champ.

"No. No. No. No!" Autumn's voice grew animated as the challenger took Blane to the mat and used his legs as leverage to flip Blane onto his stomach.

"I don't think it's over yet."

Autumn glanced at her before returning her attention to the television. Blane's legs were secured and his back bent at an uncomfortable angle as he writhed and fought to get out of what Trinity recognized as a popular submission hold, even if she couldn't remember the name.

"How can you say that? What can Blane do to get out of that?"

"Just watch."

Even as she spoke the words, Blane raised up to his forearms and painstakingly pulled himself toward the edge of the ring. No matter how much his captor struggled against it, Blane's size allowed him enough movement to drag himself to the ropes and take hold with one hand.

"One. Two. Three. Four." The referee counted until the challenger freed Blane from the hold.

Autumn, who'd moved to the edge of her seat, slumped against the back cushions. "What just happened?"

"It's a rule. Touch the ropes. Get out of the hold. The wrestler doing the holding has until a count of five to let their opponent go or be disqualified," Trinity answered as Blane took advantage of his competitor's frustration in the ring.

"Oh! Blane's got him now!"

Trinity laughed. For someone who wasn't any more a wrestling fan than she was, Autumn was really getting into the show. Trinity couldn't blame her though. Her own not-a-fan status had wavered quite a bit since meeting Blane.

It wasn't long before Blane geared up for his finishing move. By the time he ran across the ring at his opponent, the stadium was whipped into a frenzy chanting his name.

Trinity's muscles tensed in anticipation. In her periphery, she could see Autumn was reacting the same way.

Boot connected with face, dropping the challenger to his knees and then the mat. Blane covered him while the referee counted. On three, Trinity and Autumn jumped up at the same time in a victory cheer. Popcorn flew like confetti as the bowl bounced from its place on the sofa.

"He won!" Autumn exclaimed punching her fists in the air. "Woo-hoo!"

Trinity laughed at her friend's antics. But, truth be told, she felt the same way every time she watched him win. Concerned voices from the television drew her attention back to the ring. What were they saying? And why was Blane lying on his back in the middle of the ring?

"I'm not sure, Scott. I think our champion's arm could be seriously injured."

"I believe you could be right, Tony." Scott agreed with a nod. "Let's take a look at that sneak attack by Titan after his old tag team partner took the loss. Maybe Titan's trying to mend fences."

"It will take more than taking out Blane Sterling to heal those old wounds."

"Oh, no." Autumn sank onto the sofa.

Images of Titan, almost as big as Blane, running into the ring and attacking Blane while his back was turned filled the screen. The man grabbed Blane around the waist, hoisted him high in the air, and fell back launching Blane to the mat. Titan stood, glowering, before helping his old partner from the mat and up the ramp leading backstage.

Trinity righted the empty popcorn bowl and returned its contents from under their feet. "It's nothing to worry about. Happens all the time. It's just another part of the storyline."

As medics were called from the back, Trinity halted her

popcorn pickup. Despite her reassurance to Autumn, a sliver of worry crept in. True, the medics could be for show, but the way Blane remained motionless on the mat didn't sit well with her. The show cut to commercial. The commercials interrupted the otherwise silent room as the probability of real injury rose.

Blane's entrance music sounded from her phone. Only those who might contact her with the UWO had that tone. The suffocating bands across Trinity's chest loosened allowing her to breathe as she grabbed it to answer. Seeing Pamela's name where Blane's should be, tightened them once more.

"Hello?"

"Hello. Trinity? This is Pamela. Do you remember me?"

Her voice was calm, normal. Nothing could be wrong if her voice sounded like she was calling for a friendly chat, right?

"Yes, of course."

"Blane said you'd be watching tonight's match. Was he right?"

"Yes."

"Then you saw what happened after Blane won?"

"Yes." Couldn't she get to the point? People didn't call if nothing was wrong. Then again, maybe they did. What did she know? Pamela could be trying to put her mind at ease.

"I know you understand some injuries are … embellished for the sake of the story."

"Yes."

"Such an injury was supposed to happen tonight, but there was an accident. Titan didn't have enough control of the move, and Blane couldn't recover from it. He came down wrong and was knocked unconscious for several minutes."

Trinity, needing to hear more but not sure she could, sank to the arm of the couch. "Is he all right? You said he was unconscious. So, he's awake now?"

"He's awake." Her voice sounded hesitant. "But he's

suffered what appears to be a pretty severe concussion. Now, I don't want you to worry. He's getting the best possible care. I called because he would want you to know. Have you ever been around someone with a severe concussion?"

She shook her head. "No. I mean, I've had to watch people for signs of one. Jay fell at a friend's house once and had a mild one. He couldn't remember what happened, but other than that he was fine."

"The effects of Blane's concussion will likely be more severe than that. If he calls you over the next couple days, he may be confused or unable to concentrate on one thing too long. That's normal with injuries such as these. If you'll give me your email address, I'll send you some information from our team about concussion symptoms, concerns, and treatment."

Trinity hoped she gave Pamela the correct email address and remembered to thank her for calling, but she couldn't say for sure. She hung up, then startled to find Autumn right behind her on the couch.

"Did you hear all that?"

Autumn nodded. "I'm sorry. I know this was the last thing you expected when you invited me over tonight."

"You're right, but I'm glad you're here."

"Want me to stay?"

Trinity nodded, trying to swallow around the lump her runaway emotions forced into her throat.

"Want me to pray?"

Another nod.

# 20

"Eewww!" Autumn's voice carried across the bus station parking lot. "I'm going back to the car if you two are going to keep being gross."

Trinity stepped out of Blane's embrace knowing full well her friend was kidding. There's no way a public appropriate kiss and hug from Blane was causing Autumn any discomfort. She turned toward her friend, staying beside Blane. He draped his arm around her shoulders.

"Oh, please," Trinity gave attitude back to her. "I've seen you do worse in the church parking lot."

Autumn huffed. "I was thirteen!" She glanced toward Blane. "It was my rebellious phase. Any actions taken during that time of my life have reached their statute of limitations and in no way reflect my current state of faith."

A television announcer listing side effects for the newest heartburn medication couldn't have said it any better. The expression of confusion on Blane's face was priceless, like he didn't know how to handle Autumn's humor. Trinity's

HEATHER GREER

laughter must have eased his concern because his own friendly smile replaced the frightened deer look on his face.

"Blane, I'd like you to meet my best friend, Autumn. Autumn, Blane."

Hand extended Blane went in for a shake that didn't materialize. Instead, Autumn's impetuous nature ran to the front of the line, resulting in a squealing hug.

"Finally." Autumn stepped back, smiling up at Blane. "It's so good to meet you. I've been ready for this since the day Trinity first told me about you."

A brow raised. "And when was that?"

Trinity shot her friend a warning look that was promptly ignored.

"The day you met."

Another look directed at Autumn only brought out her friend's fluttery-eyed look of false innocence.

"Autumn."

Blane glanced between the two women with a devious smirk. "And what did Trinity have to say about me?"

"Autumn," Trinity warned with her best mom voice.

"Only that you were so sweet," Autumn continued, unaffected by her tone. "That you'd worked out everything to give Jay the experience of a lifetime."

Trinity relaxed when Autumn stopped. At least she hadn't veered into the completely embarrassing.

"Oh, and that you were super tall, super big, and super cute."

Heat rushed up Trinity's neck and flooded her cheeks. "Autumn!"

Hands outstretched to the side, she shrugged. "What? You did."

Blane's laugh rolled across the parking lot. "I think you and I are going to get along just fine."

188

Though some of her ire had floated away with Blane's laugh, Trinity knew she had to keep up a strong front. "After this, you two are not allowed to be anywhere near each other."

"Please." Autumn rolled her eyes. "You can't dictate that. I'm the one who arranged for Blane to stay in my brother's basement while he's here. My. Brother's. Basement. I have free rein to visit there any time I want."

"Fine. I can't keep you apart."

"You wouldn't want to anyway."

When had Autumn become so sassy? Oh, yeah. She'd always been that way. It just hadn't bothered Trinity before. She glanced between her best friend and her boyfriend, both looking as self-satisfied as the Cheshire Cat. Truth be told, it didn't bug her too much. It was a relief to know the two friends she was closest to were on the fast track to friendship themselves.

But she refused to acquiesce aloud. "Whatever. Let's get going. After all, Blane is recovering from a major concussion. He rode a train and bus to ensure he got here safely. We don't want him to have a heat stroke on top of everything else by making him stand in the sun during the hottest part of the summer."

Without waiting for an answer, she picked up Blane's bags and headed for Autumn's car. When she reached the locked trunk, she looked over her shoulder to Autumn following with Blane at her side. After hearing the click, she raised the trunk and stowed the bags inside. By the time she closed the trunk, Autumn was standing next to the driver's side with Blane waiting at the rear passenger door.

"Come on slowpoke. We're waiting." Autumn faked an impatient pout.

Trinity shook her head and went around to the front passenger door. Noticing for the first time how small Autumn's car was, she wondered how Blane would fold himself into the back seat.

"Why don't you sit up front? You can move the seat back and be more comfortable."

Blane looked from her to Autumn and back again. "It's fine. I can sit back here."

"Trinity, catch." Autumn called right before tossing her keys over the car.

Not prepared, and never good with hand-eye coordination, Trinity cringed at the incoming object. She thrust her hand out in the general direction and managed to touch the keys with her fingertips before they flew past her and landed on the pavement.

"What was that for?"

"You drive. Blane sits up front, and I'll take the back."

Blane opened his mouth, but Autumn held up a hand to ward off arguments.

"Nope. As owner of this car, I get full say about who rides where. Now, Blane, if you would kindly move, I need to get in. Thank you."

Retrieving the keys from the ground, Trinity couldn't help a bit of pride in having Autumn as a best friend. Always a great judge of situations, she saw Blane's hesitation but worked out everything to keep him comfortable. They'd gotten along great in the few minutes since they'd met, but they were practically strangers. Riding up front with her and trying to keep up conversation could have been awkward for him. Trinity would have to thank her privately.

With everyone settled into their new positions, Trinity pulled out of the parking lot. "Do we need to stop anywhere on the way to Mike's place?"

A quick check of the rearview mirror showed Autumn shaking her head. "Not me. What about you, Blane?"

"To tell you the truth, I could use something to eat. I haven't had anything since breakfast. But, if it's okay with Autumn, we don't have to stop. A drive-though is fine with me."

"Sounds great. Burgers and then we head to Mike's."

———

Everyone agreed a movie night sounded like the perfect way to hang out and let Blane take it easy. So, while Mike showed Blane to the finished basement, Autumn and Trinity made themselves at home in the kitchen on the house's main level.

"Will you pass me that box of brownie mix?" Trinity asked as she retrieved a bowl from the cabinet. Being best friends with Autumn made Mike like an adopted older brother, and she knew his kitchen as well as her own from many movie nights the three of them had shared.

Autumn handed the box to her before opening a phone app to order pizza. They wouldn't eat for a few hours, especially since Blane had just finished off a bacon double-cheeseburger, large fries, and a soda. But if they got everything ready now, they wouldn't have to worry about it later.

After adding the required egg, water, and oil to the bowl, Trinity grabbed a spatula to stir the mix. "You and Blane seem to like each other well enough, right?"

Order finished, Autumn set down her phone, and leaned back against the kitchen counter. "You like him. Isn't that what matters?"

"Of course, it is. But I'd like to know my best friend and my boyfriend are getting along. Knowing whether or not they can stand being together in the same room for more than a few minutes is important."

"I can't speak for Blane." Autumn grabbed a pitcher and

lemonade mix from the cabinet. "But I think he's a great guy. He's kind, funny, and giving. And he's obviously got it bad for you. Plus, he shares your faith, and he laughs at my jokes. I'd call that a winning combination."

Trinity slid the brownies into the oven and set the timer. "You are so full of it."

"That's why you love me."

"Love is one word for it."

Autumn cocked her head to one side and raised an eyebrow. "You know you love me. And I don't think I'm the only one you love either."

Trinity's gaze flew to the doorway as she put a silencing finger to her lips. "Shhh. You can't say things like that."

"Say things like what?" Mike's voice made an appearance seconds before he and Blane did.

"Nothing." Trinity jumped in with a headshake for emphasis before Autumn could speak. "Just girl talk is all. Why don't you two wait in the living room while we finish up in here? Maybe set up the card table for some board games until time for dinner and the movie?"

"Sure. Come on, Blane. I can tell when we're not wanted." Mike motioned for Blane to follow him, and the pair went to choose the evening's games.

Trinity waited until they were out of earshot before turning to Autumn. "Please, please don't say anything like that again. You and I both know how I feel, but Blane doesn't. I mean, we've not said those three little words to each other yet. I'm still wrestling with whether or not a month and a half is enough time to really know that yet, or at least to admit it."

"I think you know exactly how you feel. I think you're scared to take that step, to tell him how you feel and see what happens."

Trinity shrugged. "Well, he hasn't exactly professed

undying feelings for me either. What if I say something and find out he's not there yet?"

"Then you die of embarrassment, talk it out, and keep moving forward in your relationship."

"Oh, is that all? Easy enough."

Autumn laughed. "I know, right? What's a little life-ending embarrassment between a man and woman in love? Or I guess, not in love. Or, well, you know what I mean."

"Are you girls planning on joining us any time in the near future?" Mike hollered from the living room.

"Keep your shirt on!" Autumn rolled her eyes. "We're talking here. We'll be there in a minute."

"Maybe we should cool it on the yelling and just join the guys for games." Trinity, an only child, never acquired the taste for the obnoxiously loud conversations Autumn and Mike engaged in on an almost daily basis.

Autumn sashayed ahead of her. "And I know the perfect game. How about a little Truth or Dare?"

"Seriously," Trinity hissed, even though Autumn was joking. "Don't even think about it." At least, she was moderately sure it was a joke. Following Autumn into the living room, Trinity realized she was about to find out.

# 21

Blane sat on the patio's hanging swing beside Trinity. "Do I pass inspection?"

"This isn't a test. When I suggested you come up here to relax during your recuperation, that is exactly what I meant. I don't want you stressing about whether or not my friends like you."

He stayed silent.

Under his scrutiny, she folded. "Yes. Autumn and Mike seem to like you a lot. If they didn't, they wouldn't have beaten you so mercilessly at Monopoly."

"I'll be sure to make note of that. When one of your friends treats me poorly, it's a sign of acceptance?"

Trinity snorted. "No. I wouldn't say that about everyone, only Autumn and Mike. If anyone else is that way, you better watch out. Autumn and Mike are a different breed of friend."

"How much older is Mike than you and Autumn?"

"Autumn and I are the same age, but Mike is three years older than us."

"Hmm."

"What does that mean?"

He shrugged. "I was just thinking."

"No. That wasn't a thinking 'hmm'—that was a questions-are-rattling-around-in-that-concussed-head-of-yours 'hmm.' Out with it."

A quick glance was all she received before he turned and stared into the dark back yard. Trinity nudged the swing back and forth. The subtle squeak of its chains mingled with the chirping frogs from her neighbor's pond.

Eyes still focused on the emptiness ahead, he answered. "You and Mike are pretty close. At least it seems that way. Did you guys ever get together?"

*What?* No. No, they never dated. Why would Blane even ask that? Did he think they were flirting or something? Trinity ran through the evening in her head and came up empty.

"Never mind. It's none of my business."

Hearing his soft reply, Trinity realized she hadn't actually answered his concerns. And he sounded so unsure. It was baffling to think a man with everything going for him could still be less than confident. Then again, experiences might have driven in the lie that he wasn't good enough. Hurts like that could make scars that ran deep.

"No. Mike and I never saw each other like that. Tucker and I dated all through high school. Before that, Mike and I antagonized each other like siblings because that's what we considered ourselves. After Tuck, well, you're the first man who has snagged my attention."

Glancing at his profile, she noticed a hint of a smile. "Like I said. None of my business."

She rested her hand on his knee. It remained there when he looked at her. Doubt shone in the depths of his blue eyes. Hopefully her words could remove it once and for all.

"I don't mind. It's got to be awkward coming into my world

and seeing me around people I've known for forever. But I can assure you, Mike is family, an older brother. That's it. The three of us hang out together all the time. I don't call and vent to him like I do Autumn, and we don't hang out by ourselves. My friendship with Autumn is the glue that holds our strange little family together. And she's even the one who suggested you stay here and called to set it all up."

Blane nodded. "Remind me to thank her for that. I'll be a lot more comfortable here than in a hotel room. I'm surprised he doesn't rent the place out."

"He's considered it. But I think he likes having it open for friends and to offer guest speakers and others from church who might need a short-term space."

"Admirable."

The single word lacked any jealousy. Maybe Blane took her at her word and refused to feel threatened by their friendship. Autumn and Mike, more than even the rest of her church family, kept her strong throughout the grieving process. She owed them much, and she hated thinking about them not getting along with Blane.

Blane leaned his head back against the swing and yawned. Trinity checked the time on her phone. It wasn't too late. Then again, Blane might tire more easily with a concussion. She'd never been around someone recovering from a serious one and had no idea how the body reacted.

"What do you say we call it a night? You've had a full day between bus and train travel and then games and movies tonight. Besides, I've got a few small details on my latest illustration project to finish up. If I get them done tonight, we can have all day tomorrow for me to show you around."

Standing, Blane held out his hand. "Let me walk you to your car."

With her hand enveloped in his, she felt protected as she

stood and walked with him. He opened the door with his free hand before she faced him. She didn't want to let go.

"I could get used to this."

Even with the dim lighting, she saw the shadows of his dimples and his full smile. "You and me both."

Trinity raised on tiptoes as he lowered his lips to meet hers. His hand slid up her neck into her hair. Her head fit perfectly in the curve of his palm. He pulled her tight against him for only a moment before releasing her with one more feather-light kiss at the corner of her mouth. Blane sighed.

"Tomorrow morning, then?" He confirmed.

"Tomorrow." Slipping into the driver's seat, she looked up at him as he shut the door and retreated to the basement.

Trinity pulled out of the driveway. While she wasn't thrilled that Blane was dealing with an injury, it was wonderful having him with her in her hometown.

"Yes, I could definitely get used to this."

———

Blane closed the patio door and took in the view of Mike's backyard in the morning light. The steepness of the hillside making up his backyard was impressive. The grassy slope slowly gave way to businesses in what Trinity called the historic downtown area. Beyond those, the waters of the Mississippi River flowed, dotted with the occasional slow-moving barge.

He couldn't see the historic district's businesses, though he could make out a couple of church spires. Trinity had assured him there wasn't anything better than grabbing a bite to eat before wandering in and out of the eclectic variety of downtown shops. As soon as she arrived to pick him up, he would find out for himself.

"There you are." Trinity called as she came around the side of the house. "I hope you're hungry."

"Starving." It wasn't far from the truth. Mike invited him for breakfast that morning, but the man obviously didn't know how many calories it took to keep a professional wrestler going. Then again, not many people did.

In minutes, Trinity found a parking spot on a side street and led him down the steep sidewalk toward a red brick building. At least, the two-thirds of the structure was red, the bottom third was painted dark gray. Spaced evenly down the top half, long, narrow windows paired perfectly with windows along the gray portion.

The recessed arch above each of these contained what looked like an old-fashioned oil lantern. The lights flickered with the consistency of the electricity that powered them. A sign edged with a row of flashing lights deemed the place Katy O'Ferrell's Publick House. Traditional Irish music filled the street in front of the restaurant, inviting people in.

"I thought we'd start your trip with one of my favorite places to eat. You game?" Trinity asked, standing beside the entryway.

Blane held open the door and waved her in. "Lead the way."

Sitting at a high-top table next to a front window, it was easy to see why Trinity liked the place. The décor tended toward typical pub ambiance. Darker interior, televisions showcasing whatever sport was currently on, and a long bar taking up one side of the narrow room were all expected. Everything else in the room spoke of Ireland.

The menu was snatched from his hand without warning. A mischievous grin filled Trinity's eyes with happiness.

"Do you trust me?"

"Trust you about what?"

"Let me order for us. If you don't like it, you can order something else. I'll take home your leftovers for later."

Blane shrugged. "Why not? Go ahead."

The waitress returned with their sodas. "Your pub chips will be up shortly. Do you know what you want to order?"

Trinity nodded. "We want two shepherd's pies, and after that we're going to need an order of bread pudding. What ice cream do you have today?"

"Salted caramel."

"That's fine. That flavor is perfect with it."

The server accepted the menus from Trinity. "I'll be back in a moment with your appetizer."

"Shepherd's pie, huh?"

"You're going to love it."

"And bread pudding?"

"You can't come here and not get the bread pudding. That would be wrong on so many levels. Even if you're stuffed full, you make room for the bread pudding."

Blane smiled. "I'll try to remember that for next time I'm in town."

"Next time? Who knows when that will be with your schedule, Mr. UWO Champion. I think you should find all the restaurants in all the cities that sell bread pudding, try them, and tell me how they rate. What do you say?"

"Sure." Blane agreed quietly. He'd do that when he got to go back on the road. *If* he got to go back on the road. The medical staff was being cautious, and it didn't look like he'd be cleared for a return any time soon.

"Blane? Are you okay?"

He looked up from the bead of sweat tracing a path down his glass and forced a smile. "I'm good. Why?"

"You got quiet all of a sudden. Are you certain you're okay?"

Not really. But he couldn't tell her that, could he? He could always get another job if he was forced to retire due to an injury, but he didn't want to. Wrestling was what he was wired to do. Would Trinity understand how hard this job was on the body? Did he want her to have the full picture? She didn't need to worry about him every time he got in the ring. Concerns weren't limited to him being able to continue wrestling or not.

"Blane? What's wrong? Are you feeling sick? Do we need to leave?"

The fear for his health was nearly tangible. Her eyes were wide as she twisted her napkin into pieces. He had to put her mind at ease, at least on that account.

"It's nothing like that. I'm fine. Really. Just a little tired is all."

# 22

Tired? Blane wasn't tired. He was perfectly fine when a fan stopped him for an autograph on their way into the restaurant. Chatted with him for a minute before they continued on their way. Something was bothering him, and he didn't want to tell her. Trinity knew it as surely as she knew the meal would be delicious, but she couldn't force him to open up. Lucky for her, she had an eight-year-old. Pretend was a way of life at their house, and patience was a virtue in high demand.

"Okay." She knew he wasn't. He knew she knew he wasn't. But he had to come to her of his own accord.

Before things could get awkward, the waitress brought their food. After Blane blessed it, there wasn't much need for conversation until the empty dishes from the shepherd's pie were removed and all that remained on the bread pudding plate was a dollop of whipped cream that Trinity had forgotten to tell the waitress to hold.

Sliding her debit card into her purse, Trinity stood. "Want to take a walk with me?"

Blane laid a hand across his middle. "I probably should. I'm going to get fat and lazy without my regular routine."

Trinity laughed. "There is no way you're getting fat or lazy. But if you want to work out, we can swing by my gym. I have a special membership that allows me to take a guest. I mean, it's probably not what you're used to, but it'd be better than nothing."

"I'm sure it would be fine."

"Wait a minute. Should you be working out at all? They put you on medical leave. Does that keep you from working out too? How long can you go without a workout before it starts to affect you?"

He reached for her hand. It had been a long time since Trinity had felt this content. Walking hand in hand down the sidewalk with someone she cared about almost made her forget the way he avoided her earlier questions. Not even the subtle stares of people they passed shook her peace. Blane was a huge guy, and his size was bound to get attention.

"I can work out. We find out early on what we can and can't do. Plus, we know what to watch for that could indicate additional problems. For me, it's more about making sure I don't take a hit to the head again any time soon."

The bluesy tones of a saxophone, harmonica, and bass guitar filled the air as they neared the main parking lot for the shopping area. On the corner across the road a trio played for all the shoppers passing by. Blane's expression displayed his appreciation, but they kept walking past the shop-lined streets to the riverside.

"Do you come down here often?" Blane asked as Trinity led him to a bench where they could sit and watch the barges pass.

"Not as often as you'd think. It's sad." She listened to the sounds of the river mixing with those of the street musicians.

"Maybe it's a matter of taking for granted what I have readily available. I forget how equally full of life and peaceful it can be sitting and watching life happen

all around you."

Though a few people walked by, and many could be heard in the distance, no more fans approached them. Left to themselves, Trinity and Blane were content to stare out over the water. Trinity made a mental note to enjoy the area more often. Maybe she'd bring Jay down. He would love to watch the barges and the gulls swooping in the distance.

"I've got to be honest with you." Blane's tone put Trinity on edge.

"About what?"

"When I told you nothing was wrong earlier, that wasn't the entire truth."

"So, there is a problem?"

"It doesn't feel like a problem for me. But for you, yeah, it might be. The more I think about it, the more I feel like we need to talk about it."

Trinity fought the urge to stand and pace. "Then, let's talk about it. Whatever it is."

"What did Tucker do for a living?"

That was so far from where Trinity thought the conversation was going. "He taught computer science and math at a local private high school."

"I'm guessing that's a pretty secure job?"

Trinity shrugged. "I guess so. He agreed to teach summer school over the summers. So, it was at least a constant source of income. We didn't have money pouring in or anything, but we always had enough. Why? What does Tucker's job have to do with anything?"

"My job's not like that." Blane ran his hand through his

hair. His ponytail fell over his shoulder, and he shoved it back into place. "The wrestling world isn't like teaching."

'Duh' sprang to her mind, but Trinity had the good sense not to say it. "I'm aware the two are nothing alike. I didn't expect they would be. Is there a reason this might be a problem?"

Elbows balanced on his knees, Blane rested his chin on his clasped hands and stared out at the river. "It could be. You're used to security. Wrestling is hard on a person's body. Sixty-five isn't the typical retirement age for someone like me."

"What do wrestlers do when they … stop wrestling?"

"Some go into acting or build up other areas of interest to pursue as their time in the ring gets short."

"Is that what you'll do?"

"I'm not sure yet. I've never had an interest in Hollywood. Training up-and-coming wrestlers is a possibility I've considered, but nothing is certain."

She laid a hand on his arm, hoping to offer comfort through her touch. "You'll figure it out. You've got time."

He sat back and looked at her. "That's the other issue. I may not have the time."

"What do you mean?"

"Wrestling can be dangerous. One wrong move, and you're sidelined with a concussion. This is my second one this year. They take that pretty seriously, but it's still an injury I'm expected to recover from completely and return to the ring in a few weeks."

Trinity frowned. "That's a good thing. Isn't it?"

"For me? For this time? Yes, it's a good thing. But what about next time? The wrong injury, and I'm out for good. A severe neck injury has ended more than a few wrestler's careers. That's something I knew going into this profession. I love it, and it makes the risk worth it. But you have Jay. You need to know the person you're with will be able to take care of you. I'm not sure I'm that guy."

Pressure in Trinity's chest held the oxygen captive. "Are you saying you don't think we should be together?"

"I don't know what's going to happen, Trinity. I don't want you in the position of taking care of one more person in your life because I get injured in the ring. It's not right."

Trinity closed her eyes and forced a calm, deep breath past the tightness. "No. I didn't ask you to tell me the future. I want to know one thing." She raised one finger while looking him in the eyes. "One thing. Do you want to be with me and Jay?"

"Of course, I do. But ..."

"No." She shook her head and hoped the hurt she felt didn't translate into a glare. "I asked, you answered. Now, you're going to listen to me. When I had doubts and worried about Jay possibly getting hurt due to our relationship, it was you who told me to stop worrying about the 'what-ifs.' It was you who reminded me that life is full of unknowns, and we can't stop living it because we're afraid of what might come. Where is that man now? Or is what's true for me not equally true for you?"

Blane pushed up from the bench and walked to the river's edge. "It's true. But I can't put you and Jay in that position. It wouldn't be right."

"You're not God. You're Blane Sterling. And last time I checked, the ups and downs of my life were not in Blane's control, but God's. If you want to walk away, I can't stop you. But I don't know that I can go back to being friends with someone I've fallen in love with either."

Blane spun around with surprising speed. "What did you say?"

"I said I don't think I can go back to being just friends with you."

He drew closer. "After that. Your reason."

Trinity swallowed. She hadn't meant for it to come out this way, especially with Blane talking about leaving. "I said it's hard to go back to being simple friends when you already love someone. I can't do it because I love you."

In the movies, he would have swept her into his arms and kissed her like he meant it, whispering his love for her into her ear. All talk of leaving would be forgotten, and they would begin happily ever after as the ending credits rolled. Trinity wasn't surprised when none of that happened, but she would have liked some response other than Blane staring at her with an indecipherable look on his face.

She bit her lip, waiting. Maybe she should have kept her feelings to herself, but it was too late to take back her words. "I know that doesn't fix our situation. Maybe you even think it complicates matters, but it doesn't have to. You want to be with me. I want to be with you. The only question you need to consider is whether or not you're going to take your own advice and trust God with all the what-ifs. So, what's it going to be?"

"You can do that? You're comfortable going forward even knowing all it takes is one injury to take me out of the ring forever?"

"If that day comes, we'll deal with it knowing God has a new plan for you, for us."

"Even if it cripples me for the rest of my life?"

"I'll happily help you live life however that may look for as long as we're together. I won't abandon us because it gets hard. I've done hard. And I've lost a lot. It was worth the pain then, and I have a feeling it will be again if the what-ifs happen."

Her willingness wasn't the cure all to the situation. She

knew why he wanted her answers, but everything circled back around to the one question he had yet to answer.

"I'm at peace in our relationship, come what may. I know God is going to be there with us. Now, it's your turn. One last question for you to answer. Will you trust God to handle the what-ifs in our relationship, or are you going to walk away?"

His eyes slid shut as he contemplated the question, his lips moving in silent prayer. Sounds of the town and river went on around them, ignorant of the choices being weighed. Trinity tuned them out as her own heart lifted a silent petition for God to show Blane which path he should take by allowing peace to settle over him. She didn't realize she'd closed her eyes until a shadow darkened the light behind her eyelids.

When she opened them, Blane stood only inches from her. Her gaze met his.

"No more fear." His voice was quiet but sure. "I choose us, and I choose to let God worry about tomorrow."

His thumb grazed her cheek wiping away a tear. With his palm cupping her cheek, he lowered his head. His kiss was sweet, warm, full of promise, and totally in view of anyone walking by. Trinity stepped back with a smile. Better to keep some things private.

Looking into his eyes, Trinity saw only peace. Not even a trace of the fear he'd expressed remained. Fear. Who would have thought the giant of a man standing before her could be rocked by the same doubts she faced? Apparently, it didn't matter who you were. Trusting God with the unknown could be a challenge for anyone.

Trinity smiled up at him. "Then, come on. We've wasted enough of the afternoon. I want to show you my favorite antique store."

Warmth radiated up her arm as Blane took her hand, letting

her lead him away from the river to the rows of riverfront stores. Listening to the street musicians play and buzz of activity around them, contentment should have settled on her shoulders like a warm blanket. Only one thing put the tiniest cloud in her blue sky. Her 'I love you' hadn't been returned.

# 23

"I don't want to talk with you about it," Blane stressed for the third time.

Pamela was unruffled on the other end of the call. "It's personal then."

It wasn't meant as a question. Whether it was meant to create guilt over his hesitance was yet to be seen.

"Yes, it's personal. I've given you an update on my recuperation and detailed everything I'm doing to stay in shape for my return to the ring. My trainers have even been working with trainers here to make sure what I'm doing is bringing the results I need while keeping me safe. I've still not been cleared, but they're even handling that virtually with people here. As soon as I'm cleared, I'm back to work."

"But there's more. It's personal. And you're not going to speak with me about it. That's fine, but you need to talk to someone. I can tell something is weighing on your mind. Call your pastor or your father or I don't care who. If I can tell you're wrestling with something, no pun intended, you probably need to get it off your chest. I'll be praying for you, Blane."

She didn't wait for an answer before the call ended. With anyone else, he would be concerned they were angry. Matter of fact was simply the way Pamela operated. Maybe she had a point, though.

Considering his options, he turned the phone over in his hands. Settling on a man he knew he could trust to lead him the right direction, he pulled up the number and hit call. His dad's voice filled the silence, apologizing for not being available.

"Hey, Dad. Just checking in, letting you and Mom know everything's okay. I'll talk to you guys later."

He ended the call and tossed the phone on the patio swing next to him. Since the day by the river, he and Trinity had spent most of every day together. He loved her excitement in showing him her favorite parts of her hometown. They'd even taken an afternoon to see the neighborhood where she grew up. Her childhood home was still there, but when she moved out, her parents sold it, preferring a small apartment in a neighboring town where upkeep was easier.

Plans were made for the two of them to visit Trinity's parents in a couple of weeks. It would be great getting to know the people responsible for raising such a caring, strong woman. For now, he needed to figure out what to do with himself. Dad was unavailable. Trinity was taking the day to finish a project. And he was at a complete loss.

The sound of the patio door sliding open jerked Blane's attention away from the potential pity-party playing in his thoughts.

"Mind if I join you?" Mike said as he held up two bottles of soda. "I brought drinks."

Blane jerked his head toward the empty chair across from

the swing. Mike sat before extending the soda toward him. Unscrewing the top as soon as he had it in his hand, Blane took a gulp of the fizzy drink.

"Thanks."

A nod was his only response. Silence hung heavy in the space between them. Mike drained his bottle.

"Do you play pool?"

Blane shrugged. "A bit. I'm not very good at it."

"I've got a table up in the game room. Want to play?"

"Sure."

Blane let Mike lead the way. They'd eaten dinner together three of the last five days, but with Autumn and Trinity there as well, the men had little time to get to know each other. They talked a little over coffee, which Mike had ready each morning, but that was the extent of their guy-time so far.

"You and Autumn seem tight with Trinity," Blane commented as he chose a cue from the rack on the wall.

Balls knocked together as Mike placed them in the rack and positioned it on the felt. "Yep. She and Autumn have been friends for as long as I can remember. Of course, she and I had the same love-hate relationship siblings do growing up. She was in our house as much as her own. Have you met her parents?"

"No. We're supposed to soon. Should I be concerned that she hasn't introduced us yet?"

A crack filled the air as Mike sent the cue ball into the others. "Nope. I wouldn't have expected anything else. I'm kind of surprised she's introducing you at all."

"She doesn't talk about them much." Blane lined up the cue ball with a solid one across the table.

"She won't. First, God got in the way. Then, Tucker."

"I thought she was pretty much raised in church?"

Chalking the end of the cue, Mike shrugged. "She spent

213

weekends with her Granny. That woman was a saint. Took her to church every Sunday and made sure she had a ride to youth activities with us every Thursday. She's responsible for Trinity being raised in church."

"Huh. I figured with a name like Trinity, her parents would be Christians."

Mike shook his head. "Nope. Just thought it sounded cool. God knew better though."

Blane took another shot. "So, she doesn't talk to her folks much?"

"Not really. But this isn't my story to tell. If you want to know more, you'll have to ask Trinity."

Appreciation of Mike's protectiveness played tug of war with jealousy. Trinity told him there was nothing between them. Without knowing it, Mike confirmed feeling the same just minutes earlier. There was no reason to be jealous at all. She loved him, had told him so less than a week ago.

Blane tensed at the thought, causing the shot he lined up to miss completely. Instead, the cue ball veered toward the eight-ball sending it toward a corner pocket where it teetered on the edge before stopping.

"Lucky shot. You just about lost that one." Mike set up his next turn.

"Yeah."

Poised to take his shot, Mike frowned up at Blane. "Something on your mind?"

Could he talk to Mike? He knew Trinity. Then again, he knew Trinity. "I don't want to put you in the middle of anything."

Mike sent the cue ball across the table and straightened. His jaw tightened as he stared at Blane. "Are you breaking up with her?"

Blane grimaced. "No, I'm not breaking up with her. It's just ... never mind. I can't talk to you about this."

While the tension eased, wariness filled Mike's face. "She loves you. You know that, don't you?"

"She told you?"

Mike shook his head. "Doesn't have to. I've known her long enough to know. But from your tone, I'm guessing she's had that talk with you."

"Yeah." If only he didn't sound so unsure, so guilty. Then again, maybe it was all in his head.

"But you don't love her?"

Not all in his head then. He rubbed his hand over his mouth. How much should he share? He wanted to talk to someone, and Mike knew Trinity well. He could have good insight. But he knew Trinity well, and his loyalty would go to her.

"You don't. Do you?" He sounded resigned to the thought and hurt for what he knew it would do to his friend.

Blane opted for the truth. "I do love her. And I want only God's best for her and Jay."

"So, what's the problem? There's a but at the end of that sentence."

"I haven't told her yet."

Mike's mouth fell open while his brows raised in surprise. He might be as big as a bear, but the incredulous look made Blane feel like a small child who accidentally broke his neighbor's window playing catch.

"She told you she loves you, and you ..." Mike threw his hands out to the side. "What? You ignored it?"

"I didn't ignore it. I wanted to say it back, but something stopped me."

Mike put the cue back on the rack on the wall and dropped

onto a nearby chair. Blane followed suit. Whether the game was finished or not, it was officially over.

Leaning forward with his forearms balanced on his legs Mike studied him. He wasn't angry, at least not that Blane could read on his face. There may have been a little worry, but mostly, he seemed thoughtful. Scrutiny was a twenty-four seven happening in Blane's life. However, sitting quietly while one of Trinity's best friends weighed his words was a foreign feeling. One that threatened to put him on edge.

"Are you afraid of something?" Mike didn't move, didn't even blink.

"No. We talked about all the what-ifs, and we both believe God is capable of handling them."

"Maybe you're not as sure of your feelings as you think?"

Blane shook his head. "I'm positive I love her. Jay too. I started to respond. To tell her I love her, too, but I couldn't get the words out. There was no peace until I stopped trying."

Mike leaned back. "God? Do you think God stopped you?"

There was no derision in his tone. Nothing that would indicate Mike thought it was a copout. Convinced the question was sincere, Blane decided to plunge ahead. "I really do. I'm not sure what to make of it though. What reason could there be for God to prevent me from reassuring Trinity? It just doesn't make sense."

"You've prayed about it?"

Blane nodded. "Every waking moment since she told me. And nothing."

"Then, as hard as this is for me to say considering I know what Trinity must be thinking, you've got to be obedient. But I have no idea why He would ask that of you or what good could come of it. Sorry, man."

The vibration of his phone drew Blane's attention to the

screen. His dad's image flashed across it. He picked it up and swiped as he glanced at Mike. "It's my dad."

"Say no more. I've got laundry anyway."

Blane managed a parting nod as he greeted his dad. "Hey Dad. Thanks for calling me back."

"Just returning your call. Did you need something?"

*Did he?* The conversation with Mike didn't yield definitive answers, but it did confirm his direction. Obey and trust that God would tell him when a declaration of love was right.

"Nah, I got it figured out." Blane made his way from the game room to the basement while they spoke. "But while we're talking, I can tell you about how my trip's going and plans for my return. Got the time?"

"For you, Son? Always."

# 24

Butterflies flittered through Trinity's stomach as she turned off the ignition. The men and women of Riverview Church brought her to faith, helped her grow, and carried her through the worst storm of her life. Now, sitting in the church parking lot with Blane beside her, there was no denying it. She wanted her church family to love him as much as she did. To accept him as readily as they'd accepted her when she first came with Granny.

Why she thought any other outcome was possible was beyond her. She was being silly. Of course, they'd accept Blane into the family. A good, Bible-believing, faith-living man like Blane would have no issues fitting in with her congregation.

"Your church is Riverview Church?"

Trinity frowned at his obvious observation. "Yes."

He looked out the windshield and both front windows. "There's no river to view here. When you told me the name, I thought we'd be on the riverfront or at least somewhere near it. It's like you drove in the opposite direction."

The confusion in his voice sent her butterflies packing.

"When it first started, it was. The church relocated something close to fifty years ago. They moved away from the river but for some reason, kept the name."

"Hmm."

She dropped the car keys in her purse. "Ready to meet my church family?"

Every eye turned toward them as they walked through the doors. Curiosity laced each expression. Many knew she was seeing someone, but only a handful knew more than his name and that they'd met on her Tennessee trip.

Trinity shifted her attention to the preacher and his wife, waiting to greet them. "Pastor Hood, Laura, this is Blane Sterling. He's visiting while recovering from a work injury."

"It's so good to meet you, Blane." Pastor Hood welcomed him with a handshake. "I hope you'll find our little congregation welcoming."

"I'm happy to be here. Trinity speaks often about how much the support of your church has meant to her and Jay." Blane nodded with a smile before shaking Laura's hand as well.

"I hate that it had to happen because of an injury, but I'm thrilled to get to meet you." She placed a hand on her husband's arm. "I do hope you'll be here a while. We'd love to have you over for dinner while you're in the area."

Trinity nodded when Blane looked to her before turning back to Laura. "I am, and we look forward to it."

"And don't you think for a minute you'll get through this trip without coming over to my house for afternoon tea and a proper chat." A woman's voice interrupted from behind them.

"Miss Gertie!" Trinity smiled so big her cheeks ached. "I hoped you'd be here today."

The short, elderly woman swatted her arm. "Land sakes, child. Where else would I be on a Sunday morning but in God's house getting ready to worship Him with all His other children?"

Trinity laughed. "You're right. I don't know what I was thinking."

"You weren't thinking. Leastways not about worship, I'd wager." She looked up at Blane with a sly grin and a quick wink. "I'd guess her mind's on this strong, handsome stranger she has yet to introduce me to. Where were you when I was young and single?"

Blane laughed, his eyes sparkling with joy. "I have a feeling you'd have given me a run for my money back then. And since Trinity's not doing the job quick enough for you, I'll see to it myself." He stuck out his hand. "Blane Sterling. It's a pleasure to meet you, ma'am."

Miss Gertie waved her hand through the air. "None of that handshake stuff. We hug around here."

Without a moment's hesitation, Blane folded the slight woman into a loose hug. His ease with her surprised Trinity. Not that he'd care, but without knowing it, he'd just earned a boatload of brownie points with her church grandma. Maybe he'd even earned a few extra with her too.

"And what is wrong with you, calling me ma'am like that? That's for old people. I may have wrinkles and spots, but inside I'm a spring chicken. From now on, you can call me Miss Gertie like everyone else."

"Yes, ma'am, um, Miss Gertie," Blane answered.

Giving Trinity a pat on the arm, Miss Gertie smiled up at Blane. "I think this one's been raised right. Might want to think about keeping him."

"I'll see what I can do."

Miss Gertie looked at her watch. "Goodness. Look at the time. I've been standing here gabbing when I should be getting snacks ready for children's church." She smiled at Blane. "Good to meet you." She looked at Trinity. "And you be sure to call me. We'll get together this week."

Confident Trinity would do as she was told, Miss Gertie flitted off toward the children's church rooms without waiting for an answer. Trinity led him down to her seat, but before they made it to her usual pew, six rows back left side, Theresa Cavins met them in the aisle. At one time, she would have been taller than Trinity. Age left her diminished in size. But nothing, not even age, would have the audacity to dampen her forward personality.

"Does Eric know you're back from your trip? I'm sure he's anxious to see you again." Her sweet smile directed at Trinity belied the true meaning of her inquiry. Her attention's subtle shift to Blane before returning to her erased any possible misconception.

"Oh?" Trinity cleared her throat. "I'm sorry he didn't tell you, Miss Theresa. Things didn't work out with Eric. Shame on him for not letting you know."

As she craned her neck, hawkish eyes met Blane's gaze. "I couldn't help overhearing your conversation with Pastor Hood and his wife."

Trinity fought a giggle. There was no way she could miss it. Miss Theresa sat at the end of the pew right where Pastor Hood and his wife greeted people for that very reason. Her position there made it easy to slip into the aisle and interrogate people when she heard juicy news. Nothing that happened in the sanctuary would ever slip by her. Trinity returned her attention to the woman.

"I am Theresa Cavins. Mrs. Cavins to you. I hope you don't find this intrusive, but you mentioned recovery from an injury. I just wanted to say, I hope it's nothing serious."

A groan would garner Miss Theresa's displeasure. For that reason, Trinity stifled hers. This was a ploy to draw out information. A quick wink from Blane assured her that he knew it as well and apparently didn't mind.

"That's so nice of you. To check on me, I mean. I'll be fine in a couple weeks. Just trying to recover from a concussion is all."

Miss Theresa's sharp intake of breath coincided with the time-worn hand she placed on her chest. "A concussion. Oh, my. What dangerous line of work are you in Mr. Sterling?"

Blane chuckled. "It's really not like that, Mrs. Cavins. I'm a professional wrestler, and I took a hit wrong. Nothing to be overly concerned about."

Suddenly, Miss Theresa bore a striking resemblance to the little monkey in one of Jay's favorite animal books, the one with eyes that swallowed up his face. With her current expression, Miss Theresa could be its twin.

"Oh. Well, that's nice. I should let you find a seat and scoot back to my own."

Without giving time for a reply, she hurried back to her seat. Blane glanced at Trinity who shrugged and shook her head. Growing up in a small church, one got used to a variety of characters taking their places in the pews. And Theresa Cavins was nothing if not a character. She had a heart of gold underneath all her nosiness, but it took a little mining to find it.

Leaning down, Blane whispered. "Do I need to watch out for Eric? Will we have to have a little talk?"

This time, Trinity did groan. "Not at all. Most men have been content to leave me alone, but Miss Theresa has determined I need to get together with her great-nephew. Grieving got me out of it for a while, but right before our Tennessee trip, I finally gave in. I figured it was the only way the hounding would end."

"And it didn't go well?"

A smile played at the corner of her lips. Maybe it shouldn't, but knowing Blane didn't assume he was the best thing going in her life made her feel that much more special to him. "No. It was a disaster I'd rather forget."

Several found time to introduce themselves. After all, greeting newcomers was the polite thing to do. However, other than an exchange of names and the expected, "Nice to have you with us," there was little real conversation.

Sitting in the pew with Blane beside her, Trinity felt every look from the other church members. She turned discreetly several times only to find whispered conversations end with too-innocent smiles.

Blane leaned down close to her ear. "It's because I'm new and a little bit different. Give it time."

Blane was right. She tried to relax into the pew. All they needed was a little time to get to know him, and the congregation would see the loving, Christian man she saw every time she looked at him. Besides, they were here to worship, and that's exactly what she intended to do.

Service ended as it always did. Everyone milled around while gathering their Bibles and rambunctious children. While most didn't make it in early enough to chat before worship began, they weren't averse to staying a few minutes after.

The pastor's message of encouragement helped lift Trinity from the funk that surrounded her when they first sat down. The new perspective fought back her earlier trepidation leaving a genuine smile as the youngest Thompson son approached them.

"Hey, Miss Trinity! Where's Jay?" Spencer spoke to Trinity without his eyes ever leaving Blane.

"He's visiting his grandparents. It's his special month with them before school starts. He'll be back in a few weeks."

The boy nodded, but Trinity doubted he heard a word she

said. She laid a hand on Blane's arm. "And this is Jay's new friend, Blane. Blane, this is Spencer Thompson."

Blane squatted in front of the boy and held out a hand. It was so reminiscent of his first meeting with Jay, doing all he could to put himself on the same level as the boys. She doubted he even realized he did it. The caring move was a natural part of Blane.

"It's good to meet you, Spencer."

"Jay said he's your partner." Spencer eyed Blane skeptically.

"That's right." Blane saw the statement for the question it was.

"He said you took him in a limo too."

"I did." Blane nodded. "We took one on the way to the stadium before our match."

Jay's best friend chewed on his lip for a second before leaning toward Blane. His hand came up to shield his mouth from prying eyes, though hers were the only others present. "Jay says a limo is cooler than the sports car David's dad has. I think it is too. But we can't say anything. It could hurt David's feelings."

How could Blane keep a straight face when Spencer was so adorable? Trinity raised a hand to her mouth. It wouldn't do to have the boy think she was laughing at him.

"I promise not to tell," Blane whispered back.

"Spencer, there you are." Mrs. Thompson appeared out of nowhere and clutched her son's hand in hers before Blane could stand back up. "Let's leave them alone."

"Oh, it's fine," Trinity assured her. "We were just talking about Jay and introducing him to Blane."

The woman flicked a glance in his direction with a hesitant smile. "Yes, well. Nice to meet you." She propelled her son forward with a hand to his back. "Come on, Spencer. We should get home. Lunch doesn't end up on the table by itself."

Trinity watched her usher the child through the thinning crowd, stopping briefly to speak with Anne Carter. The elderly woman looked across the church toward her and Blane, shifting her gaze immediately when they made eye contact.

A change in the direction of her thoughts was needed to keep her post-message outlook. She slung her purse over her shoulder.

"Are you hungry? I know this great little Italian restaurant if you're up for it."

Warmth spread through her as Blane's hand rested on the small of her back. "Lead the way."

After saying their good-byes to Pastor Hood and his wife and agreeing to Sunday lunch the following week, Trinity squelched the urge to say anything until she and Blane were headed to the restaurant. She was still fighting for the positive attitude she felt after the message but hurt for Blane made staying silent on the matter impossible.

"I am so sorry." She looked briefly from the road as they stopped at a stoplight.

Blane's brows dipped in confusion. Maybe he hadn't been making excuses back at the church. It was possible he fully believed the other member's reactions were completely normal. This was one time she knew better.

"My Riverview Church family is a great group of believers. They've helped Jay and me through so much. I don't think we would've experienced healing after Tuck died without them. They helped me pick up the pieces, even more so than my real family."

"They seem like a great group of people."

"Really? That wasn't anywhere near where I was going with this. Besides, can you honestly say that after the kind of welcome you received? Pastor Hood, Laura, and Miss Gertie were fine, but would you really call the way everyone else treated you welcoming?"

He had the nerve to smile that gorgeous smile, dimples peeking through his beard and all. People on the street stared. Fans approached for autographs and pictures, but those who didn't were distracted by Blane's size. What happened at the church that morning was not the same. It felt different because it was.

"They were fine. I'm not what they expected. Give them time."

Trinity shook her head. "No. I've seen many new people come through those same doors. Not one of them was treated like you were. I don't get it. They welcome everyone and love on everyone the moment they come in. Why should you be any different?"

"I think you're reading too much into it." He held up a hand in response to her intake of breath. He had more to say. "But, for the sake of argument, let's say you're right. Why would your church family react the way you believe they did?"

"I don't know."

"Yes, you do. Just a few minutes ago, you told me how important they are to you. How much they supported you and Jay after Tucker died. They're invested in you, in your lives. They hurt with you and helped you heal."

"So, now I'm not supposed to move on? First my in-laws and now the church? Don't I get to be the one to decide when I'm ready to date again?"

Trinity pulled into the main riverfront parking lot and found a space. The restaurant was a few blocks away, but nervous energy coursed through her making it impossible to sit in the car to finish the discussion. She got out and locked the car when Blane followed her lead.

Rather than waiting for her to come to him, Blane went around the car and took her hand in his. As they reached the intersection and waited to cross, he picked up their conversation.

"I'm not sure that's the issue. That Mrs. Cavins lady set you up with her nephew. I don't think they have an issue with you deciding to date again. Besides, you alone determine when you're ready and who to give your time to. And while we're on the subject, if I haven't said it already, thanks for deciding that now is a good time and that I'm the right guy."

Tingles ran up her arm at the gentle stroke of his thumb on her hand. It amazed her that someone could possess such great physical strength and yet be so incredibly gentle. And he chose her. Yes, she might have decided to start dating again, but just as important was the fact that Blane picked her. And really, that's what happened. If he'd not approached her first, she might not have taken the leap. And thank God she had, because now, she knew the protectiveness of his strength and the comfort of his gentleness.

She raised their entwined hands and placed a kiss on the back of his. "Best decision I've made in a long time."

"But that isn't what I meant about their reasoning. No one faults you for dating again, at least not that I could tell. The problem is, I am not Tucker."

"What? Who could expect you to be?"

"Think about it a minute. What was that guy you were set up with like?"

She grimaced. She didn't want to think about him. "Eric? He was not a pleasant person."

"But what did he look like? What did he do for a living?"

"He was shorter than you. Average height, I guess. Slim. Clean cut. And I think he worked at a bank."

"So, while he might not have had Tucker's personality, if

someone were to make a mold of the Tucker look, the guy might fit? And he's got a regular job? And I assume with Mrs. Cavins pushing him, he goes to a local church?"

She hated to compare Eric and Tucker at all. Other than the superficial, there weren't any similarities. But looking at the outer veneer, she could see Blane's point. "Sure. He has certain qualities that might be in line with Tucker's, but not on the important things."

"Now look at me." He paused. "It's a night-and-day difference. From what I can tell, Tucker and I don't share interests or hobbies, other than maybe wrestling. You said yourself I don't look like him. And my job is nothing like his."

"So?"

"So, maybe because you loved and were loved so well by him, people have this idea that whoever you date is supposed to be Tucker 2.0. Must be a shock to prepare for a new Tucker Knight and find Blane Sterling standing in front of you."

Could it be as simple as he made it sound? She had to admit, he was the last thing she expected. Why wouldn't he be a surprise to those who loved her?

"Sounds plausible."

"Sure, it does. I bet you this time next week, I'll be old news. People will adjust their expectations, and your church family will be back to normal."

Trinity opened the door to the restaurant before Blane took it from her and waved her ahead of him. Always a gentleman. Tucker would be happy to know she'd found someone to treat her as the precious gift he'd always told her she was. And if what Blane said was true, her church family would see it soon enough. Why, then, did she have a sliver of apprehension piercing her bubble of peace?

# 25

"Definitely makes exercise more appealing," Autumn mused from the treadmill beside Trinity.

"I can't argue with that," Trinity answered without looking away from the scene in the weightlifting section of the gym. She loved the way Blane's muscles moved and worked as he lifted a barbell with more weights on each end than she would have thought possible.

"Still not sure it makes getting out of bed at 4:30 any better."

The good-natured grumble mirrored Trinity's thoughts on the matter. If her phone would've survived, she might have heaved it across the room when her alarm shattered her peaceful sleep that morning. As much as she enjoyed watching Blane workout, she wasn't sure they'd be making this a tradition.

"Blane and I tried to come at a more reasonable hour last week, but even the less-busy times have too many people for him to get anything done." Trinity punched the arrow on her treadmill to quicken her pace. "There are more wrestling fans in the world than I would've thought."

"So, you've been getting up at this awful hour since then?" Autumn nodded her head toward the men. "Look. Mike tries hard, but my brother is no Blane Sterling."

Trinity watched as Mike lifted the bar, minus several weights, while Blane spotted him. "No. Blane has either come alone, or he's come with Mike. Honestly, your brother seems thrilled to come with him whether he can lift the same amounts or not."

Autumn snorted a laugh. "Not. I don't think we have to worry about him catching up to Blane any time soon. But if he's enjoying the guy time, more power to him."

"You watch. Blane has been teaching him technique, and I even saw him studying a copy of Blane's workout routine and diet information the other day when I was over there. One of these days, he's going to walk into church looking all fit and strong, and people are going to think we have a new member."

Autumn slowed her machine to a crawl before stopping it completely. Trinity did the same, then motioned to the rowing machines. Wiping a small towel across her neck, Autumn dragged herself toward them.

"Speaking of church, how did it go on Sunday? Was your new man a big hit?"

Trinity adjusted the machine to her needs and grabbed the handle loosely in her hands. "He's always big. But a hit? I'm not so sure."

"Why? What happened?"

While the two kept an easy pace on the rowing machines, Trinity gave her the details. "I can see his point, but I don't know. It felt like something more to me."

"I'm sorry we weren't there to help. Mom insisted we

attend Aunt Lydia's church since her big birthday celebration took place right after service. Ready to quit?"

Trinity glanced at the guys. Bench presses complete, they'd moved to a different type of weights. She had no idea what they were, but both men seemed focused on whatever it was they were doing.

"I think the guys need a bit more time. What do you say we hit the showers and head to the gym's smoothie bar? They have a great chocolate banana one. We can finish our conversation while the boys wrap up their workout."

Fifteen minutes later, Trinity sat at a small table at the smoothie bar and handed Autumn her drink. The guys were finishing their session with some stretches, so they had time to enjoy their smoothies without sucking them down quickly enough to induce brain freeze.

Autumn licked a stray dollop from her lip. "You really think things at church went beyond everyone expecting another Tucker?"

Trinity thumbed a sweat droplet from her cup. "I wish I knew. I've never seen them act like that. Of course, as far as I can remember, most of our visitors have been friends and family of people who already attend. I can think of a few transplants over the years, but they've been mostly from our sister churches."

"And most of them don't stand out in a crowd quite as much as Blane does."

"That's true too." She took another sip of her smoothie. "What does it sound like to you? Think Blane is right, and it's just about him not being another Tucker?"

One shoulder lifted in a shrug. "It could be sour grapes from Miss Theresa. You did turn down her nephew. But Blane's theory is possible and maybe even more probable. No one else would really care if you and Eric didn't hit it off. Tucker was an integral part of the church for a long time. And his illness really brought the church body together. But you were also on edge bringing someone new to services. It could also be nothing more than being overly sensitive to reactions."

"Should I say something? Maybe ask Pastor Hood about it tonight at small group?"

"Nah. I'd wait until Sunday and see if there's an issue."

The guys exited the locker room and headed their direction. Trinity gathered up the empty smoothie cups and deposited them in the garbage can. "I guess you two finished proving who's the bigger he-man?"

"Like there could be any contest." Mike rolled his eyes. "Blane's bicep is as big, if not a little bigger, than my thigh. I'm not even going to pretend I could hold my own in a battle of strength."

Blane slapped him on the shoulder, nearly knocking him off-balance in the process and proving Mike's point. "You don't have to be my size. My job, however, depends on it. Might have been different if I was hired as one of the smaller guys, but my look plays a huge part in my character. I'm not going to mess with that."

Trinity glanced at her phone. "Speaking of work, we'd better get going. You have a conference call starting soon."

"Finding out if you're back on the roster?" Mike asked.

"Yep. I'm feeling good. Now, if only the medical staff and trainers will agree with me, I can get back to work."

Autumn fished her keys out of her purse and looked at her brother. "Well, then, we'd better get out of their hair. I'll take you home before I head out to get my morning shot of caffeine and get to work. Do you want a ride, Trinity?"

She shook her head. "No, thank you. I think we're going to head down to the riverfront. While Blane has his call, I'll have some quiet time with God and enjoy the view."

The quartet walked out together and said their goodbyes in the parking lot, agreeing to meet for mid-week small group that night at the church. Trinity drove straight to the riverfront so Blane wouldn't be late for his call.

Taking her phone from her pocket, she found an empty bench and opened her Bible app. It was nice being able to take her quiet time on the road when needed. A glance down the river confirmed Blane was already on his call. She looked back at her screen. Time to find out what God had to say to her today.

Encouraged by the short devotion, Trinity took time to listen to a song it recommended before turning her heart to prayer. Blane was pacing between the river and the large flood wall. Even with the distance between them, she could tell he was running his hand through his hair. Not a good sign. Good thing she was there to pray.

"Lord," she began quietly. "Thank you for this time with Blane. I know he didn't expect it, but You did. And You know the outcome of the call. Blane has enjoyed this time too, but he's anxious to know everything is okay and get back in the ring. Whatever happens, whether we see it as good or bad, help us understand You will use it for our benefit."

Her conversation with God continued until she felt the bench shift under the weight of someone sitting beside her. Opening her eyes, she offered Blane a tentative smile.

————

Curiosity filled Trinity's blue eyes, already darkening with the tension of the situation. But which direction did she want this to go? Was she ready for him to return to the ring? Or was a tiny part of her hoping he'd have to stay?

He watched gulls swoop behind the barge-churned water

of the Mississippi River, feeling a little like the unsuspecting fish. Until this injury, life was fine. A little churning of the waters every now and then, but nothing had threatened to derail his life plan. God stayed with him through the rough patches and always brought him back to calm waters a little more faithful than he'd been.

"How long are you going to keep me in suspense?" Trinity tried for light-hearted, but concern weighed down her words.

Blane reached for her hand. It was amazing how even that small connection kept him grounded. "I'm sorry. The call wasn't exactly what I hoped to hear."

Her eyes dimmed with her frown. "I'm so sorry. Did they tell you why or when you might get called back?"

"No. But they did say they need me back in Nashville next week. There are a few more tests in my future. The results could give me a clearer idea of when I can get back in the ring."

Trinity's silence spoke volumes. Two bombshells in one twenty second conversation. She must need time to process. Why wouldn't she? He needed time to process everything. Three weeks wasn't a lot of time to recover, but he'd known guys who had been cleared in that timeframe.

"I love the time we're spending together. I don't want you doubting that. But I've been out of the ring for almost three weeks now. I'm ready to get back to it."

"I can understand the desire. It's what you do. Part of what makes you who you are. It's only natural you'd miss it. I missed home when we were in Tennessee, and that was during a voluntary week's vacation."

Knowing she understood was a blessing. He could think through situations and options without wondering if Trinity thought he was trying to get away from her life in Cape Girardeau. Not that he had options to sort through. His only choice was to stay out of the ring until he was cleared. That was the frustrating part.

He smacked his palm down onto the bench sending shockwaves through his arm. "I just want to get back to work. I know I'll be cleared eventually, but I'm ready now."

"It's got to be tough. You feel completely fine, but their testing says otherwise."

"I'm aware of the issue," he barked.

She didn't move on the bench, but Blane could feel the distance she put between them as surely as if she stood and walked away. He rubbed a hand up and down his cheek. It did no good taking out his frustration on Trinity, even unintentionally.

"I'm sorry. You didn't do anything wrong. I let my irritation at the situation get the better of me, and I shouldn't have spoken to you like that."

"It's okay."

"No. It's not. I can be frustrated about something and not bite your head off. You're only trying to help."

"In that case, you're forgiven. But I understand if you need some time to process before you're ready to talk about it."

Maybe a little time alone, well alone with God, was exactly what he needed. At that moment, he could feel the nervous energy of the unwanted turn of events zinging through him. Unless he wanted to keep apologizing to Trinity for snapping at her over nothing, he needed to get himself in check.

"I think I need to get back to Mike's for a bit."

Trinity nodded and stood. "Well, then, let's get you back there."

Disappointment laced her words though she tried to sound unaffected. Apparently, understanding the need and being okay with it were two different things. Did Trinity feel as useless as he did in the events?

Standing, he pulled her into his arms and placed a kiss on the top of her head before resting his cheek against her hair. In seconds, she relaxed against him. As small as she was, she fit in his arms perfectly. He could see her there for the rest of his life. Now would be the perfect time to assure her of his feelings for her. He inhaled a deep breath, but once again, felt the words lodge in his throat. *God? Why don't you want me to tell Trinity I love her?*

Peace was the only answer he received. Blane couldn't understand why, but he wasn't fighting it. That feeling of serenity had led him many times in his life, and he knew second guessing it wasn't an option worth exploring.

"You know how much you mean to me, don't you?" It was the closest he could come without disobedience.

Her arms tightened around his waist. "I know."

Whether he said it or not, he trusted that she did know. He tried to show her, even if he couldn't speak the words. "Thanks for being with me in this mess."

Her body moved from his only enough to allow her to tilt her head back to look up at him. "This is tough, more so for you than me. But I've lived through the messiest of messes. We'll make it through this one too."

This time, she stepped out of his embrace. "Let's get you home. You can call me when you're done mulling over everything and ready to talk."

# 26

Miss Gertie poured three glasses of sweet tea while Trinity plated three servings of her famous dark chocolate cake draped in velvety chocolate fudge frosting. Blane scooped two of the glasses off the counter.

"Here. Let me help with these."

The elderly woman patted Blane's forearm. "Such a sweet young man." She glanced at Trinity. "Be a dear and hand me one of those plates. We can each take two things and make it to the veranda without cake on the floor."

Trinity smiled and did as instructed. She loved Miss Gertie and her insistence on old-fashioned words. Who else called a covered porch a veranda anymore? And the first time she'd been invited to tea, she'd expected a proper English tea with cookies and dainty cups filled with the fragrant, steaming liquid. Tea to Miss Gertie was always a tall glass of sweet, iced tea, and freshly baked chocolate cake was the accompanying treat nine times out of ten.

"Just set it there, sweet boy." Miss Gertie motioned to a glass-topped patio table at the far side of the porch.

Sweet boy. Trinity fought a giggle and looked to Blane. When was the last time anyone had even considered referring to him as if he was a teen on the cusp of adulthood? His manly physique was unquestionable, and there were times his dark looks and smirk combined to give him a roguish appearance. But with his dimples peeking out from his bearded cheeks and a boy-next-door grin on his face, Miss Gertie's words fit perfectly.

If God had favorites in heaven, Miss Gertie was sure to be one. It was impossible not to fall in love with a woman whose loving, lively spirit was infused in all areas of her life. She'd been mother, grandmother, and friend all rolled up into one for as long as Trinity could remember. What her parents hadn't accepted or encouraged, Miss Gertie had nurtured through all the good and bad in her life.

"What kept you two from services last night?"

And blunt. How could she forget Miss Gertie's tendency to get right to the point? Always done in love, Trinity could accept it from her more readily than anyone else.

"It was a ..."

"It was my fault, ma'am," Blane interrupted to take the blame.

Miss Gertie pinned him to his seat with a look. "First of all, you can do away with all this ma'am nonsense. I told you before, Miss Gertie is more than sufficient. And more important, what was so important you kept my girl from mid-week church?"

Oh, mercy. Her cake-filled fork stopped half-way to her mouth. He'd stepped in it now. Trinity wished there was a way to warn him to tread lightly. Not that Miss Gertie was one to hold a grudge, but Trinity wanted her to love Blane as much as she did. And right now, he looked like a toddler who got caught with his mom's permanent markers and a tell-tale drawing on the kitchen cabinets.

"She missed for me," Blane reiterated. "I got some tough news yesterday, and it kind of sidelined me. Actually, that's exactly what it did. I don't know how much Trinity has shared with you about my work and why I'm here."

Miss Gertie placed her glass on the table. "You're a professional wrestler. While I don't understand the appeal, she and I watched a show together one night. Seems like you're very good at what you do."

"Thank you."

"She also informed me you were staying here while convalescing from a concussion."

Blane finished a bite of cake before answering. "It's my second one inside a year. In my line of work, the doctors are always careful. More so since it's so close to the last one. Yesterday's call was supposed to clear me to return. It didn't."

"I'm sorry. I know how important work is to a man. My late husband, Earl, God bless him, never handled being out of work very well." She included Trinity with a look. "Tucker. Now that man handled his situation with grace and patience. Never seen the likes of it before."

Trinity swallowed around the lump that suddenly took up residence in her throat. "He had his good days and bad. But God blessed him with peace for his path."

Their elderly host turned back to Blane. "And God will do the same for you. As young and able as you are, your wait won't be long. Until then, hold onto God and the things in life that bring you closer to Him."

"That's what I aim to do. After I got the news, God and I spent the morning together."

"Good boy."

"But Trinity and I still had to work through what I need to

do the next couple weeks. So, she packed a late lunch, and we picnicked at the park before taking a much-needed hike to burn off some of my excess energy."

Miss Gertie addressed Trinity. "Did you go to the Conservation Nature Center trail or one of your Illinois spots?"

"This time we stayed in Missouri and hit the Conservation trail," Trinity answered. "But we may take a day trip later if we get the chance. Right now, it looks like we'll be going back to Tennessee for a few days."

"Oh? Why?"

Blane sighed. "I'm afraid that's my fault too. The medical staff and trainers want me there in person for some tests before they give the green light for me to get back in the ring. That's why we didn't make it to church last night. By the time we hashed out all the details and walked the trail, we were both too spent to make it to small group."

"You've got no reason to apologize." Trinity placed a protective hand on his bicep. "We both needed a little down time after figuring things out. And we did watch an online service from one of the other pastors I enjoy listening to."

Miss Gertie pushed her empty plate out of the way. "You don't have to justify it to me." She held up a hand to stop any arguments. "Oh, I know I sounded like it. I just want to make sure my girl is in good hands and going in the right direction. Just being a Nosey Nellie is all. She's the only family I've got left."

Why did her emotions always seem to get the better of her lately? Trinity cleared her throat. Miss Gertie's love poured over her heart like ice-cold lemonade on a hot summer day, just the right amount of sweet and completely refreshing. Though they might not be related by blood, their family bond was God-given and a blessing she never wanted to take for granted.

Standing, Blane stacked the empty plates. "I'm going to let Trinity fill you in on the details, while I take care of these dishes. Anyone want a drink refill?"

Both women shook their heads. Blane arranged the cups on the stack and turned to Miss Gertie. "Soap and a dish rag in the sink?"

"The rag's in the sink, but the soap is in the cabinet underneath. Maybe we should come in and help."

"You'll do no such thing. We've enjoyed your hard work. The least I can do is take care of the aftermath. You and Trinity just sit back and relax." He made his way to the kitchen without another word.

Worry about whether Miss Gertie would accept him dissipated. Knowing his offer was genuine and not an attempt to score points with their hostess made it even better.

Miss Gertie fanned herself with her hand. "Goodness, girl. If I were a few years younger, I might fight you for that man. Good looking, godly, and he does the dishes? Where was he when my Earl died?"

Trinity laughed. "Miss Gertie, I have a feeling if you wanted to fight me for him even now, you might just win."

An emphatic shake of her gray head countered the statement. "If you believe that for a minute, you must have lost your sight along with your heart. That boy is positively smitten. It's written all over his face. There won't be anyone taking him away from you any time soon. Now, what is this about a trip?"

The abrupt change of subject did nothing to erase the warmth her words of Blane's devotion brought. "Blane took a bus and train up here. He didn't want to take unnecessary risks with so fresh an injury. But since Jay is still with Tucker's parents, I offered to drive him back for his tests. We'll leave on Monday and be back by Thursday or Friday evening."

"That was sweet of you. I'm sure having your company will make the time go a bit swifter."

Trinity grinned. "I guess it wasn't completely unselfish. I've got to admit, I wasn't fond of not seeing Blane for a few days. I'd rather spend the time with him now, while we can."

"I see your young man isn't the only one smitten in this relationship."

"And how do you feel about that?" Trinity tried not to fidget. Miss Gertie's approval of Blane meant even more than that of her parents. Which reminded her, she should confirm next week's visit with them before long.

Miss Gertie's papery hands layered over hers on the table. Trinity met her eyes and saw exactly how much she was cared for.

"I couldn't be prouder of you and the choice you've made. He makes you happy. From what you've said, Jay loves him. He loves God, and that boy positively adores you. He's not what I expected, but he's perfect for you."

"Thank you. I think so. For now, we better get going." Trinity gave Miss Gertie a hug before heading into the kitchen.

"It was nice to meet you, young man. You take good care of my Trinity, and I expect to see both of you at church on Sunday."

Blane dried his hands on the dish towel next to the sink. "It was my pleasure. And you can count on me taking care of Trinity and both of us being at church."

"That's what I like to hear."

# 27

Trinity quietly sang along with the worship music on the radio as they pulled into the church parking lot. The anxiousness Blane expected wasn't present at all.

"You're in a good mood this morning," he observed.

Trinity looked up at the sky through the windshield as she turned off the engine. "It's a beautiful Sunday morning. Why shouldn't I be in a good mood?"

He hesitated to bring up the last service they'd attended together. "Honestly? I thought you'd be a little worried."

The grin she gave him looked anything but concerned. "Nope. After visiting with Miss Gertie, I realized you're right. My church family needs to get to know you better. That's all. You've already got allies in Mike and Autumn. Miss Gertie was won over the moment you did her dishes. I'm sure after services today and lunch with Pastor Hood and Laura, you'll be well on your way to winning over the rest of the congregation."

He chuckled. "No pressure or anything."

"Don't be ridiculous," she said as she got out of the car. "Just be yourself. Everyone will love you soon enough."

It didn't take long to find out Trinity's optimism was misplaced. Autumn, Mike, and Miss Gertie greeted him with open friendship. Though more restrained in their communication, the pastor and his wife were friendly enough. A few of the men even greeted him with reserved handshakes. But there was a tension in the sanctuary Blane couldn't explain that left him uneasy.

The sense he was being watched crept up the back of his neck before worship began, and it didn't leave throughout the service. Paranoia. That was the only reasonable explanation. Trinity's nerves from the previous week somehow put him on the defensive. The people in the pews were Trinity's church family. They were the loving, supportive people who helped her through Tucker's loss.

Determined to give them the benefit of the doubt, Blane forced his attention on Pastor Hood delivering the message from behind the pulpit. He was still the new guy in the congregation. That was bound to cause some ripples to the status quo.

———

After services, Trinity met Blane at the church door. "I hate to do this, especially since we're supposed to have lunch with Pastor Hood and Laura today, but apparently a special meeting has been called for Bouquets of Hope. Would you mind waiting while I see what's going on?"

"Don't worry about Blane," Laura spoke up from across the aisle. "We can give him a ride, and you can meet us after the meeting. If that's all right with him, that is."

A slight dip of his chin assured her he would be fine with the arrangements. The confirmation freed her to attend the meeting without concern over him waiting alone.

"That sounds great. I'm not sure how long the meeting will last since I'm not aware of why we're meeting in the first place. But I will join you guys just as soon as I can."

"You don't know why you're meeting?" Laura frowned. "You're still the coordinator, aren't you?"

Trinity laughed off the concern. "Maybe there's been a coup, and I'm being overthrown. Seriously, it's probably something about a need that came up unexpectedly. Nothing to worry about."

Cutting through the sanctuary, Trinity made her way to the fellowship hall. Bouquets of Hope meetings always took place around one of the folding tables. She smiled at Miss Gertie behind the long serving counter that separated the main part of the room from the kitchen area. Some things would never change. Miss Gertie was always the last to leave because she was the first to volunteer to clean up the coffee cart the church provided to those who arrived early. With Jay in tow, Trinity rarely got to enjoy the perk.

Assuming her seat at the head of the table, Trinity nodded a greeting to each of the ministry members gathered around. "Thank you all for coming. Let's start with prayer."

Every head bowed while Trinity asked the Lord to be in the business they were there to conduct. After the amen, she looked to Eve Thompson. "Eve, I'm going to turn it over to you since you're technically the one who called this meeting."

Eve nodded, only briefly making eye contact. "As Trinity said, thank you for coming."

Odd. In all the time she'd known Eve, Trinity had never considered her mousy. Politely quiet and reserved, but not the nervous sort. Why was her voice shaky?

"What we're discussing today isn't easy, and I want to remind everyone to please think before reacting."

Where was this meeting going? Trinity looked around the

table. A few women looked directly at the table in front of them. A couple shifted in their seats while their gazes bounced from place to place, never landing for long. And Theresa Cavins sat like a statue at the opposite end of the table, hands folded in front of her, eyes glued to Trinity. The smile Trinity tried to give her brought no response. Trinity's stomach tied in knots as she returned her attention to Eve.

"This is a wonderful ministry. God has blessed it time and again. To know we are helping those who are facing the hardest battles of their lives is rewarding for each of us. But it is also a responsibility we must take seriously, if we want to see it continue to thrive. We have to be above reproach in everything that takes place."

Trinity's confusion prompted her to action. "I agree. We need to guard the reputation of the ministry through living what we believe every day. But I'm not sure where this is coming from. Did something happen while I was away that I've not heard about? Or was it something more recent?"

Eve swallowed hard. "Well, yes. Sort of. Maybe both, I guess."

"What are you talking about Eve?"

"You." Theresa Cavins shot the single word like a bullet from a gun. "She's talking about you and that new man in your life."

Now she knew what the coyote on those old cartoons felt every time an anvil dropped on him from the sky. Pain radiated as the weight of Theresa's words stole her ability to breathe. "Blane?"

"Yes, Blane," Theresa clarified.

"I don't understand. What does he have to do with this? With Bouquets of Hope?"

Someone cleared their throat, pulling Theresa's attention from Trinity momentarily. When it returned, the change was undeniable. Theresa's posture softened, and a pity smile turned her lips.

"I know this is hard to hear, but we only bring it to you because we care. About you and about Bouquets of Hope." The hardness in her tone melted leaving only saccharine and the bitter taste it inevitably left behind.

Dancing around the subject was getting them nowhere and making Trinity's head hurt. "Please, just tell me what Blane has to do with anything."

"We're concerned you're going down a dangerous path. This Blane fellow is charming enough, but he's not the type of guy you should allow into your life. Think of Jay."

Trinity squared her shoulders. "I think of Jay every day, thank you. And Blane has been a wonderful addition to his life."

Theresa sighed. "That's what I was afraid of. You're so blinded by your grief over losing Tucker that you've let it lead you into a relationship that isn't good for you or Jay. You're not equally yoked, as they say, and it's going to drag you away from God in the end."

"Blane is not dragging me away from God." The urges to scream and vomit came simultaneously. Trinity refrained from giving in to either.

Eve looked at her for the first time since Theresa began her tirade. "You did miss small group on Wednesday. You never miss small group."

Though her voice was quiet, it felt like a nail being driven into a coffin Trinity hadn't known was being fashioned. Trinity closed her eyes and took a steadying breath.

"There were extenuating circumstances on Wednesday. I'd be happy to explain if it will help."

"There's no need to explain." Theresa waved her hand.

"That's how it starts, the slippery slope. Excuses that sound good come more frequently until you're absent all together."

Fire pulsed through Trinity with each beat of her heart, and part of her wished she could breathe it like a dragon directly toward Theresa Cavins. This attack was unprovoked.

"Blane is not causing me to fall away from God. He's a good, godly man."

Theresa had the gall to snort in disbelief. "Good is relative and of no use to God. Our good is nothing compared to His. As for godly, think about it clearly for a moment. Consider the way he looks. The way he demands attention every time he enters the room. It's pride."

Trinity folded her arms across her chest. "No. It's size. Blane doesn't demand attention, but his size singles him out for it. And he looks fine. Just because he wears his hair long and doesn't wear the same style clothes as everyone else in the congregation doesn't make him a sinner."

"But his profession might. The man is a wrestler. He makes his living fighting other people. And that's not the worst of it. I've heard stories about some of the things that happen in that world. I've seen pictures of some of the women. No one could be in that line of work and call themself a Christian."

"Blane is a godly man."

Theresa was oddly calm. "And that is the crux of the matter. You're blinded to the truth. We've come to you, hoping you'll see where you're straying. But if not, we have to deal with it for the sake of the ministry."

Trinity's mouth dropped open. "Deal with it? Are you asking me to step down from the ministry I started in my husband's honor?"

"Not yet. We're asking you to remember your husband and ask how Tucker would view this new development in your life.

If you can't see it, if you refuse to accept this loving correction, then we will have to make some changes."

"And this is how you all feel?" Trinity looked from person to person. Eve and at least one other person nodded slowly without looking at her. No one else gave an answer. Theresa sat at her end of the table, the only one to make and keep eye contact.

That's where it fell then. For reasons only God could judge, Theresa Cavins was riled up about Blane and must have railroaded the rest of the group into following her lead. With a powerful personality, she and Trinity had butted heads in the past. It wasn't unusual. But nothing like this had ever taken place. If you asked Trinity a month ago, she wouldn't have thought it possible.

The pity mask returned to Theresa's expression. "We're not doing this to hurt you. We want what's best for you and this ministry. We want you to be happy, even find a suitable man to be part of your life. We know you'll need time to seek God. Remember, He always forgives us when we come to Him in repentance. We'll be waiting for your decision. Meeting dismissed."

Trinity didn't wait for anyone to speak or pause to say goodbyes before racing to her car. She slammed it into gear and pulled from the parking lot, only getting as far as the nearest shopping center parking lot before she had to stop. Pulling in away from the crowd of cars, she sat in stunned silence.

This wasn't happening. This couldn't be happening. Her church family loved her. They were good, Christian people. One person could not have turned the whole group against her.

She slammed her hand onto the steering wheel. Theresa Cavins. That woman had been a thorn in her side more than once. And what was that about a suitable man? Of course, this had nothing to do with Blane's faith or lack thereof. An easy target. That's what he was.

This had to do with her choice of Blane and her dismissal of Eric. How ironic was that? Theresa called Blane ungodly, but Eric, who looked like everyone thought a Christian should look, got a pass for deplorable behavior. Ugh! People like Theresa Cavins gave Christians everywhere a bad name.

But she couldn't lose the ministry. And she didn't want to lose Blane either. Couldn't God make this go away? Maybe even make Theresa suddenly decide to leave their church? It didn't have to end poorly. No one had to lose. All God had to do was remove the one person who stirred the pot more frequently than anyone else she knew.

Riverview Church would be better for it. She knew it. There was no doubt that without Theresa there, the remaining church body would take up any slack in ministries. She'd be happy to take some of it on, if God would only make Theresa back off or leave completely. No ministry needed to suffer because of the loss, especially not Bouquets of Hope.

"Why, God? Why this? Why now?" Trinity's questions broke the dam holding back her tears. "Lord, I love Bouquets of Hope. Are you asking me to give it up? I don't want to, but they're not giving me a choice."

Sobs wracked her body as she considered losing what God placed in her heart after Tucker's death. Even the possibility of stepping away from it left her feeling like Tucker was being taken all over again. And just like before, she had no say in the matter.

"Only I do have a say this time." The realization of what it might cost to keep the ministry caused a fresh wave of tears. "Please, don't ask me to give up Blane. I love him, and You know they're wrong about him. He loves You. He lives for You. Please, I can't take any more loss. It's not fair."

When her tears dried up, Trinity was left with a stuffy nose and silence. She sat, stunned until her final cries came to mind again.

"It's not fair." Only this time it was an indisputable fact instead of the cry of a breaking heart. "It's never going to be fair. People fail."

They'd always failed, and that wouldn't change in the future. She could refuse to forgive them, but it would only hurt her in the long run. Besides, she'd needed forgiveness enough times in her life to nudge her toward giving it to others.

"Honestly, I probably need it after some of the things I've thought today," she scolded her reflection in the rearview mirror.

Taking a moment, she silently confessed her attitudes. She couldn't let them distance her from God. The only way she would find the answers she needed was to keep communication between her and God uncluttered by sin. And if there was one thing she needed to help solve this mess, it was God's undeniable direction.

With a final prayer for clarity, Trinity felt like she could move again. The weight that settled on her body didn't lift completely, but it eased enough to keep her breathing. Though her mind felt a bit swampy, and her tears left her exhausted, Trinity pulled her car from the lot and headed to Sunday lunch at the pastor's house.

# 28

"My goodness," Laura commented as she opened the door to Trinity's knock. "That was certainly a long meeting. I hope everything got worked out. We were just sitting down at the table."

Blane turned in his seat as Trinity entered the room. His smile froze in place as he took in her appearance. At the church, optimism radiated from every pore. What happened in that meeting to leave the worn-down woman in front of him?

Well-taught manners kicked in despite his concern over her appearance. He stood and pulled out her chair before reclaiming his own.

"You made it right on time. I shared my testimony with Pastor Hood and Laura while she put the finishing touches on the meal. We both finished up, and the pastor said grace not two minutes before you knocked."

A joyless smile curved her lips. "Great. I'm starving." She looked to Pastor Hood. "I found Blane's testimony beautiful. I'm anxious to hear what you thought of it."

Pastor Hood scooped a healthy helping of mashed potatoes

onto his plate before passing the serving bowl to Blane on his left. "It is a powerful testimony of God's relentless pursuit of a wandering heart, even when that heart seemingly didn't want anything to do with Him."

"It is a moving testimony," Laura added as she accepted the bowl making its way around the table. "It really shows God's mercy. There were days when a testimony like that made me wonder about my own."

What could a woman like Laura have done to make her question her testimony? True, he didn't know her well, but he could see she was a gracious and giving woman with a calming spirit.

"What did it make you question?" Blane decided answers were better than speculation.

Her fork stopped before she could empty it of the green beans she'd speared. "I think it goes without saying that your testimony isn't like mine. And I'm not referring to wrestling, though I've not done that either. I grew up in church."

Ah. Now it made sense. Her story was that of the good girl who rebelled in her late teens only to return later. Blane didn't know God in childhood, but he could imagine the guilt that would accompany walking away and having to return like the prodigal.

"I loved God from an early age, and my faith never wavered. Oh, I experienced times when I didn't feel God's presence as clearly or hear His direction with assurance. There were times I sinned, and times I grew. Even in the distant times, I had my faith."

It wasn't what he expected.

"What's wrong with your testimony?"

The smile she gave him was serene. "Absolutely nothing. But I didn't always feel that way. It felt boring and uninspiring. I'd hear testimonies like yours, and they were so powerful, moving. Mine was more like, 'Church girl gives heart to Jesus and stays in church.' How could God use that?"

"You don't feel that way anymore, though. What changed?"

She placed a hand over her husband's. "God brought us together. My husband was raised in church but didn't commit his life to Christ until his early twenties, right before we met."

Pastor Hood wiped his napkin over his lips before taking over the story. "Like many teens, I pushed my limits. I saw the boundaries I'd been given as attempts to make me remain a child instead of seeing how they were making me a better man. After I gave my life to Christ, I regretted many of my decisions. When I met Laura, I had to face many of those choices and the physical consequences they brought into our relationship."

Blane could see Laura's gentle squeeze of his hand. He looked at her again. "How did his life change your opinion of your testimony?"

"I realized, because of the faith I lived from an early age, I was spared those tough conversations. I wasn't perfect, but because of God in my life, I avoided some of those life-changing sins and wouldn't have to deal with the fallout every time I entered a new relationship. I saw it clearly in romantic relationships, but the principle carried over into each area of my life."

"I don't think I've ever considered that perspective before. Put like that, I'm pretty sure you've got a stronger testimony than any of us."

Laura laughed. "That's the most amazing part. God needs each story. There are people who will be moved by your story, and they might not be the same ones who need to hear mine. God reaches us in different ways, and that's why I've come to understand my testimony is as usable as anyone else's, when I offer it up for God to use."

Conversation flowed through the meal until the final piece of pie and cup of coffee was enjoyed. Not one time in their afternoon together did Blane get the feeling he was being tested. Pastor Hood and Laura's interest and the friendship they extended came without strings attached.

With promises to get together again, Blane and Trinity said their goodbyes. Blane waited until they were half-way back to Mike's house before breaking the uneasy silence that shrouded Trinity from the moment she joined them for the meal.

"You might as well spill it. You're going to anyway."

Her thumbs tapped an erratic beat on the steering wheel. "I don't know what you're talking about."

"You do too. Something happened at that meeting. Whatever it is left you completely shaken. Out with it."

"Do you mind if we don't go home right away? I mean, if you do, I understand. We could both use some time to pack for the trip tomorrow."

"Whatever it takes to get you to tell me what's going on. It won't take me long to pack."

Trinity drove down the busy highway without speaking. The silence chafed worse than a mat burn under a tight-fitting pair of jeans. When they crossed the bridge over the Mississippi and out of Missouri, Blane wondered how far she'd run before dealing with whatever weighed her down.

"Trinity?"

His quiet question prompted a silent shake of her head. Still not ready to talk about it then. Worry snaked its way through his body. Trinity was a talker. For something to render her silent, well, he wouldn't have imagined it possible. Even when he needed silence to process, he could feel Trinity's desire to talk it out filling space between them. This was something new, and he wasn't sure how to deal with it.

*Lord, Jesus, I'm lost. I've never seen Trinity like this, and I have no clue what happened. Whatever took place in that meeting, Lord, let her know You're with her. Help me comfort her and offer godly encouragement.*

The silent prayer continued as miles passed while he looked outside the passenger-side window. It was close to an hour before she turned onto a country road that snaked its way up a tree-enclosed hill and emptied into a parking lot where trees gave way to a wide-open field. Wide open except for a visitor's center and an enormous white cross.

"What is this place?"

Trinity opened her door. "It's Bald Knob Cross. I found it one night after Tucker died. At night, the lights come on, and it almost glows. It was so peaceful and still. I sat under it, soaking it in while I prayed. I learned later the full name is the Bald Knob Cross of Peace."

"Fitting." He followed her through the parking lot toward the cross.

"I've only come back a handful of times."

"I'm guessing you come when you need some peace?" Turning in every direction, he whistled. "It's a beautiful view. You can see for miles up here."

"They say you can see three states from here. I'm not sure if that's three in addition to Illinois or including it. I guess it really doesn't matter."

Autumn at the cross would be gorgeous. Too bad it was summer. Still, he couldn't fault her for her choice in places to get away from everything. "Not as long as you find what you're looking for. Want to talk about it yet?"

Trinity sat, legs bent in front of her, at the base of the cross and looked at the vast landscape around her. "They want me to step down, Blane."

He dropped to the ground beside her. "From Bouquets of Hope? But didn't you start the ministry?"

"Yes, but it's not my ministry. It's a ministry of Riverview Church, not Trinity Knight."

"I get that, but it seems strange to ask the person who started the ministry in the first place to step down."

Her jaw was tight as she nodded. "Yep. I've not seen it happen before."

"Did they give a reason?"

"Yep."

"Care to share? I'd love to hear what's prompting this outlandish request."

Pain and regret filled the eyes she turned on him. "You sure about that?"

"Of course, I want to know. There can't be a justifiable reason for this."

She picked at the grass in front of her. "It's you. Well, you and me."

"What do you mean, 'it's you and me'?"

"Exactly what I said. They informed me they're worried about me. My choices of men to associate with are less than godly. And it's the kind of behavior that could be harmful to the reputation of Bouquets of Hope."

Bile crept up his throat. The idea that his presence in her life could cause her to lose the ministry she loved made him sick. To keep from gagging, he swallowed hard. His head swam worse than when he got the concussion.

"Wait. Your choice in men? Me? Why am I not Christian enough for them? Or for you or whatever? Never mind. It doesn't matter. We can fix this. I'll come speak with them, answer any questions they have. They'll see the truth, and everything will be fine."

"No. It won't." She swiped tears from her cheeks with her fingertips. "They don't want to talk to you. They've made up their minds. The way you look. Your job. Even the way you carry yourself and grab the attention of everyone in a room. It all goes into their opinion that you're not a godly man."

The acid churning in his stomach refused to dissipate. He swallowed again. This couldn't be happening. He'd heard the arguments before. He'd silenced them again and again in his personal life. Hashing through the specifics and offering rebuttals would do no good. If the women wouldn't listen, he couldn't stop Trinity's hurt.

"And they all feel this way?"

Trinity shrugged. "Some more than others. It only takes one strong-willed, bitter woman to lead the way. Once she convinces a few others that she's in the right and that they're making this decision for the good of a sister-in-Christ and the ministry, the idea snowballs out of control. I have a feeling there are several who don't agree, but they aren't going to buck this one either. They'd rather deal with the splinters they get from sitting on the fence."

"Who?" Blane held up his hand. "No. Don't tell me. I don't need to know. Isn't there anything you can do?"

Tears flowed as she nodded. Blane reached to wipe them away. His breath caught when she leaned away before feeling his touch.

"I have a choice. Give up Bouquets of Hope or give up you."

Hearing it so bluntly expressed ignited anger Blane didn't realize was simmering under the hurt he felt for Trinity. He was on his feet in one move, staring down at Trinity. "They have no right!"

"Be that as it may—"

"No! You can't simply lie down and take this! It's wrong!" He stalked back and forth in front of her.

"I agree, but—"

"What do you mean 'but'? There is no but."

Trinity stood and he nearly shook off the hand she placed

on his bicep. Instead, he stared at where it rested, offering comfort he had to refuse. His jaw ached from the tightness that crept into it. Trinity bit her lip and let her arm fall to her side.

"I know you're upset. I am too." Her voice was quiet, calm. Unreasonably so in his opinion.

He reached for her hand, forcing himself to relax. "It's not at you. You understand that don't you?"

"Of course, I do. Believe me, I threw my own hissy fit in the car on the way to lunch today. Hopefully there weren't cameras in the shopping center parking lot. If there were, someone got a show."

Her chuckle disarmed his anger. He tugged her into his chest and wrapped his arms around her, laying his cheek against the top of her head.

"I ..." He wanted more than anything to say the three words he knew would bring comfort. Still, they refused to leave his lips. He improvised instead. "I'm sure whoever saw it understood there were bigger issues going on. If they hadn't, I'm sure the cops would have shown up before you were done."

The rumble of her laugh worked through his chest like a massage, relaxing him for the first time since the conversation began. He could stay in that place forever. Hold her tight while the rest of the world buzzed around them. Only, they both knew it was impossible. He held her closer as if doing so would make the uncertainty of her next answer less daunting.

"What are you going to do?"

Her arms tightened around him as she burrowed further into his chest. "The only thing I can do." He felt her shudder. "I'm going to step down from Bouquets of Hope."

How could an answer be everything he wanted and nothing he wanted for her at the same time? "Trinity? You'd give up Bouquets of Hope?"

"That's going to be the easy part."

"Giving up the ministry of your heart is the easy part? What's the hard part?"

She tilted her head back. With her lips twisted in a frown and eyebrows drawn together, she looked adorable. He wouldn't consider pointing that out at the moment, but still, it was true. Tears filling her eyes brought him back to the weight of the conversation.

"What am I missing? What else is going to happen?"

"You don't see it? I'd choose you a hundred times over, Blane. But in doing so, the ministry isn't the only thing I'll be giving up."

"But that's what they want? That's what they said, right?"

The top of her head dropped against his chest. The shudders he felt where his hands rested on her back signaled the restart of her tears. He moved one hand protectively to stroke her hair.

"It's going to be all right."

"No. In choosing you, I'm going to lose the ministry *and* my church family. I can't do it, Blane. As long as I'm with you, I'm *persona non grata*. I'm the woman at the well before she met Jesus, living in sin and outcast. It's not just Bouquets of Hope. They won't find me fit to serve in any ministry. I can't stay in a church that sees me that way."

The depth of what she was giving up for him hit hard. "But not everyone feels that way. Maybe it won't be that bad. Maybe you can stay."

Her head moved against him as she shook it. "No. I can't. There would be a few to stand up for me, but I'd always have to fight that battle. Besides, what they're doing is wrong. You said it yourself. I don't think I could continue worshiping in that environment."

Stepping away from her, he held her shoulders. "That's it. You need to take it to Pastor Hood and Laura."

"I don't know. I'm not into the whole tattling on the playground vibe."

"It's not the same thing. They are the church's shepherds, and if there's something making the flock sick, they need to know it."

She caught her bottom lip between her teeth. He waited, wondering if she would see the wisdom in his words. It felt right to let the pastor know of the issue.

"Maybe you're right about telling them. I'm not sure. What I do know, is I need to start looking for a new place to worship. Even if this situation is dealt with, it doesn't mean the person changes. It means the behavior stops. Knowing those lies are going to be whispered behind my back is too much."

"I can't ask you to leave your church."

"You're not. And my mind is made up."

Relief that she'd chosen to believe in him, in their relationship, was short-lived. The rest of her solution didn't sit right. There had to be another way.

# 29

The next morning, Trinity pulled into Mike's driveway. Blane shut the trunk of Mike's car as she put hers in park and got out.

"You think it's going to be so lonely around here with Blane leaving that you can't stick around either?" she joked. "Don't worry. I'll bring him back in a few days."

An unsettling feeling came over her as neither of the men laughed or even smiled at her joke. What was going on? She wasn't late picking up Blane for their trip to Tennessee. Her phone showed no missed messages or voicemails to inform her of a change in plans. The uneasiness grew when Mike patted Blane's shoulder.

"I'll give you two a minute."

"No. You finish up. We'll be back soon." Blane gave the cryptic instructions before gesturing around the house with a jerk of his head. "Can we talk?"

No. She wanted to scream the word at him. No, they couldn't talk. She didn't want to talk. In fact, it was the last thing she wanted to do. Nothing good would come from it. She knew it as surely as she knew Blane's bags filled Mike's trunks. What she didn't know was why. She opened her mouth expecting the two-letter word to shoot from her lips like a bullet.

"Sure." Even her mouth and mind had turned traitor. She followed him around the side of the house. At least he'd chosen the side without a neighbor close. She had a suspicion whatever was about to transpire was better just between them.

"You can't imagine what these last few months have meant to me."

"Stop."

"You and Jay have brought so much joy to my life. And knowing you'd choose me. I can't tell you how much I'll treasure knowing that."

"No. I said stop it. Now." He hadn't even said the words yet, but her body cued the tears anyway. "Don't do this. Please."

The last word sounded strangled. She didn't care. Blane couldn't do this to her, to them. They'd come to an agreement less than twenty-four hours ago. Why would he go back on that?

He reached out to take her into his arms, stopped before touching her. His eyes slid shut as his arms dropped to his sides.

That was it. An acknowledgment of what was between them would make leaving harder for him. It would give her time to change his mind. She stepped toward him and slid her arms around his waist. One breath. Two breaths. Before the third could pass her lips, she felt the warmth of his arms closing around her.

"You're not making this easy." His voice was hoarse and rough.

"Good. Because you're not doing what I think you're trying

to do. Now, we have to get on the road if we want to make it to Tennessee before it gets dark."

He held her tighter. She felt the sharp rise and deep fall of his chest under her cheek. It was going to be okay. She relaxed her arms around him. When he pulled away from the embrace, she realized her mistake.

His cheeks were wet with tears. "No. We're not going anywhere. Trinity, I ..." What was it with this verbal hang up? "I can't let you lose your church family. You can stay and work it out with them. I know it. But you can't do it with me in your life. I know you made your choice, but I've made mine too. Your church is your family. They've carried you through so much heartache already. They'll be there for you again. I know it."

"No." The soft word sounded pathetic to her ears.

"You know I'm right."

"What about Jay?" It was a desperate attempt, but one she'd employ without shame if it changed his mind.

He shook his head. "I don't know. It's something we'll have to work out once he's back home. Until then, I'll keep up the once-a-week calls while he's with his grandparents. I want to be there for him, but ultimately, that will be up to you."

Trinity huffed. Up to her? What a joke. If anything was up to her, they wouldn't be having this discussion. "Fine."

"Trinity, please."

She raised her chin and fought to keep it from quivering. "No. You can't leave me and then tell me not to be upset about it. You're breaking my heart, Blane. I love you."

"You're right. I can't ask that of you any more than I can allow you to give up your church family for me. Please ... just ... I don't know. Just please remember, this isn't easy for me either. I don't want to lose you, but me staying is selfish. I want the best for you, and right now, that isn't me."

She refused to look at him. His reasoning made sense, but she didn't care. Didn't want it to. Blane Sterling in her life. That's what she wanted, but he wasn't going to accept that.

"Good-bye Trinity."

———

The path around the house and back to the car felt twice as long. Every muscle in his body ached to return to Trinity, crying on the other side of the house. To take her into his arms where she fit so perfectly. But he couldn't. It was bigger than him, bigger than them. She didn't understand it now, but she would. And her church family would be there to help her start again, as they had been before and, without him, as they would continue to be.

Mike looked at him over the top of the car. "Are you sure about this?"

He didn't trust himself to speak. A nod would have to do. He opened the door and slid into the passenger seat. Staring out the windshield, Blane barely registered Mike getting in and starting the engine.

When he'd explained the situation to Mike at midnight the previous night, Mike hadn't liked the outcome but said he'd help. Mike's assurance to stand beside Trinity and make sure Blane's leaving healed the breech between her and the rest of the church meant more to him than the ride to the bus station. At least he could leave knowing someone else was there to take care of her. The fact that it couldn't be him cut deep into his heart.

They arrived at the station with only a few minutes to spare. Mike grabbed a bag from the trunk and followed Blane into the white block building waiting with the small group of passengers milling around while Blane moved into the ticket line.

Blane returned shoving a ticket into his pocket before reaching for the bag Mike held. With a bag in each hand and the announcement of the bus's arrival blaring over the speaker system, Blane felt this last disconnect to Trinity and the friendships he'd made with her.

"Make sure she's okay?"

"You don't even have to ask."

"And don't let her hold your helping me against you."

"Never. Autumn wouldn't allow it."

Blane smiled despite himself. "Good. Thanks for everything, Mike."

"Take care of yourself. And don't be a stranger."

"I won't. Now, get back home and check on Trinity. I have a bus to catch."

Blane shuffled with the other passengers toward the bus. There was a long, slow road ahead before he would reach home. But worse than that, he couldn't even begin to guess how many miles he'd need between him and Trinity before the ache lessened. Even if he couldn't say it, he loved Trinity. That's the only reason he could take the heartache and board the bus that would take him away from her for good.

# 30

From her blanket cocoon on the couch, Trinity watched Autumn. She focused on a spot behind Trinity's self-made fortress of solitude and silently pleaded for help. Not even a hint of movement. Mike was apparently not taking the bait from the kitchen doorway where she assumed he stood like the sentry to a castle. She'd seen the two of them in action enough times to know how it all went down. The only difference was, this time it was directed toward her.

Autumn's lips pursed as her brows rose. *Uh oh*. Mike was in for it now. *The* look. The one that brooked no disobedience and bent the strongest of wills to her desires. A rustle sounded behind Trinity moments before Autumn's mouth dropped open in disbelief.

If she felt at all like smiling, Trinity would have mustered up the wryest smile on the planet to celebrate Mike's mutiny. But she didn't feel like it. Not at all.

"You shouldn't be surprised."

Narrowed eyes turned on her. "Oh, now she speaks."

Trinity lifted a blanket clad shoulder in a shrug. "It's the first time I've had something to say."

"And I wasn't surprised."

"You're not a good liar. I saw it all over your face. You thought he would cow to you, and he didn't. What you seem to forget is that in all the years I've known Mike, he's never been one to dip a toe in the pool of emotion. And if I had to hazard a guess, I'd say we're about to skip straight from wading to jumping in the deep end without a lifeguard. Even your powers of persuasion aren't a match for that."

Autumn's hands braced against her hips. "Very poetic. Now, get off the couch and let's go to lunch. You said you would."

Trinity scooted further into the cushions. "No, I didn't."

"Yes, you did."

"No, I didn't. I said I *might* be up to going to lunch. I'm not."

A huff filled the space between them. "You can't keep doing this. It's been five days since Blane left. You've not left your house, and I'm not even sure you've changed out of your PJ's."

Trinity lifted the edge of her blanket and looked inside. "Of course, I've changed. Yesterday's PJ's were blue. These are green with little smiley faces. *Smiley faces.* See? I'm perfectly fine. With Jay at his grandparents' house, there's no need for me to do more than that. No crisis here. You can stop playing emotional EMT now."

Arms crossed against her chest, Autumn raised an eyebrow. "And *I'm* the bad liar? Don't even try to pull this stuff with me. We've been friends for forever, and I can promise you, I know you. Maybe even better than you know yourself. Blane broke your heart, and you're content to sit here wallowing in the pain."

Trinity blinked and sniffed as her words landed squarely in her heart. "I'm not wallowing."

A sigh accompanied Autumn's relocation to the other end of the sofa. "Trinity, sweetie, I know this is hard. The first time you put yourself out there after Tucker's death, and it ends like this."

Dropping her head onto the cushion behind it, Trinity stared at the ceiling. "But why? Why did it end? I loved him. I still love him."

Though her blankets kept the warmth from seeping through to her skin, the pressure of Autumn's hand on her arm gave a little comfort. She closed her eyes in a futile attempt to stem the flow of tears.

"I know you do."

"And," Trinity hiccupped. "And I thought he loved me."

"I'm not sure you want to hear this," Autumn's voice was soft, "But I think he does, even if he never told you."

"How can you say that after what he did?"

"Right or wrong, I think he did it for you. He understands how vital your church family is to you. He removed himself from the equation to try to rectify the situation."

Trinity felt her jaw lock in place. "He wasted the choice. I don't think I can go back and pretend this never happened."

"No one is asking you to. But don't count God out yet. He can still do a work and bring something good out of this, for you and for the church as a whole."

"It would take a miracle."

"It's a good thing we serve a God who specializes in miracles then."

Autumn's smile was sure. The faith it exhibited bolstered Trinity's, working to reassure her that everything would work out. While the situation was far from redeemed, she still found the strength to offer a small grin in return.

The shrill ring of Autumn's phone caused her to jump. Grabbing her purse from the floor beside the couch, Autumn dug through the contents until she pulled her cell out and swiped across the screen.

"Hello?"

A pause.

"Yes, we are, but her phone died and is charging in the other room."

Autumn placed her open purse back on the floor beside her while the caller filled the silence with words only she could hear.

"I'll let her know. See you tomorrow." She hung up the phone and dropped it back in her purse before turning back to Trinity. "That was Laura. She said she tried to call but couldn't get through. She wants you to know there is another Bouquets of Hope meeting tomorrow after services."

"I'm not going."

"Trinity ..."

"No. I can't be around those women. They want me gone. They think I'm some sort of fallen woman, and they ran Blane out of my life. I don't want anything to do with any of them." Her fist pounded emphasis into the couch cushions.

Several heartbeats passed while Autumn simply looked at her. Seeing pity or disappointment, maybe both, in her friend's eyes, Trinity raised her chin but couldn't keep it from quivering. She would not cry. Not this time. She was angry, not hurt, and that didn't warrant tears.

"You know I'll stand beside you no matter what," Autumn reasoned. "But this time, I think you're wrong."

Trinity's mouth fell open. Heat rose into her cheeks in rhythm with her growing irritation. Autumn, however, looked unruffled and unfazed. The long-term friendship between them served as a guarantee that Trinity's best friend knew the warning signs. The only uncertainty remaining was if the information would inspire a course correction to the conversation.

"You're upset. And rightfully so. But you know this isn't the answer. Don't let this drive you from the ministry and church. Don't let Blane's sacrifice be for nothing. You've already lost enough in this mess."

Trinity turned her face from Autumn though it did little to hide the confusion and never-ending flow of tears. "I don't know. I'm not sure I have the strength for that."

"You have the strength," Mike's voice sounded from behind her.

When had he returned? And why? Emotionally compromised women were not his forte. All three of them knew it, and it was never an issue. Mike was who he was, and they accepted it without question or push to change him.

Lost in her musings, Trinity didn't hear him moving until he stood in front of her. Whatever brought him back into the conversation must have been a powerful motivator. Not only was he joining the intervention, but he also knelt in front of her, putting himself directly in her line of sight.

"I've seen your strength," he began. When she started to look away, a shake of his head stopped her. "No. I want you to listen to me. We watched you care for Tucker from diagnosis all the way to the end. You hurt and were scared. Suddenly, all your dreams were gone along with the man you loved. Jay needed you when you felt you had nothing to give. You gave it anyway. You made it through."

"This is different."

"Yes, it is. But you're going to make it through this, just like you did then, with grace and strength."

"And just like before," Autumn began as she moved to sit on the floor beside her brother, "we'll be there with you. And not only to help you deal with losing Blane. We'll be there for whatever fallout comes at church as well. You've done nothing wrong, and I believe, somehow, God is going to make that clear."

Mike nodded. "But even if no one listens and things don't get better, we're with you. And you'll be able to move on knowing you've done all God would have you do."

Trinity sniffed and stretched out from her blanket to enclose both Mike and Autumn into a group hug. With her head resting on the bridge of their shoulders, she felt their strength and courage seeping into her soul.

"You guys are the best."

"Enough of this mushy stuff," Mike announced as he pulled away.

"Huh uh, mister." Trinity said strengthening her hold on him. "You've waded into this pool of emotion, and you aren't getting out of it that easily."

A groan from Mike elicited a laugh from Autumn. Her amusement was contagious and both Mike and Trinity joined her. The action was enough to ease the weight Trinity carried. She sat back on the couch, her blanket cocoon abandoned behind her.

Autumn stood and looked to Mike. "We'd better get home and let Trinity get some rest. We've all got church tomorrow." She glanced at Trinity. "Pick you up?"

"Sure."

Trinity accompanied them to the door. Autumn gave her a quick hug before heading to their car. Having had enough of the emotional stuff, Mike was content with a hand to her shoulder before stepping onto the porch. As he hit the first step, he turned back.

"Not sure if it helps or not, but Autumn's right. I don't know if it was the right move or not, but Blane must have thought it was the best thing to do. He didn't say much, but I know he cares about you."

As he joined Autumn and started the car, Trinity closed the door behind them. Finding herself rooted to the spot, she leaned back. The hardness of the door against her head threatened to make it ache, but Trinity didn't move. Did thinking Blane loved her make any of this better?

Maybe one day it would. Right now, it offered little comfort. Tomorrow, as she faced her church family, Trinity was convinced there wasn't great enough love in human existence to comfort her through that trial. Good thing she had God's love to step in. She was going to need it.

# 31

Trinity would never understand, short of God's intervention, how she made it through the worship service and message without breaking down or throwing up. From the time she woke up, her emotions played pinball inside her, leaving her discombobulated and restless.

"Ready?" Autumn asked next to her on the pew after the last amen.

"No."

"I'll be right beside you the whole time. And Mike says he's staying. Says he's always wanted to be the getaway driver, and this is the perfect opportunity."

Despite the butterflies swarming her middle, Trinity laughed. "Fine. Let's get this over with."

She really couldn't ask for better friends. Autumn wasn't even part of the ministry. Support was the single part she played in this drama. And Mike didn't have to wait around, but Trinity hadn't even asked him to stay. With them by her side and God going before her, she might make it through this in one piece.

Confusion pushed gratefulness out of the picture as she looked around the meeting table. In addition to all the Bouquets of Hope regulars and Autumn, Laura and Miss Gertie sat at the head of the table where she usually took up residence. At least she wouldn't have the choice of maintaining or ignoring eye contact with Theresa this meeting.

Good thing too. She sat at the end trying to look unaffected by the oddities of the meeting's attendance. Instead of in control, she looked more like she'd sucked on a lemon. Apparently, unlike last week's ambush, this meeting was a surprise to her as well.

Laura's smile as she indicated an empty chair with the wave of her upturned hand conveyed assurance that all would be well. Claiming the seat was easy. However, the confidence Laura extended was lost to Trinity. Autumn plopped into the seat next to her.

"This is highly irregular," Theresa attempted casual concern but couldn't fully manage to sand the sharpness from her tone. "Bouquets of Hope has no issue accepting new members, but there is no need to call an extra meeting to do so."

Laura's serenity didn't waver. "That's wonderful to know, but I didn't call this meeting to induct new members into the group. However, since I know, like me, you're all waiting to get home to your pot roasts, let's open with prayer. Then, we can get down to business."

Every head bowed as Laura invited the Lord into the day's meeting. As she spoke of the Holy Spirit speaking to each heart, leading them closer to God and farther from self, Trinity knew they were getting hints of the meeting's subject matter. A warning flickered in her heart that things were about to get uncomfortable.

"I believe it's always nice to start a meeting, not only with prayer, but with God's word. A short devotion. I understand Miss Gertie isn't part of this group, but she was instrumental in the calling of this meeting. So, I've asked her to join us today and share a short scripture with us. Miss Gertie?"

Flipping to a cloth marker in her well-worn Bible, Miss Gertie began reading from 1 Samuel 16. Starting with God's rejection of Israel's current king, Miss Gertie told the familiar story of God's call on Samuel to anoint a new king from the house of Jesse. As the oldest of eight brothers passed in front of Samuel, the prophet knew this must be God's anointed.

Miss Gertie's slight pause arrested the attention of everyone around the table, though they knew what came next. "'But the LORD said to Samuel, 'Do not look at his appearance or at the height of his stature, because I have rejected him; for God sees not as man sees, for man looks at the outward appearance, but the LORD looks at the heart.'"

Looking once more around the table, she continued. "And what, exactly did God see when he looked at young David, future king of Israel? Did He see perfection? We know from David's story, the man fell short. Adultery and murder top his list of sins against the God he served. Yet, even knowing what was to come in David's life, God made a declaration about him. And He made it even before Samuel anointed him."

The crinkle of pages filled the silence as Miss Gertie flipped to another passage. "First Samuel thirteen tells us, 'The LORD has sought out for Himself a man after His own heart, and the LORD has appointed him as ruler over His people.' King Saul's heart didn't belong to God. He didn't trust God to go before Him. David never wavered in his faith. Yes, he sinned like any other man or woman who has ever lived."

A few of the metal chairs scraped the floor as their occupants squirmed. Gertie paid them no mind. She wasn't done speaking.

"And when he did, he came to God with a broken heart for forgiveness. In good and bad, David craved God's presence. I want to be that kind of person. I want to desire God in my life before all else, even when I fail miserably. I want God to look at me and see a woman after His own heart."

Silence. The temptation to scour the room judging the number of guilty consciences pulled at Trinity. But no. She couldn't stoop to that level.

"I asked Miss Gertie to share this passage," Laura explained, resuming control of the meeting, "because I want all of us to keep it in mind as we deal with today's business. This past Monday, Miss Gertie asked to speak with me and my husband. Though not part of it, she heard several things discussed in a meeting that concerned her. The details she shared disturbed us too. After much prayer, your pastor and I determined it's an issue that needs to be met head on. That's why we're here today."

Theresa huffed. "Let me get this straight. Someone overhears something she's not even part of, runs and tattles, gossips, mind you, and you just take it as gospel and decide it needs intervention? That doesn't sound very godly to me."

"That is precisely why I called this meeting. I don't want to take anything I hear secondhand as the truth." Laura remained unfazed by the judgment. "And since it was presented as a group issue, I'm addressing the group to find the truth. Would anyone care to tell me what exactly happened at last week's meeting?"

Theresa didn't break eye contact with her. "We had an internal issue, and we dealt with it."

"First, I appreciate that each ministry of the church enjoys a level of autonomy. It removes the need for the pastor to hear every little detail. However, this issue, as I understand it, called into question a person's suitability for serving in the ministry.

And the belief that she is not walking with God prompted an ultimatum of sorts."

Silence fell over the table as she spoke. As they had during the previous week's meeting, several sets of eyes remained focused on the very uninteresting plastic tabletop in front of them.

"Accusations," Laura continued, "calling into question a member's spiritual state are beyond the reach of the individual ministry groups and should be brought to the leadership for direction in handling. With that overlooked, I'm here to ascertain whether anything remains to be done. But first, I need to know, is this what happened?"

"It wasn't exactly like that," Theresa spoke again.

"Then, what exactly was it like?" Laura looked at each person.

They couldn't see it with their heads down, but Trinity didn't doubt they could feel it. Laura's gaze stopped on Trinity. She wanted to plead with her to stop the meeting. Let everything go back to normal. Laura's eyes conveyed a need to trust.

"Eve? You were here, weren't you?" Laura addressed the woman who looked up from the table.

"Yes." It was barely a whisper.

"Would you, please, take me through the events of the meeting. What prompted its calling? How did it progress?"

After a shaky intake and exhale of breath, Eve began. "It was concern for Trinity. Mrs. ..." Her gaze flicked to Theresa before she continued. "Um, someone was worried about the choices Trinity had recently made."

"Bouquets of Hope choices?"

"No." She shook her head. "That man she's dating. He's not a godly choice. She said she'd talked to several others. Everyone felt the same way. She said we should confront

Trinity with the truth. Give her a chance to see the error of her choice and cut the sin out of her life. That's why the meeting was called."

"And you spoke with each of these ladies too?"

Eve frowned. "No. But Mrs., um, the person who approached me, already had."

"Go ahead. What happened at the meeting?"

Theresa Cavins slapped her hand against the table. "I'll tell you what happened. I called the meeting. We confronted Trinity with the sinfulness of her choices, and she chose to keep her sin rather than cut it from her life. Still, we wanted to give her a chance. We encouraged her to pray about it and give us an answer this week. It was up to her. Deal with the sin or step down from the coordinator role in the ministry."

"And the sin running rampant in her life?"

"Choosing to let that man in her life," Theresa spat back. "I don't care if he pretends he's a believer. He swaggers into the house of God like he owns the place, getting attention for himself rather than giving it to God. And if that wasn't enough, he's a professional wrestler. That career is no place for someone who truly loves God. Turn on one of those programs sometime. You'll see what I mean."

"And you all feel this way?" Laura swept the room with a glance. A few heads lifted with discomfort written on each face.

Eve spoke up. "It makes sense. Why would anyone who follows God work in such an ungodly place?"

Laura nodded. "I can only think of one reason."

"See? That's what I mean." The words shot from Theresa's mouth like a fatal bullet.

"I see it in the story of Joseph living, working, and practically ruling in godless Egypt. Or in the story of Daniel or

Shadrach, Meshach, and Abednego." Laura went on as if she and Theresa were on the same wavelength.

Trinity knew they weren't, and she believed Laura knew it too.

The wry twist of Theresa's lips announced her displeasure. "Apples and oranges. That's what those comparisons are. Those godly men were forced to live in those lands. They didn't have a choice."

Laura's head tilted to the side. "True. How about missionaries? They go into godless societies all the time in an effort to shine God's light in the darkness."

After a moment of silence, Laura, again, picked up the thread of conversation. "My husband and I had the pleasure of speaking with Blane at length last Sunday. We were blessed to hear his testimony and asked him why he works in the industry he's chosen. Other than Trinity, have any other members of Bouquets of Hope reached out to him? Asked him about himself beyond the barest of facts?"

Slow, silent shakes of heads started up around the table. Trinity appreciated what Laura was trying to accomplish. This issue was bigger than the specific situation she faced. If it wasn't tied into the overall spiritual health and well-being of the church, Laura never would have intervened so publicly. At the same time, listening to her speak of Blane and her conversation with him was too much. Her heart was too battered to handle it.

The metal folding chair scraped across the flooring, grabbing the attention of everyone in the room as Trinity abruptly stood and snatched her purse from the back of it. Autumn rose more hesitantly beside her.

"I'm sorry. I have to go." She addressed the room before turning to Laura. "I know there are issues to untangle and deal with here, but I'm not in a place to do it right now. I trust your judgment."

Autumn laid a restraining hand on her arm. "Are you sure you don't want to stay?"

She swiped a tear from the corner of her eye. "I hope God uses this situation to grow each of us and make the ministry stronger. I really do. But the man I love walked out of my life less than a week ago in a misguided attempt to salvage my relationship with everyone gathered for this meeting. Ultimately, I'll need to come to terms with everything. But today can't be that day."

Without stopping to find out if Autumn was following, Trinity fled the room. Once she reached the church's front stairs, she stopped long enough to suck in a ragged breath. The prospect of listening to Laura recount the testimony Blane shared with her in a beautiful, vulnerable moment was too daunting. Her fractured heart and frayed nerves were already searing from the emotions of the day. Laura and Miss Gertie would fill in the details, and she'd decide from there her next step.

The door opened behind her. Trinity didn't turn. Autumn came to stand beside her, bumping her with her shoulder.

"You sure know how to make an exit."

Trinity's laugh held no joy. "Ministry coordinator loses mind. Forced to resign. Details at five." Trinity raised her hand and swiped it across the sky like an invisible banner as she spoke.

Autumn ran a hand through her hair before using the other to shift her purse higher onto her shoulder. "I don't know. After you left ..."

"Please, I can't talk about it anymore."

"Then, let's get out of here," Autumn said as she looped an arm through hers. "I've got the perfect cheer-up plan."

# 32

"Come sit by me," Mike suggested, patting the empty cushion beside him.

Trinity plopped down into the spot and leaned against the back of the couch where he'd draped his arm. Far from the first time they'd sat next to each other like this, Trinity knew without any doubt it was nothing romantic. No hidden agendas rested under that arm, only a bit of friendship.

The effort was appreciated, though it recalled other arms. The strength she found physically in Blane's arms translated into emotional strength as well. She missed his broad chest behind her head, supporting her in every way. No. Movie night was about forgetting everything that turned her life upside down and inside out over the last week. She was determined to let it accomplish its work.

"Autumn, get in here with the popcorn!" She playfully ordered her friend.

"I'm coming. I'm coming." Autumn entered from the kitchen behind them and took the final seat on the couch. "Good grief, you're impatient."

Trinity snatched the bowl. "No. I'm hungry and ready to get this movie started."

"Hey!"

"I'm in the middle. I should hold the snacks." Trinity shrugged before stuffing a handful of popcorn in her mouth.

"Whatever. Mike, start the movie."

"Aye, aye captain."

With one of her favorite rom-coms starting on the big screen TV and the three of them fighting for handfuls of popcorn from the same bowl, Trinity started to relax. Comfort may not have come from the arm draped over her shoulder but enjoying a night of normal with her closest friends started her tattered emotions in the right direction.

"I can't believe women fall for that kind of stuff," Mike announced at the end of the movie. "I mean, seriously, the guy totally duped her pretending he wasn't the one closing down her mother's bookstore. Completely shady if you ask me."

"No one asked you."

Autumn's retort paired with an arm swinging in front of Trinity who barely ducked back far enough to miss getting hit with the decorative pillow in her hand. Mike, however, didn't move quickly enough and got a face full.

"Hey! Don't get mad at me for pointing out the man was not on the up-and-up dealing with her, and he's the hero. I just don't get it."

Taking the empty popcorn bowl with her, Trinity headed for the kitchen. It never failed. Autumn and Trinity ate up the romance in their favorite films only for Mike to point out the flaws. Only their favorite of all time, *The Princess Bride*, escaped criticism. The addition of pirates and fencing to the romance tempered his views on that one. And his acceptance of the film allowed him to retain movie night privileges when they chose a rom-com.

"We've explained it before," Trinity called over her shoulder. "Viewers aren't meant to dive deep into each nuance and plot device. You've got to suspend disbelief and enjoy the ride."

"Besides," Autumn joined in. "there are just as many holes in the superhero and sci-fi ones you watch. You just don't want to admit it."

"Not hardly ..."

Trinity moved beyond hearing the rest of the retort in favor of heading to the bathroom. Two glasses of lemonade and a two-hour film created a need more pressing than being part of the debate. Besides, the arguments wouldn't be new. Both sides emphatically employed the same ones every time they got together for movie night.

Trinity stopped in the hallway on the way back to join Mike and Autumn in the living room. Was that someone else she heard? Maybe it was just the television. She listened until someone spoke again. Miss Gertie. While she really wasn't up to additional company, Trinity knew going home after church without checking on her would have been tough for her honorary grandma.

"Hey, Miss Gertie." Trinity's greeting stuck in her throat as she entered the room. Miss Gertie was there with Autumn and Mike. So was Eve Thompson. And after she'd worked so hard to keep her mind off the day's earlier events.

If Miss Gertie noticed the abrupt end to her welcome, she ignored it. "Sounds like you've had a relaxing evening with these two troublemakers. I'm glad to hear it. But I do have to ask if we can sit and talk for a minute or two. I think Miss Eve has a few things she'd like to discuss with you."

*No* sprang to mind, but that would be rude. Not to mention very unforgiving. Trinity had no desire to make things worse by choosing either path. The slow, deep breath she allowed herself before answering helped calm thoughts.

"Sure. Do you mind talking in the kitchen?"

"Not at all. Lead the way."

Trinity glanced at Mike and Autumn. "Are you guys staying?"

Unspoken communication passed between them before Autumn answered. "I think we'd better get home for the night. Call me if you need anything."

Trinity nodded. "It's just us then. The kitchen's over here."

Miss Gertie and Eve followed. Trinity thudded against the wooden chair as she sat. When had her body become so tired? Probably about the time she sat down for that Bouquets of Hope meeting a week ago. Why did it feel like longer than that?

When her guests were seated on either side of her, Trinity looked between them. Should she say something? What was the protocol for hosting unexpected guests in your home, especially when one might even be a little unwanted? Hospitality might be a neutral starting point.

She cleared her throat. "Can I get either of you something to drink?"

"No," Eve answered. "I think it would be better if I just say what needs said. If I don't do it now, I may not get it out."

Trinity's stomach clenched. What happened after she left? And was Miss Gertie here to offer emotional support to her when Eve delivered bad news or for Eve to have strength to share what was on her mind? If the news was bad enough she had to ask, did it even matter who Miss Gertie was there for?

The older woman patted Eve's hands resting on the table. "It's like a bandage. It'll sting a bit, but you've got to yank it off anyway."

"I need to apologize to you." The words came out on a

heavy exhale of breath. "I didn't mean to hurt you, but I know I did."

Speaking to ease the tension was out of the question. Jumping in with a quick 'I forgive you' or 'it's all right' would be an easy way to effectively end the uncomfortable discussion. But would she mean it? Probably not. And if she offered forgiveness without meaning it, the issues would continue to simmer below the surface waiting to explode at the next opportunity.

Eve's mouth twisted to the side as she bit the inside of her lip. Discord was never a chosen path for her. Normally, her discomfort sparked a bit of empathy in Trinity. Today? Not so much. Maybe if she hadn't been on the receiving end of the hurtful behavior.

That wayward thought had to be silenced. Trinity closed her eyes. It remained, tattooed on her eyelids, where it scrolled across her mind like a weather announcement crawls across the bottom of a television screen. But Eve came to apologize.

*Lord, help me forgive. Give me the strength to let this go, for my own sake and for Eve's.*

"Maybe," Miss Gertie cut into her prayer, "you should start at the beginning, Eve."

"Okay." Her voice sounded as brittle as dead leaves in the fall. "When you brought Blane to church last Sunday, I was shocked. He's such an imposing person. I'm ashamed to even say it, but I wasn't comfortable when I saw Spencer talking with him."

Her head bent low under the weight of her admission. Trinity didn't know whether to scream or cry. Had her church family so misunderstood Blane? He'd never been anything but caring toward her and Jay. She pictured the way Blane knelt in front of Spencer, getting on his level to make him comfortable.

How could anyone fail to recognize the kindness that flowed into everything he said or did?

She recognized it the first … wait. The image of her standing next to Jay and pulling him close to her side crashed into her condemnation of Eve's actions. Meeting Blane for the first time, her natural reaction was one of caution. They were in a public place meant for fan interaction. He had dressed the same way then as he did at the church. And still, she'd felt that same intimidation due to his size and style. How could she fault Eve for doing exactly what she'd done?

"I understand. I was the same way when Blane first approached me and Jay." The comfort flowed from her lips without hesitation.

Hope flickered in Eve's eyes as her gaze snapped away from the table to meet Trinity's. Seeing the woman's actions through her own opened the door to mercy Trinity thought permanently sealed shut.

"It's true. We were in a safe place, meant for interaction with the wrestlers. It didn't matter. When I saw this bear of a man approaching Jay and me, I shielded my son. I think it's a mother's natural instincts. My trepidation didn't last long, though, because Blane's kindness and gentleness were evident from our first conversation."

Eve bit her quivering lip, as Miss Gertie dug through her purse, producing a tissue. Eve accepted it and dabbed her eyes. Sensing wadded tissues from the bottom of Miss Gertie's bag were not going to be enough, Trinity stepped away from the table to retrieve a box from her bathroom counter. With reinforcements sitting in the middle of the table, she took her seat.

"Thank you for being understanding," Eve began. "But you did something that I regret I didn't do. You were hesitant but took time to hear Blane out. I did the last thing I should have done. I walked away without giving him a chance. And if that wasn't bad enough, I went off and talked to others about my misgivings."

Trinity couldn't excuse Eve's choice to gossip as right, but realistically, she knew it wasn't an unusual practice. If she wanted to think about her own life, it wouldn't take long to come up with examples of similar behavior. How easy it was for these 'little' sins to sneak into a person's life pulling them down a dangerous path away from God.

"I probably don't need to guess what happened at that point. I think I may have lived it."

Eve wadded the tissue in her hands. "You're right. And that's what causes me the most shame. I took it to others who validated my concerns and fed them. Over that week, one individual reached out to me several times. It never occurred to me that her seeking me out was unusual. She confirmed my worst fears and assured me everyone else in the group shared them."

Regret showed in her eyes. "'It's for Trinity's spiritual good' became the mantra giving us the courage to call that meeting. I told it to myself often enough, I began to believe it. Not even the pain it caused you was enough to snap me out of it. If the whole group believed it, it had to be true."

Trinity's steepled hands covered her mouth as the admission drew a sob from deep inside. Part of her wanted to demand the name of the pot-stirrer, but she already knew. Besides, gossip created this problem. It wasn't going to be the answer to fix things. If anyone had stood against it, the problem might not have progressed this far.

The group, including Eve, had let a woman working in the weaknesses of a powerful personality entice them away from what they knew was right. Standing up against that kind of push wasn't easy. But maybe, for Eve, this was the beginning of knowing it had to be done.

"I'm so sorry, Trinity." The apology accompanied more tears. "When Miss Gertie read about Samuel in the meeting today about looking at the heart, it hit me. Hard. And when she spoke of David being a man after God's own heart, I looked at my own. I realized it looked nothing like God's in this situation. I want that though. And admitting my sin to God, to you, and trying to make amends is my starting place. Please, forgive me."

Trinity sniffed. She didn't feel like forgiving. Then again, it wasn't about what she felt. Eve's desire to have a heart after God convicted her of that truth. If she was going to be a person after God's heart, unforgiveness wasn't an option.

"I forgive you. I know coming here, sharing all this, was hard for you. I appreciate that more than you know. I can't say I'm not still hurt and even a bit angry about all this, but I choose forgiveness."

"Thank you. Please know, I'm determined to learn from this and not allow it to happen again." Eve said as she reached into her purse and retrieved what looked like a stack of envelopes. "After Miss Gertie's devotion and Laura sharing Blane's testimony, many of the Bouquets of Hope women were convicted as I was. We texted our families to take care of lunch and chose to spend our time in prayer."

She slid the bundle across the table. "Before we left, I asked Miss Gertie if she would accompany me to speak with you after evening services. After the way the meeting went, I knew you wouldn't be there, and I didn't want to wait a week to say what needed said. Some of the others overheard me talking about it, and tonight, they gave me these to pass along to you."

Trinity fingered the edges of the envelopes. The messages

would be read when she was alone with her thoughts and reactions. "Thank you."

"Well," Miss Gertie said as she abruptly stood. "It's time Eve and I leave you be. Everything needing said has been said. Now, you both need time to sort through it. We'll show ourselves out."

Eve nodded and followed Miss Gertie's lead. She stopped in the doorway, turning to face Trinity.

"One last thing. I'm sorry about Blane, and I'll be praying for you."

Trinity's head dropped to her arms on the tabletop as Eve continued her exit. Whether her tears were born of relief or emotional exhaustion was undecided. Rather than trying to stem the flow, Trinity allowed everything she felt to pour onto the surface before her.

When the box of tissues was emptied and Trinity cried enough to dehydrate herself, a shaky peace rested on her soul. The evening's events were necessary for healing. If only restoration came immediately.

As she shifted to straighten her stiff back, the pile of envelopes rubbed her arm. She stared at them considering her options. She was tired, but her emotions were already wrecked. If she looked at them now, they couldn't cause more pain than she already faced. If she waited, they could reopen the wound instead of prepping her soul to heal.

She untied the string binding them together and slid the top envelope from the stack. Turning it over in her hands, it seemed impossible that something so innocuous had the potential to break her heart all over again. It was now or never. Trinity wedged a finger in an open spot in the seal and ripped it open.

Tightness filled her chest, as she unfolded the paper. *Please,*

*God, help me deal with whatever I find in these notes. And help me find mercy to extend if anyone asks for forgiveness.*

Knowing the women wrote of their own volition, Trinity was certain there would be few, if any, that continued the condemnation of her choices. As she finished the last letter, relief loosened the bands that held her lungs hostage throughout her reading.

The same story was woven through each page. While some seemed to negate their own choices, tending to follow their confessions with 'but this' and 'but that' finger-pointing, she knew they were trying. She prayed God would continue working in their hearts.

Most of the letters were hearts bleeding onto the page from the self-inflicted wound of sinful choices. The honesty and introspection of those letters mirrored that of Eve's kitchen table confession. The same understanding God brought to her in dealing with Eve flooded her heart for these women as well. Forgiveness, while not easy, was a given.

There were a few names missing from the list of those who had reached out. Trinity determined it wouldn't keep her from extending forgiveness even to those. If they ever asked, she'd be able to honestly report it was done long before.

God would heal the damage to her church family. It would take time, but she trusted He would do this work so the church could bring Him glory. Trinity could take comfort from that, even as she prayed. He would do the same in her relationship with Blane.

# 33

"Leave it alone, Pamela," Blane ordered with a glare.

Her eyes narrowed. "Fine. For now. But don't think you scare me. You never have, and you never will. This discussion will happen."

The downside of friends knowing the real Blane Sterling was that he could no longer keep well-meaning busybodies in their place with a look.

"Whatever." He would put her off again when the time came. "For now, we have work to do."

A dramatic sigh paired perfectly with an exaggerated eye roll. "And that's my point. Since you came back, you've thrown yourself into work with a vengeance. You're not unaffected. Technically, you're fine."

"Then leave it at that. If I'm doing my job and doing it well, that's all that matters."

"No. It isn't. You come, you wrestle, you leave. I know you still love the job, but you left part of yourself behind when you left Trinity."

"Don't. Talk. About. Trinity."

Her manicured hand raised in front of her like a stop sign. "Fine. Just please, talk to somebody. You've got to deal with this. Three weeks isn't a long time, but I'm worried about you."

"No need."

Before she could respond his phone vibrated. The number displayed was unfamiliar. Strange. His number was only given out to family and friends. And his cell service did a good job weeding out the potential spam. His finger hovered above the screen where he was about to hit the ignore icon. The area code looked familiar. What could it hurt to check?

"Hello?"

"Is this Blane Sterling?" A familiar voice came across the line.

Blane smiled, though he knew there was a reason for the call as well as he knew he probably wasn't going to like it. "Miss Gertie, is that you?"

"Oh good. It is you."

"How did you get my number? Did Trinity ask you to call?"

As soon as Trinity's name was mentioned, the flurry of Pamela's activity behind him ceased. Of course, she'd homed in on a conversation regarding Trinity. That was all she seemed to talk to him about lately.

"Last question first. No. Trinity doesn't have the foggiest idea I'm calling. As to how I got your number, let's just say that girl has never been careful with her cell phone around Autumn and leave it at that."

Subterfuge. Somehow it seemed to fit Miss Gertie in a harmless sort of way. Still, it didn't bode well for the topic of discussion if she felt she had to resort to trickery to get his number from Trinity.

"What can I help you with, Miss Gertie?"

"It's time for you to come back and patch things up with Trinity. She needs you here."

Straight to the point. He respected that, though he couldn't agree. There was too much at stake for her to deal with his re-entry into her life.

"I can't do that to her."

"And why not?"

How much did she know about why he left? Knowing Trinity saw her as a grandmother and spiritual mentor, he'd guess she'd been made aware of all of it. But what if he was wrong.

"Trinity faced some difficult choices with me around. Choices she shouldn't have to make. I left to remove the need to make those decisions." He silently congratulated himself on keeping it vague.

"Very diplomatic. But I know about all that nonsense with the church. While I respect your attempt to protect Trinity from loss, the whole decision to leave is nothing but hogwash."

He didn't have time to argue this with her, especially not with Pamela more than likely lurking around somewhere close enough to eavesdrop with a clear conscience.

"I disagree. Trinity has suffered enough loss, and she can't lose the people who have been family, friends, and support system through the hardest parts of her life."

"You are not listening to the words coming from my mouth." Her tone was laced with impatience. "All of that is taken care of. It was just one woman's refusal to look at the situation without bias. She made up her mind, and then, she made up everyone else's minds too. It's been dealt with, and the issue isn't an issue anymore."

Hope flickered. Could he return? A large part of him wanted nothing more than to hop in his car and head back to Missouri.

But he'd left for her good. Would returning open the door to more hurt for Trinity?

"I'm sorry, Miss Gertie. Knowing Trinity has patched things up with her church family means more to me than you know. But going back is too great a risk. Accepting the idea of me is one thing. It's easy with so many miles between us. Acceptance of the reality of me in Trinity's life is different. I don't want a repeat of this for Trinity. I can't go back."

"You're making a mistake. Trinity loves you."

The words cut into his chest without mercy. He knew that. He was trying to forget that. Move on with his life as he hoped Trinity would.

"I can't. It kills me to say it, but I can't."

"I guess I have to respect your decision." Her disappointment was almost tangible. "Good-bye, Blane."

With shoulders weighed down by the conversation, Blane returned the phone to his pocket. He wanted nothing more than to return to the woman he loved. No, that wasn't true. The reason he left in the first place was to safeguard the relationship she had with her church family. That was his top priority. To risk her support system for the sake of him being with her would be selfish. Wouldn't it? And last he remembered, love wasn't selfish.

Movement to his right drew his attention. Pamela stood behind one of the announcer tables, shuffling through a stack of papers. She watched him as if determining his need for a listening ear. It wouldn't be the first time their shared faith and friendship, not to mention their constant proximity to each other due to the job, gave him the opportunity to talk through his problems with her. Pamela had shown wisdom time and time again.

Blane raised his hand to wave and forced a smile. "Be back in a bit."

"Bye," she replied as she returned the wave.

A perfectly sculpted, raised eyebrow left him with little doubt Pamela wanted to ask about the phone call. Someday soon, he might oblige. Today was not that day. He fished his keys from him pocket and headed to the door.

# 34

"Welcome home!" Trinity's voice joined those of Miss Gertie, Autumn, and Mike who joined her for Jay's annual coming home party.

Jay rushed her, nearly tackling her to the floor with his hug. "I missed you, Mom!"

First, she squeezed him. Then she attacked his ribs until his giggles turned to shrieks. Loosening her hold, she kissed the top of his head. "I missed you too."

"Mo-o-om." He whined as he scrubbed his hair with his hand, leaving it to stand on end like it did each morning when he woke. "Stop it."

Half pleading, half warning, his eyes were wide. The message was clear. Don't embarrass me in front of everyone with your kisses. She could wait. Bedtime would come soon enough, and she could smother him with all the kisses she wanted. Oh, how she'd missed him.

Tucker's mom laughed from the doorway behind them. "I remember when your daddy felt the same way about my kisses, Jay. But one day, he realized they weren't so bad after all."

Hefting the suitcase in front of her, she stumbled into the house. A hand to her lower back reminded Trinity the woman wasn't getting any younger.

"Here, let me get that Mrs. Knight." Mike stepped around Trinity and Jay to take the heavy case.

She patted his cheek. "What a sweet gentleman you've turned into. I was surprised Trinity didn't set her cap for you after Tucker passed."

Mouth gaping, Trinity stared at her mother-in-law. Mike was rendered speechless, and she couldn't blame him. Mrs. Knight took in everyone's reactions with a sigh.

"But then, that spark never appeared. Did it? There's only one man who has arrested my daughter-in-law's attention since my son. And I don't see him anywhere."

"Rita," Trinity hissed in a tone leaving no room for argument. "I told you what happened. Now is not the time to bring things like that up."

Rita glanced at Jay whose attention jumped from adult to adult gauging the situation. With a smile meant to reassure him, she focused back on Trinity.

"You're right. Now is about Jay. There will be time later to discuss matters further."

The correct time, as Trinity found out, was three hours later. With Jay tucked in and his bedtime routine completed, the adults gathered around the table for coffee and what was supposed to be chit-chat. Though Mike had to excuse himself, the others stayed. Trinity's cup was still half-full when the conversation veered in a less than desirable direction.

"I'm not sure I see the issue," Rita commented.

Trinity stifled her groan. "You and Tate don't even like

Blane. Jay almost missed out on his summer visit because of it."

"That was before we got to know him." Rita clasped her hands on the table in front of her with a dramatic sigh. "Do you know that he didn't once miss his weekly bedtime call with Jay?"

"And Jay regaled us with stories about everything you guys did together on your trip to Tennessee," Tate added. "Seems the young man went above and beyond to make your trip special."

Rita's one raised finger caught Trinity's attention. "And it wasn't just to score points with you like we thought it might be. Blane made Jay feel important and needed. I could hear it in my grandson's voice. Not to mention the mood boost that came with every phone call."

"When he asked to speak with me before hanging up one evening, I wasn't sure what to think." Tate took a sip of his coffee. "I figured he might try to sway me by telling me how great he is. Instead, he made sure we were okay with the calls. He didn't want us feeling like he was trying to take Tucker's place in Jay's life. Then, he asked me if there was anything I wanted to know about him."

Trinity went to the sink and poured out the remainder of her coffee. After rinsing the cup, she filled it with water. The last thing she needed as she tried to sleep after this conversation was caffeine.

"That's all well and good, but it doesn't change anything. Blane and I are through."

"You don't have to be." Miss Gertie shrugged from her place at the table.

"That is true." Autumn nodded her agreement.

Tate emptied his cup before joining in. "From what I've

heard, the barriers standing in the way of this relationship have been removed."

"You told us yourself that the church group reached out to you asking for forgiveness," Rita added. "With their understanding of how wrong their attitudes were, I know they'd give Blane a chance if you'd let them. Problem solved."

"Problem not solved." Trinity smacked both palms on the tabletop then caught herself. She lowered her volume so as not to disturb Jay. "You all seem to forget that while I love Blane, admitted as much to him, he left. I know his reasoning. I even respect it. But the truth is, while I could reconnect with him, there would be no point. As long as he thinks it's for my good, I would be in danger of having him walk out all over if something like this took place in the future."

"But he loves you," Autumn reasoned. "Doesn't that make it worth the risk?"

"It might," Trinity conceded. "Except we don't know that he does."

Autumn rolled her eyes. "Yes, we do. It didn't take perfect vision to see it. I think it would have been visible from space."

Every head around the table nodded. All of them but hers. She tried reminding herself that they interfered because they cared. Still, it was frustrating that no one listened to her side of things with an open mind.

"It might have looked like love. I'll even admit that at times it felt like love. But if he had multiple opportunities to say it and didn't, shouldn't that give me pause? If I said it to him and he said nothing in return, don't you think it's possible the omission was because he doesn't feel the same way?"

Silence answered the question as each person fidgeted in discomfort. No, they didn't like that possibility any more than she did. But they had to admit her theory carried weight.

Thankfully, she was saved from further introspection when

conversation moved from her love life to safer topics. By the time her friends and in-laws said their good-byes at the end of the evening, Trinity was grateful for the time she spent with them. Once Blane was removed from the picture, they were able to enjoy each other's company.

Gathering up empty cups from the table, Trinity let her mind wander back to the taboo. Her in-laws accepted Blane. It brought a sense of relief. Their epiphany didn't aid her relationship with him, but it would mean less subjects to avoid with them in the future since Blane indicated he would remain part of Jay's life.

She filled the sink with hot, soapy water and started washing the cups and dishes from dinner. As she finished cleaning up on autopilot, she gazed out the window at the night sky. The black canvas was sprinkled with a thousand points of light. The only other time she could remember seeing the sky so clear and filled with stars was one of the nights around the campfire at Blane's house.

Distracted, she placed wet, soapy hands on the edges of the sink. In bringing up Blane earlier had her friends unknowingly opened a Pandora's box? Would thoughts of Blane now seek her out, tempting her in her alone time with thoughts of what she couldn't have? Would she be hounded in every waking moment with the memories that hurt her heart most?

Her eyes slid shut as another thought occurred to her. Were the hauntings going to stop at her conscious times or would they follow her into sleep? There had to be a way to gain control and purge him from her thoughts. She pulled back her shoulders and stared at her reflection in the darkened panes of glass.

Life had dumped plenty of hard tasks in her lap, and she'd completed each one. This was no different. Blane Sterling would no longer be allowed to hijack her thoughts.

# 35

"How's Jay getting along at school this year?" Autumn asked as she took a seat across from Trinity at the small round coffee-house table.

Trinity stirred her smoothie with her straw. "It's only been two weeks, but he really likes his teacher this year. I still can't believe I have a third-grader. Time flies."

Autumn sipped her iced latte. "What's his favorite subject this year? And you better not say recess."

"While he does enjoy his free time, the only assignment he's talked about at this point is an English assignment. It'll probably change a hundred times before the year's end, but right now, I'd say English is the winner."

"What was this super special assignment about?"

Trinity's phone rang. The perfect excuse to avoid delving into an uncomfortable discussion since the assignment was about Jay's summer. The paper ended up reading like an ode to Blane. She picked up the phone without looking at the number and swiped to answer.

"Hello."

"Hello. Is this Trinity Knight?"

Her nerves went on the defensive. The cold that swept through her as she recognized the voice would rival the temperature in the dead of a midwestern winter.

"Hello, Pamela," she greeted the other woman while simultaneously trying to avoid eye contact with Autumn across the table.

"Oh, good. Is this an okay time to talk?"

*No.*

"As good as any."

"Great. I'll get right to business since I know you must be busy."

"I appreciate that."

"The UWO needs Jay to come down for a photo shoot. It's part of the whole Champion in Train promotion."

*Double no.*

"I'm afraid that isn't going to work for us. Jay has already started school, and I don't think it's wise for him to miss." It wasn't a lie, but she wasn't going into the rest with a near stranger.

"Don't you worry about that. I figured as much and told my bosses so. That's why we would like to do it over Labor Day weekend. That gives you guys this week to pack and prepare. If you drive out on Friday, it would be a fairly late night when you arrive. So, we'll push the shoot until Saturday afternoon. Then you'd have Sunday to sightsee or drive home. Either way, Monday you'd be back at home relaxing before school resumes on Tuesday."

Pamela had certainly covered all her bases. And when she agreed to allow Jay to be the Champ in Training, she'd committed to working with the company for additional promotional needs. She couldn't go back on their agreement because personal issues interfered.

"That sounds fine. We'll be there Saturday for the shoot."

"I'm so happy to hear it. I really want to get this shoot done before holiday-related needs take precedence. I'll send you an email with the specifics. Bye."

The call ended. Though she didn't voice the question on her mind, Autumn's single raised eyebrow did it for her.

Trinity sighed. "How do you feel about a trip to Tennessee?"

———

"But I want you to come too," Jay whined from his seat in the back of her car.

Trinity gripped the steering wheel until her knuckles turned white. He doesn't understand. The thought had played on continuous loop since she broke the news that morning at breakfast that they'd be visiting Blane in Tennessee after she picked him up from school. He was bound to be excited. It was only natural. And he didn't have any framework to understand the workings of adult relationships.

To Jay, this was a chance for them to see their new friend again. The concept that she wouldn't be as thrilled to see Blane was foreign to him. When he left for his grandparent's house, the three of them were the best of friends. He wouldn't have any idea that Blane hung up from his weekly bedtime calls without speaking to her.

"I know you do," she explained. "But this time, I'm going to let Aunt Autumn take you to see Blane. She's never been in a wrestling stadium. I need you to show her around."

"But why can't you come too?"

"It's time to go Jay," Autumn interrupted the circular conversation. "Hurry and get unbuckled. We don't want to be late for your pictures."

"Fine."

The monosyllabic answer stated his mood clearly without the pursed pouty lip paired with it. But Jay unbuckled and followed Autumn into the stadium without further argument. Trinity closed her eyes and rested her head against the headrest. Now, if she could only survive the next hour without her thoughts obsessively returning to the man inside the building taking pictures with her son.

The blank canvas of her mind did nothing to stem the flow of her thoughts. Instead, it turned traitor, painting an image of Jay posing with a giant of a man with his long hair contained in a ponytail and dimples showing through his dark beard.

The dimples gave away his secret. Fierce and intimidating as Blane Sterling was in the ring, once those dimples showed up, the truth was known. His eyes would sparkle like a precious gem, and anyone watching knew the beast in the ring was really a teddy bear.

Trinity groaned. This was not helping. Maybe she should take a walk. She didn't know the area well and wasn't sure it was safe. But was it any riskier than staying in her car dreaming about the man she loved but couldn't have?

A knock sounded on the window. Trinity jumped, opening her eyes to the intruder. Outside the glass, Pamela stood wearing a sheepish grin. Trinity turned the key and rolled down the window.

"I think there's been a misunderstanding," Pamela's friendly smile turned to an apologetic grimace. "When taking photos with a minor, we have to have an adult present."

Trinity frowned. "That's why I sent in his Aunt Autumn. Is she not with him?"

"Oh, yes, she is. However, the adult must be a parent or *legal* guardian." She stressed the word legal as if it might be beyond Trinity's ability to comprehend.

If Trinity wanted to, she could take offense. But Pamela was only doing her job and covering the company's legal rear end. She might not like it, but she understood. Still, she didn't want to go inside, where running into Blane was a certainty.

"Couldn't we stretch the rules? Just this once? If I sign something stating Autumn has my permission to act as guardian in my place?"

Pamela's eyes grew round. "Oh no. That wouldn't do at all. I could get in a lot of trouble. The company could too."

Trinity rubbed her hands over her eyes. There was no way around it. Refusing would disappoint Jay, and she wasn't prepared to do that. She would have to go in. Too bad her heart wasn't ready to do that.

"Fine," she relented. "Lead the way."

# 36

Trinity stood in the empty stadium after Pamela dropped her off, promising the crew would be in momentarily. It was cavernous when there were no fans filling the seats or wrestlers in the ring. The ring. What did Jay see when he was in the ring with Blane? What did Blane see every time he wrestled?

She glanced around. No one was there. Listening carefully, she detected no footsteps drawing closer. Inching close enough to feel the smooth canvas mat under her fingertips, she walked the length of the side until she stood in front of the steel steps on the corner. Those steps would give her entrance to the ring if she wanted to do that. She listened again, hearing nothing.

Before she could talk herself out of it, she climbed up the steps and through the ropes. She moved to the center of the ring and turned in a circle, looking out at the stadium. Closing her eyes, she tried to imagine what it must look like to the performers.

"What are you ..."

Trinity spun toward Blane's voice calling out from behind

her. Tucking her bottom lip between her teeth she watched him approach. The frown he wore made him look more like a warrior and less like the friend she'd come to know. He'd asked her a question though, at least part of one.

"I, uh, I just wanted to see what you and Jay saw when you were in the, uh, the old squared circle," she stammered with a nervous laugh trying to use the unfamiliar terminology. "I'll get out now."

As she moved toward the corner to exit, Blane made it down the ramp. Her escape stalled as he climbed the stairs she planned to use, blocking her path. The frown was still in place. She looked down, focusing on his chest rather than his eyes. At least it couldn't intimidate her. Unlike his face, his chest didn't reflect his mood or his intensity.

"You don't have to go." His voice was rough and low. "I thought you were a reporter. I didn't know it was you, until you turned around. Why are you here, Trinity?"

His question brought her eyes to his. She'd not been told about a reporter, only the photo shoot. And why did he act like she was the last person he expected to see?

"I'm here for the photo shoot. Pamela called. Said we needed to do one more set of promotional shots." His frown grew. He wasn't happy to see her. "I wanted to wait in the car. I sent Jay in with Autumn, but Pamela said I had to be here for legal reasons. Please, don't be mad."

"Mad? I'm not mad."

"You seem mad. Your expression is two steps away from the enraged beast in the ring look."

Blane laughed. "Enraged beast, huh? Nice to know how you see me in the ring. But I assure you, I'm not mad. Just confused. Pamela scheduled an interview today, but she never mentioned anything involving Jay."

"You didn't know we'd be here?"

"Nope." He shook his head before ducking to navigate his way through the ropes and into the ring.

Trinity stepped back, allowing him room, and trying to maintain enough distance to keep her rebel heart from pounding. He straightened only a few feet from her. The confusion dissipated taking with it the intimidating glare and leaving behind an intensity that beckoned her closer. A warning siren blared in her mind, reminding her that Blane's was not a love she could have.

She licked her anxiety parched lips. "I'll find Pamela and straighten this out. Tell her Jay and I are leaving. I'm sorry she ambushed you with us."

"Please, don't do that."

Though he didn't make a movement toward her, his request for them to stay drew them closer. Was she not the only one feeling the desire to stay close?

"Are you sure?" She had to know.

"Positive," he answered. He searched her face before averting his gaze. "Jay would be so disappointed. I don't want to do that to him."

Her world folded in on itself as she registered his meaning. It was all for Jay. Whatever she thought she saw in his eyes was a romantic dream. She blinked away traitorous tears.

"Devastated is more like it." For her and Jay, but she couldn't say that out loud. "I'll see where they've gone."

If only she could hold herself together until she moved far enough away from him. She stepped around him, heading for the stairs. He grasped her hand as she passed, causing her to pause. Should she free her hand and run from the sweet torture of his touch?

"Wait."

His low, gravelly voice sent hope flying through her. Was disappointment waiting to shoot it from her sky with his next words? Against her better judgment, she remained next to his side. When she didn't move, Blane gently pulled her to stand in front of him.

He released his hold on her hand leaving it numb with the absence. The brush of his fingers up her arm awakened her senses with warmth. She closed her eyes against the desire to enjoy the moment, forgetting the inevitable crash to come.

"That came out wrong. I don't want to disappoint Jay, but I want you here too. Every day since I left, I've worked to convince myself this ache will pass. Since Miss Gertie's call, I don't know how many times I've stopped myself from leaving everything behind and coming to you."

"Why did—wait." His words registered, derailing her train of thought. "Miss Gertie called you?"

Blane smiled as he nodded. "You might want to watch your phone a little closer. I think some of your friends may have figured out your password."

She made a mental note to have a talk with Autumn as soon as opportunity arose. "Why did she call?"

"She wanted to make sure I knew your issues with the church were worked out and encouraged me to come back."

Hope plummeted to earth. "But you didn't."

"No." He shook his head. "There were a couple reasons. I left so your relationship with your church family wouldn't be destroyed. Miss Gertie told me the change was genuine. But sometimes it's easier to accept a hypothetical than the real problem standing in front of you. I couldn't chance it that their change only lasted until I returned."

"I can assure you; the soul-searching and change are as real as they come. But you said there are a couple reasons. What else kept you away?"

He took her hands in his and waited for her to look him in the eyes. His shoulders rose as he inhaled. "I left you. What if I came back and you'd moved on? What if you just didn't want me anymore? I couldn't take that."

"I wanted you. More than anything I wanted you."

———

He dropped her hands and took a step back. Throat tight, he tried to swallow. He cleared it in an attempt to unclog the disappointment lodged there.

"Wanted. That's in the past. What about now?"

She shook her head and shrugged. "I don't know."

Is this how she felt when he left her? Blane looked away from her to stare over her shoulder into the empty stadium. Once again, he cleared his throat. He blinked against the salty sting of tears. The moisture still found its way to his cheek.

"It's okay." A raspy whisper was all he could manage.

"Please, let me explain," she pleaded. "I did a lot of soul searching after you left, even more after reconciling with my church family. Like you, I realized two things. The first was that as much as I love you, I couldn't reach out to you. You left. I understood why. Strangely, part of me even felt cherished."

She understood his reasons. Blane couldn't help a smile of relief. It faded with her slight frown. Had he gotten the wrong idea.

"But the truth is, we should have decided what to do together. You wanted my best, but I get a say in that. If we ended up going the wrong way, we'd acknowledge the mistake and learn from it. I couldn't come to you, because I couldn't take the chance that you'd do the same in the future."

He rubbed his hand across his mouth. How could he have been so stupid? Her explanation left him no doubts he was in the wrong.

"I am so sorry. I never meant to make you feel like you

didn't have a say. I honestly thought I was doing what was best for you and that's what mattered most. I was ignorant. I was wrong, and I would never do that to you again knowing what I know now. Can you forgive me?"

He'd apologized, but she didn't have to accept it. Every word was true. And he'd never meant to remove her ability to choose. Would she see that? Could she move past it and extend mercy?

"Of course, I forgive you."

He blew out the breath he'd been holding. One hurdle down. One to go.

"The other thing?"

"What?"

"You said there were two things. What else kept you from calling?"

"It doesn't matter."

"Of course, it does."

He knew it. She knew it. If it was standing in the way, it mattered. What could be so bad that Trinity didn't think they could work through it? What would keep her from trying? His stomach tied itself in knots as he considered the only thing he could think of.

"You've moved on." Just saying the words sucked the air from his lungs.

"What?" Her brows dipped low as she frowned.

"You couldn't come to me," he started before pausing to take a calming breath. "Because you've found someone else who fits better in your world."

The confused look remained. "No. That's not it at all."

He wanted to believe her. There was no reason not to. Trinity wasn't the kind of woman to say things to placate him.

"Then, why?"

She looked away. Her lips trembled and her shoulders shuddered. Ignoring her tears, she turned back to him.

"I couldn't come to you because even though I love you, I had no assurance that you felt the same."

A sucker punch wouldn't hurt as much as Trinity's doubt of his feelings. Then again, he'd never said the words.

"I hoped you'd know. I tried to show you every day we were together."

It sounded weak, even to his ears.

"You were wonderful to me. I thought you might love me. But you never said. Then, you left. After that, I didn't know what to think."

He stepped closer. "Is that the only thing stopping you now?"

Hope shined from her eyes, even as they begged him not to play games with her heart. Slowly, she nodded. She needed the real Blane, not the performer who played to the crowd in that very ring.

Her skin was soft and warm against the hands he raised to frame her face. Ignoring the temptation of her full lips, he brought his gaze to hers.

"Trinity Knight, I love you. More than I ever dreamed possible."

The joy she felt was unmistakable. Her smile was brighter than the lights that filled the stadium during the shows. As his attention dropped to her lips, the desire to pull her into his arms returned.

"Kiss her already!" Autumn's voice shouted from somewhere behind the curtains at the top of the ramp.

Trinity's beautiful laughter was cut short as he dropped his hands from her face to encircle her waist, pulling her nearer. Happy to oblige their unwanted audience, he lowered his head until his lips were a breath from hers.

"I love you," he assured her before he gave in to the kiss.

Her sweet, responsive lips drew a stronger response from him. He tightened his embrace, allowing the promise of the moment to wash over him. A whistle emanated from behind the curtain, reminding him they were not alone. It took all his strength to break their kiss and loosen his hold on her.

A dreamy smile covered her face. Raising up on tiptoe, she pulled his head toward hers. Excitement gave way to confusion as she didn't meet his lips for another kiss. Instead, with her breath tickling his ear, she whispered, "As much as I love you."

He enveloped her in his embrace, resting his cheek against her hair. In that moment, Blane knew God restored what he thought he'd lost forever. Trinity saw beyond his sinful past to the man he was in the present. She accepted the life he felt called to in the ring, without allowing it to define him. Trinity acknowledged everything making up Blane Sterling. And a thousand championship titles couldn't begin to compare to knowing, despite it all, she chose to love him.

# EPILOGUE

*Eight months later*

"Is it time?" Jay asked for the thousandth time. "You said it was almost time. That was forever ago. And you remember what happened last time, don't you? We were late. We totally missed Maverick. We can't be late this time. Come on, Mom."

Trinity laughed. Of course, she remembered the meet and greet. They'd missed Maverick, but Blane walked into their lives that day. But this night wasn't about photo ops. Those took place yesterday. This night's event was Ring Wars 25. And they were already backstage. They literally could not be late.

She opened the door to the dressing room and took his hand. Halfway down the hall, her arm ached at the way he tugged on it in his rush.

"Slow down, Jay. I'm old and can't keep up," she laughed even as his excitement stoked her own.

Jay dutifully fell in step beside her. "You're not old. You only think you're old because you have me. And grownups always talk about how kids wear them out. But kids don't really do that. I figured out the real secret. Moms and dads make kids go to bed early. But they stay up late. Sometimes really late. They just need to go to bed with their kids. Then, they won't be tired anymore. I told Spencer and David. They think I'm right too."

"What do Spencer and David think you're right about?" Blane's voice sounded behind them.

"Blane!" Jay turned and pulled his hand from Trinity's. At the same time, he launched himself toward Blane who quickly knelt to meet him with a bear hug.

"Hey, Partner! Ready to make it official tonight?"

A quick glance up at Trinity clued her in that his question was for both of them. Her smile pushed her cheeks up until they ached. She'd never been more ready. She nodded, and Blane shifted his attention back to Jay standing beside him with a suddenly serious look.

"We're going to be partners forever after tonight. There's no going back," he parroted the words Blane used to describe what would take place after the matches were over.

"That's right." Blane nodded. "No going back. It's you and me from now on."

Jay's face broke into the biggest grin she'd seen. "You and me. When our music plays, we're going to go to the ring and we're going to win. Know why? It's cause we're the biggest and the strongest. Maverick can't beat us."

Warmth spread through Trinity at the way Blane's attention and care had shifted Jay's allegiance from the wrestling character he once revered to a real, godly man he could emulate.

"And when we win, we're going to be so happy. You can hold me up, and I'll hold up our belt. But then ..."

"I think you're getting a bit ahead of yourself," Blane interrupted. "Let's win that title first. Okay?"

She barely caught Blane's subtle wink, but it was hard to miss Jay's exaggerated one in return.

"'Kay."

As she sent Blane and Jay off to get ready, Trinity couldn't help feeling she was missing something. Maybe Blane didn't know Pamela had talked with her about the evening's post-match announcement. As she made her way to her special front row seat, she rubbed her empty ring finger.

Two weeks earlier, Blane sat beside her on the swing they shared by his backyard fire pit and asked her to marry him. The moment he proposed to her under a blanket of stars was perfect and sweet. Her 'yes' was without hesitation. Though lacking a ring to slip onto her finger, Blane assured it was not a spur of the moment decision.

Once UWO learned of their engagement, Pamela wasted no time calling her. The story of the UWO champion meeting and falling in love with the mother of his Champ in Training was the perfect way to end Ring Wars 25. But they wouldn't proceed with it unless Trinity was on board.

It was a rare thing for a wrestler's storyline to break what Blane called kayfabe, that wall that separated the wrestler in the ring from the man in real life. It was the addition of Jay as the Champ in Training making it possible now.

"Right this way, Miss Knight." One of the security personnel, stepped aside to allow her passage into the main part of the stadium. "I've got clear instructions on which seat you're to have tonight. Follow me."

"Thank you," she replied as they wound their way through the seats to one front and center to the ring.

"Let me know if you need anything tonight," he offered. "I'll be close by."

"Again, thank you."

Left on her own, Trinity scanned the stadium. Though it was early, a few people milled about. Soon, the seats would be filled to capacity. And after the show, Pamela, or whoever she designated, would announce her engagement to Blane. Trinity was still surprised she agreed to the request. Early on she and Blane had discussed the need to keep Jay from being a gimmick. Their relationship was an extension of that.

But this felt less like a gimmick and more like sharing their joy with everyone. Blane's proposal was his timing, his way. It had nothing to do with the business. But he was also a public figure. She had to get used to that. And the company saw the opportunity as a good story. She'd always been a sucker for a good story.

———

Trinity jumped in the air, cheering as the official counted "three". Blane retained his championship! Pride in his athleticism and work ethic welled up inside. He did his job well, and he enjoyed every minute of it. Exhausted as he was after a grueling match, his smile reflected the satisfaction he felt.

Running from the barricade, Jay bounded up the steps and into the ring. Blane swung him up on his shoulder. Perched there, the official had to reach to hand him the title belt. With the skill and swagger to match any wrestler on the roster, Jay held the belt with both hands and thrust it over his head. The crowd erupted in a new round of cheers.

Pamela brought a microphone to the ring and Blane lowered Jay to the ground, took the belt from him. Jay trotted over to Pamela for the microphone. Back at Blane's side he lifted it to his mouth, only to bite his lip and look up at Blane.

"You can do it." Blane nodded, placing a hand on Jay's tiny shoulder.

Trinity barely made out Blane's encouraging words as Jay raised the microphone again.

"We are the champions," his nervous voice rang out through the stadium. More cheers sounded, and Jay took a step back.

To encourage the masses to give Jay quiet, Blane lifted his hands, palms down and lowered them. Then, he knelt beside Jay, putting his arm over his shoulders.

"Is there anyone you want to thank for supporting us?" Blane coaxed.

"I want to thank my mom." His slight shoulders straightened as he looked straight at her. "My mom's the best. If they gave champion belts to moms, she'd get one every year."

You'd think the crowd was replaced with teenage girls watching a rom-com the way Jay's answer elicited a group "aww." Trinity smiled at her guys in the ring and wiped a tear from her eye, hoping to snag it before a camera panned her way.

Blane traded Jay the belt for the microphone and stood. "Would you all like to meet this championship mom?"

"Mom! Mom! Mom! Mom!" The crowd shouted in unison.

Blane motioned for Trinity to join them, and the security guard who'd led her to her seat opened a spot in the barricade to let her through. She took a deep breath and stepped toward the ring. The crowd continued to cheer as she climbed into the ring. Blane waited for her to stand beside them before speaking.

"Anything you want to say, championship mom?"

Trinity laughed as she shook her head. "Only that I hope I can retain my title when he hits his teen years."

Laughter from the crowd blended with Blane's before he quieted them once more. "I think we can arrange that. And while we might not have a belt for you to prove you're the champion we know you are, we do have something special for you to show what you mean to us. To show what you mean to me."

The crowd's silence was unlike anything she'd experienced. It was as if they were collectively holding their breath. Trinity's heart pounded as she reminded herself to breathe.

"When I met you and Jay last year, I had no idea I'd gain the greatest wrestling partner ever."

They both glanced at Jay beaming up at them.

"And finding the greatest life partner was nowhere near my radar. But God surprised me that day and gave me both. I love you more than I ever imagined I could, and I look forward to spending a lifetime with you and Jay by my side." He dropped to one knee and held out a jewelry box. Nestled inside was a beautiful opal surrounded by chocolate diamonds, set in rose gold. "Trinity Knight, will you accept this ring and share forever with me?"

As she said yes, and he slipped the perfectly fitted ring on her finger, fireworks exploded around them causing the stones to sparkle in their light. Blane stood and pulled her into his arms with a kiss that left her breathless.

The crowd's roar was deafening. Blane opened their embrace to pull Jay close. Confetti rained down on them, and Blane and Trinity stood side by side with Jay in front of them. Together, they looked out at the thousands of people cheering their engagement. People they didn't know, and who wouldn't care about them in a matter of weeks.

Movement to the side drew Trinity's attention. In moments, Autumn, Mike, Pastor Hood, Laura, Blane's parents, and Miss Gertie were climbing into the ring. Blane leaned close to her ear.

"Surprise, again."

After accepting hugs and tears from each one, Trinity stood back as they showered Blane with the same affection. God brought her a man of strength, physically, but most importantly spiritually. A man after God's own heart. She'd never expected another chance at love like this, especially not coming from the wrestling ring.

As she watched her friends and family interacting with each other and the departing crowd, Trinity laughed. This stadium had seen its share of surprises through the years. But she doubted it had ever seen love in the squared circle.

# AUTHOR'S NOTE

*Love in the Squared Circle* is a fictional story, but both Nashville, Tennessee, and Cape Girardeau, Missouri, are real places. For the sake of the story, I've created elements of each place completely from my imagination, including the Nashville hotel and Trinity's church and congregation. However, my husband and I enjoy spending regular afternoons in Cape Girardeau, and I had to include some real elements too. The restaurant Trinity takes Blane to is one we visit regularly. And while we've often heard a street musician with his bass guitar on the corner, we've yet to see a group perform.

# ABOUT THE AUTHOR

Heather Greer grew up in a rural southern Illinois town with two brothers. A little bit tomboy, she didn't mind her brothers' insistence on watching the occasional wrestling match. As a result, her friend's invitation to tag along with her husband to watch a wrestling pay-per-view wasn't as off-putting as some might think. What started as commentary on outfits, moves, and entrance music quickly developed into an appreciation for the athleticism exhibited and ability of the wrestlers to tell a story through words and in-ring actions.

Always one who enjoys a good story, Heather began watching documentaries and reading the biographies of favorite wrestlers. It was the powerful testimony in the biography of Shawn Michaels that sparked the idea for *Love in the Squared Circle*. His story of faith, combined with the contrasting in-ring and out-of-ring personalities of various wrestlers, turned the spark of Blane and Trinity's story into a flame.

But don't worry. Heather's go-to entertainment choice is still Hallmark movies and Christian romance books. No matter what framework she uses to tell a story, there's going to be strong faith and romantic elements and a cast of characters readers can laugh with, learn from, and cheer for as they find their way to happily ever after.

# ALSO BY HEATHER GREER

### Cake That!

#### Ten bakers. Nine days. One winner.

Competing on the *Cake That* baking show is a dream come true for
Livvy Miller, but debt on her cupcake truck and an expensive repair
make her question if it's one she should chase. Her best friend,
Tabitha, encourages Livvy to trust God to care for The Sugar Cube,
win or lose.

Family is everything to Evan Jones. His parents always gave up their
dreams so their children could achieve theirs. Winning *Cake
That* would let him give back some of what they've sacrificed by

allowing him to give them the trip they've always talked about but could never afford.

As the contestants live and bake together, more than the competition heats up. Livvy and Evan have a spark from the start, but they're in it to win. Neither needs the distraction of romance. Unwanted attention from Will, another competitor, complicates matters. Stir in strange occurrences to the daily baking assignments, and everyone wonders if a saboteur is in the mix.

With the distractions inside and outside the *Cake That* kitchen, will Livvy or Evan rise above the rest and claim the prize? Or does God have more in store for them than they first imagined?

scrivenings.link/cakethat

# MORE CONTEMPORARY ROMANCE
# FROM SCRIVENINGS PRESS

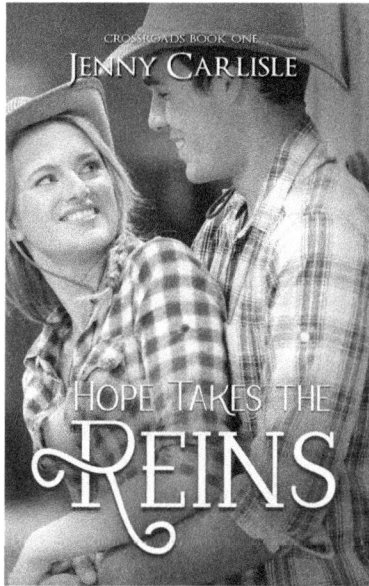

### *Hope Takes the Reins*

By Jenny Carlisle

O.D. Billings has lived in the shadow of his brothers all his life. Even his name brings him down, so he has used only initials for years. Now, his older brother has returned home from the army, rejecting the role his family expects him to assume in their pickup truck dealership, and the younger brother is intent on risking his life on the back of a bucking bull. O.D.'s fans at the rodeo love his confident swagger during tie-down roping competitions, but every trail he heads down on his own seems to wind up going nowhere.

Hope Caldwell's world is still reeling after her mom's recent death from cancer. She thrives on keeping the family's rodeo business going. Getting back to normal seems impossible when she overhears her uncle's plans to sell out. How can she continue without the only way of life she has known for all of her nineteen years? Can she rely on the help of a big-talking cowboy? Or does he have too many problems of his own?

scrivenings.link/hopetakesthereins

––––––––

Scrivenings
PRESS
Quench your thirst for story.
www.ScriveningsPress.com

*Stay up-to-date on your favorite books and authors with our free e-newsletters.*

ScriveningsPress.com

CPSIA information can be obtained
at www.ICGtesting.com
Printed in the USA
LVHW080531130422
715873LV00016B/927

9 781649 171993